SAME OL' situation

USA TODAY BESTSELLING AUTHOR

LACEY BLACK

Same Ol' Situation

Burgers and Brew Crüe, book 3

Cover Design by Melissa Gill Designs
Photographer Wander Aguiar
Model Zach Bradford

Editing by Kara Hildebrand

Proofreading by Joanne Thompson & Karen Hrdlicka

Format by Brenda Wright, Formatting Done Wright

Published in the United States of America.

ISBN-13: 978-1-951829-16-2

Isaac

"I think we should take a little break."

I stop in my tracks, her words registering like nails on a chalkboard. Slowly, I turn around and face the woman I've called my girlfriend for the last few months. Hell, off and on for the last three years. "Excuse me? A break?"

She flips her long blonde hair over her shoulder and props her hands on her hips. "Well, yeah. You know, you're always so busy with work and never have time for me," she whines.

"Always busy? I've been opening a new business, Savannah. We've been busting our asses to open Crüe Brewery these last few months. We've put everything into this new venture. I told you it was going to be intense for a little bit, but once this place opened, it would mellow out again. You said you understood that."

She wrinkles up her nose and tsks. "Yeah, well, I changed my mind. I'm tired of being alone every night because you're working."

I let out a long, frustrated groan and run my hands through my hair. "Tonight's opening night. Literally, tonight is our night to celebrate what we've accomplished these last few months. We have a building full of family, friends, and patrons all here to help us celebrate. Why are you doing this?"

Savannah shrugs her shoulders, as if she isn't ripping my heart from my chest and crushing it with her French manicured nails. "Listen, Isaac, I have to go. I'm meeting friends down at the Burberry."

All I can do is gape at the woman I've been in love with for the better part of three years. Sure, we've had our share of differences, but at the end of the day, she's the one I love, the one I plan to spend the rest of my life with.

"I'll talk to you later, Isaac. Maci is texting, wondering where I am," she states, her fingers tapping away on her cell phone. The one that's always in her hand.

When she takes off down the empty hall, black heels clicking on the tile floor, I finally seem to snap out of the stupor I'm in and go after her. "Wait! You can't just leave, Savannah. Everyone is waiting for us."

She stops and turns, an unaffected look on her face. "Everyone? You mean your friends? The grumpy bartender, the playboy chef, and that loser who plays guitar? Please," she scoffs, rolling her eyes. "You're too good for them. They use you, and you're too blind to see it."

I can't believe what she's saying. My friends—my *best* friends—and business partners are nothing but loyal, hardworking, and caring men. We built our business from the ground up, all contributing equally in different areas. Walker's the man behind the bar and has built quite a following amongst patrons, keeping them happy and entertained all week long. Jasper's in the kitchen, the creator of our menu and often makes the food himself, since he is a bit of a control freak regarding the grill. Jameson's talents include security at the bar, playing guitar on Friday and Saturday nights, and now, serving as manager of our brewery.

And me? I'm Numbers, the man in the office. The one who makes sure all the i's are dotted and the t's are crossed. I have a dual major in accounting and business management and have put them both to good use in these last five years since we started Burgers and Brew.

Five years of late nights, barely getting by at times, and stress beyond comprehension, but I wouldn't trade it for the world.

I wouldn't trade *them* for anything.

"I don't understand this," I start, trying to wrap my head around her words. I knew she didn't always get along with Jameson, but to call him a loser? He's anything but.

Savannah sighs dramatically and rolls her eyes once more. "Of course you don't. You'll never understand. You don't even try, because I'm not your first priority. *They* are."

With both hands in my hair now, I just stare in shock at the woman I love. How can she not see how important this is to me? "*They* are, yes, but so are you! If I'm not at work, I'm with you. Taking you out, making sure to spend time with you."

"It's not enough," she says bluntly. "I want more, Isaac! More than just spending time in your restaurant or bar. More than just a quick phone call on your way home from the office. You own this place. You shouldn't have to work every day."

"I've adjusted my hours tremendously since we started dating again. The only reason I've been gone extra nights is because we were getting the brewery ready to open," I counter, my blood boiling in my veins.

"Yeah, a brewery. What kind of business model is that anyway? Clearly Jameson pulled one over on you with that plan. This brewery is going to bleed you dry in no time. Don't come crying to me when you're flat broke and need a handout."

Shaking my head, I turn away from the only woman who has the ability to build me up and then strike me down with a single blow. "Jesus, do you hear yourself right now?"

"I do," she confirms, slipping her phone into her clutch and flipping her hair once more. "It's long overdue, Isaac. We're just too different. We want different things." Another annoying fucking hair flip. "I'm out of here. Good luck with your brewery, but don't say I didn't warn you," she sasses, walking right by me in her designer pantsuit and leaving through the only exit in the empty hallway.

I must stand there for ten minutes, recalling the entire conversation. We had been up in my office, making sure everything was set before heading over to the brewery. Well, I had been making sure. Savannah had been on her phone, sighing and tapping her foot impatiently while she waited.

That's the thing. Tonight's a huge night for us. She knew that. I've been talking about this invitation-only opening night for weeks. Ever since we began planning the event, it's been a top priority for us. Hell, Savannah helped me with some of the pertinent details. As an interior designer, I relied on her expertise to help with the setup of the rooms to make sure traffic flowed, that everyone had their set duties. Walker is in charge of the beer tasting, Jasper the appetizers we're serving, and Jameson and I are giving tours.

Now it's all screwed.

No, that's not true.

The night isn't screwed, just me.

I run my hands through my hair once and make sure I have my keys. It's a Friday night and Burgers and Brew is closed. Not because we don't trust our team to be able to handle the business while we're all next door at the brewery, but because we had to pull so many of them over to help. Some of our kitchen staff are working with Jasper to provide food, waitstaff is helping clear tables, and bartenders are helping with beer tasting.

In fact, not only is it all-hands-on-deck for staff, it's that way for family too. Mallory, Walker's wife, is working tonight as a server and Lyndee, Jasper's girlfriend, provided us with desserts from her bakery across the street and is in the kitchen with Jasper. Hell, even Lyndee's brother and Jameson's sister are here helping.

Why?

Because we're like a close-knit family, dammit.

The fact that Savannah doesn't see it, or flat-out insults it for that matter, downright pisses me off.

Before I can push through the door to head next door, I hear a small commotion behind me. "What are you doing out here?" Jasper asks after pushing through the swinging kitchen door, a large tray in his hands.

"Thinking," I reply, pressing my back against the wall so he can pass.

He doesn't, though. He stops directly in front of me and pierces me with an intense gaze. "About what? Everything's going fine."

I sigh, not wanting to get into what just happened with Savannah right now. It's no secret my friends haven't always been big fans of hers, but they've never not supported me. In fact, most of the time, they're quiet about my whole relationship with her. Well, except Jameson, who has made his feelings known on a few occasions. The difference is, he says his piece and then moves on.

I almost dread hearing what he's going to say when he finds out she fucking broke up with me.

Again.

"You're right, it is fine. Let's get those over there, shall we?" I state with a fake smile plastered on my face.

Now isn't the time.

Tonight, we celebrate.

Tomorrow, I can deal with this painful broken heart.

"What can I get you?"

The question startles me, mostly because I thought I was alone. I've been hiding at the corner of the bar, trying to keep my surly mood away from everyone here to have a good time.

For three hours, I smiled, shook hands, and showed off our new business like the gracious host I was expected to be. Now, as the open house winds down, I feel like I've been run through the wringer all night, my nerves frazzled, and my heart aching once again. It was easy to push the bullshit with Savannah out of my mind earlier, but now, it settles over me like a storm cloud about to let loose a downpour.

Slowly, I turn to find the owner of the voice. It's feminine, yet a touch husky, and smooth as silk. But it's not her alluring voice that grabs my attention, nor the long dirty blonde hair with bright pink streaks. Even in the low lighting in the corner I'm hiding in, I can see the striking contrast of colors. It's her eyes. They're a lighter shade of brown, like aged whiskey, but hold a hint of apprehension.

So familiar.

So gorgeous.

"Last time I saw you your hair was black," I mutter, wishing my gruff attitude wasn't so obvious.

She flashes me a quick grin. "Life's too short to stick with boring hair colors your entire life."

I nod, taking in her attire. She's wearing a formfitting green polo with our Crüe Brewery logo on the left breast, the dark ink of a tattoo peeking out from the sleeve and moving down her arm. She's paired it with black pants that do nothing but accentuate the curve of her hips. They're tight, but not overly so, and I can practically picture how her ass looks in them from the back view.

When I don't say anything else, she sighs and moves farther down the bar. Mentally chastising myself for my bad attitude, I'm surprised when she returns a few seconds later with a shot glass. She leans over the edge and slides the glass toward me. "You look like you could use one of these."

I can't stop my snort. "Only one?" I ask, reaching for the small glass.

She shrugs and watches me intently, studying me. It's as if she knows something's not right, which is crazy, considering we don't really know each other. Not well anyway. Sure we've seen each other a few times over the years, have even had brief conversations, but standing with her now, with those soulful brown eyes focused on me, it feels so much more intimate.

It's probably just the lighting.

And the shit-tastic night I've had.

I down the shot, hating the burn of the liquid as it goes, yet reveling in the harsh taste. Actually, it's not that bad. Definitely not something we keep available behind the bar. "What was that?" I ask, wiping my lips with the back of my hand.

She flashes a grin. “It’s a bottle of Don Julio 1942 tequila. Jameson thought it’d be good for after you were all wrapped up here. I figured it wouldn’t hurt to hand out one shot beforehand.”

I take in the bottle sitting on the bar top. The long, slim design with a wider base that looks like it costs more than I make in a night. And knowing Jameson, it probably does.

Leaning against the bar, she keeps her gaze locked on me. “There’s only three reasons a man like you looks as miserable as this on a pretty big night. Either he lost his job, his fancy car, or his girl.”

I snort, knowing her assessment is spot-on. “Well, my brand-new Maxima is in the parking lot out back, and, as you can see, my job is very well intact.”

Realization flashes through those whiskey-brown eyes, and she tsks. She leans forward, her mouth drawing dangerously close to my own as she whispers, “A Maxima, Isaac? Really?”

Okay. Not at all what I expected her to say, which makes me laugh.

“I’ll have you know, the Nissan Maxima has the highest safety rating, receiving the top safety pick for mid-sized sedans again this year.”

A single eyebrow arches upward. “Really? Talk about living on the edge. What do you do on a regular Saturday night? Help old ladies cross the street on their way to bingo?”

Sobering, I think back to what I’ve done the last several Saturday nights. “No. I work.”

Again, she tsks as she refills the shot glass. “All work and no play makes Isaac a dull boy.”

“The Shining?”

She shrugs, sliding the full glass back toward me. “Is there anyone better than Jack Nicholson? Really, I’m in no position to judge you for your work schedule, Isaac. I work six days a week myself, most nights until eleven or midnight."

I reach just to her left and retrieve a second glass before grabbing the tall bottle of expensive booze. Once it's filled, I push it in her direction, feeling her eyes watching my every move. "It's no fun drinking alone."

She's silent as she takes the glass and holds it between her fingers. For some reason, I take notice of her nails. They're trimmed short but painted the same color as what's streaked through her hair. Savannah always had long nails, expertly manicured by a salon two towns over.

With a shrug, she brings the glass closer to her full, pink lips. "I don't mind drinking alone. Less chance of someone hurting you that way."

I bring my glass up, positioning it beside hers. "But more opportunity to think," I counter, holding her gaze.

The corner of her lips tick. "Here's to not thinking."

"And to not drinking alone," I add, tapping our glasses together with a resounding clink.

Holding her gaze, I tip my head back, letting my second shot of tequila slide down my throat. She drinks the liquid like a pro, not even the slightest wince crossing her stunning features. We both set the empties down on the bar top, eyes locked the entire time.

What is it about her? Why am I suddenly so drawn? To her eyes, to that pretty pink mouth. Is it because of Savannah and our split? Is this what a rebound feels like? In all the times Savannah and I have taken a break, I've never felt this...attracted to another woman before. Especially not mere hours after the relationship ended.

Worse, this sudden attraction is aimed at someone I've never looked twice at in the past. Someone who has always been there, and frankly, probably always will be. Someone with very kissable lips and eyes I could drown in. Someone I shouldn't want, yet...do.

"BJ! Quit drinking my tequila!" Jameson hollers, grabbing his sister's attention, and just like that, essentially dowsing me with a bucket of ice-cold water.

Yeah, there isn't enough liquor in that bottle to help me forget how messed up this night has been.

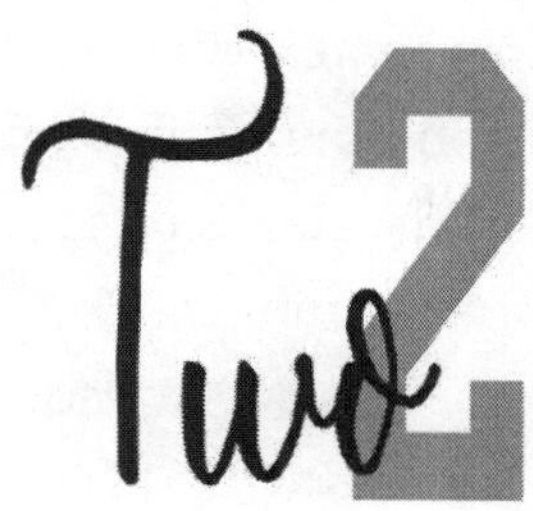

BJ

Isaac looks downright miserable, has most of the night. Even as my brother makes his way toward us, he wears his discomfort, his guilt like one of those fine suits he owns.

He flashes my brother a big smile. “Great night, wasn’t it?”

Jameson nods, though his all-knowing eyes are assessing his friend. “It was. I see you’ve started without us,” he says, eyeing the bottle and two shot glasses. Though, if I know my brother, he’s not mad about it.

“Sorry, been a long night,” Isaac replies, running his hands through his dark hair.

My eyes are drawn to his arms, to the way the shirt molds to each one and stretches tautly against his hard muscles. I wouldn’t say he’s built, not by a longshot. He’s not muscular like the meatheads that come into my tattoo shop, anxious to put a phoenix on their pec or an armband around the bulging bicep. No, Isaac is lean, but you can tell he’s fit. He works out and takes care of his body, even if he hides it behind those stuffy suits.

Tonight, it's no surprise he's dressed well. His black pants are pressed flat, his blue button-down crisp, and the black tie hidden behind a formal vest. It's probably all designer, too, costing more than my apartment rent for the month.

"Where's everyone else?" Jameson hollers, whistling for Jasper and Walker.

I turn away, anxious to put a little distance between myself and Isaac. Grabbing the rag and soapy water, I start cleaning up after tonight's party. There are glasses and small paper cups sitting everywhere, used throughout the night for beer tasting. The pilsner mugs were used after someone found a beer they liked, one of the five new beers on tap.

"What's this?" Walker asks, approaching the group with his arm thrown over his wife's shoulder.

Mallory and Walker were married last month and are expecting a baby this fall. Jameson's already head over heels in love with her daughter from a previous relationship and can't wait until the new baby arrives. My brother has always had a soft spot for kids. It comes from years of raising a sibling, thanks to absent parents.

"Here," Jameson says, sliding a shot glass over to his friends. He pours extra, handing one off to Lyndee, Jasper's girlfriend, and her brother, Dustin. He even grabs a small bottle of apple juice and throws some of that into a shot glass for Mallory.

My brother's such a good guy.

"Beej," he hollers, grabbing my attention by using the nickname only he calls me. When I turn around, he slides a drink my way too. "You're celebrating with us."

I grab my glass and try to stay out of the way. I may have helped my brother tonight, working behind the bar serving one of their new flavors of beer, but this night isn't for me. It's for him, and his three friends.

"Gather 'round," Jameson instructs, causing the group to draw in closer. By doing so, Isaac shifts behind the bar until he's standing directly beside me. Warmth ebbs from his pores, seeps through his expensive suit and wraps around me like an old, familiar blanket. Not only can I feel the heat of his body, I can smell his cologne. It's rich, but not overdone, and tickles my nose in the best possible way.

"For nearly six months, we've all worked our asses off. What started off as some hairbrained idea I had, grew into this," he says, pointing at the gorgeous warehouse where their new brewery is housed. "And it did because of you all."

"No way, man," Walker says, shaking his head in disagreement. "This beauty may have been your idea, but it happened because of *you*."

"And I couldn't have done it without my friends," Jameson replies, clearing his throat. I've known him my entire life, and I don't think I've ever seen him get this choked up before. Even that time I broke my arm when I fell off my bicycle. He carried me seven blocks to the hospital and sat with me while they set the break and cast it, watching me cry the entire time. Even then, his eyes barely watered.

He lifts his shot glass above his head and says, "To Crüe Brewery."

"To Crüe Brewery," everyone repeats before downing their shot of tequila—or apple juice, as is Mallory's case.

I lift my glass, my arm brushing against Isaac's. I'm not sure what warms me more, the alcohol invading my blood or the man standing way too close for me to be able to think straight.

I don't know what it is about Isaac that suddenly draws me to him. Clearly, he's having a rough night. By the sounds of things, he has broken it off with his girlfriend, Savannah. Again. They sound as compatible as a needle and a condom. Obviously, they don't mix.

I've always thought he was attractive. Actually, no that's not true. I always thought Walker was attractive. Isaac was always quiet, subtly watching in the background in his Dockers and fancy shirt. The guys I usually go for are more of the muscular, macho type, with a killer smile and ass. But years ago, my young girl crush on Walker passed by, leaving a friendship I can appreciate. My brother has great friends. They'd do anything for him, and by extension, anything for me.

But I was never really attracted to Isaac. Sure, I found him cute, but the suits and ties didn't really do it for me, you know? Not when I work in a tattoo parlor all night long. I've seen—and held, thanks to my piercing services—everything a girl could imagine. My type has always been a more rugged, tattooed kind of man.

Yet, I can't seem to stop from looking at my brother's friend through new eyes. He's not just cute, he's gorgeous. Sexy. Today he's clean shaven, but I can't stop from wondering what he'd look like with a few days' growth on his jaw. And more shocking, how that stubble would feel against my thighs.

Yeah, out of all my brother's friends I could develop a crush on, Isaac Thompson wasn't the one I expected.

I busy myself with clean up after the party, tossing the paper cups and stacking the glasses to go back to the dishwasher, all while trying to keep to myself. Everyone pitches in, helping to stack the rented chairs brought in for the evening and picking up trash. The entire time, the guys are sharing stories, which really turns into telling every old, embarrassing one they can remember.

When there's a break in the conversation, Mallory asks, "Hey, where's Savannah? I thought she was going to be here tonight."

I glance over just as Isaac tenses. "Oh, uh, she had plans and couldn't be here."

Everyone stops and turns. "Plans? What kind of plans? I would have thought being here was her plan," Jasper says, a bite in his tone.

Isaac sighs, rubbing his forehead. "Let's not get into it," he replies, quickly grabbing the nearest garbage can and pulling out the full bag and tying the drawstrings closed.

"Are you shitting me right now, Numbers?" my brother thunders from across the room.

Isaac doesn't turn around. "Don't start, Jameson. I'm not in the mood to deal with your bullshit too."

I close my eyes, wishing I didn't know what was coming next. But knowing my brother as well as I do, I can already see the argument on the horizon.

"My bullshit? What about Savannah's bullshit?" Jameson argues back.

"Hey, Jameson, it's all right," Walker starts, reaching over and placing a slow hand on his friend's arm.

Jameson just rips out from under the touch. "No, it's not all right. I'm fucking tired of her treating him like shit. Over and over again."

"What do you want me to do?" Isaac yells back, turning and facing my brother with anger in his eyes.

"Stay the fuck away from her. It's that simple. Realize you're too good of a person to be treated like yesterday's takeout trash," he demands, throwing his arms up in the air. Suddenly, he realizes everyone is looking at him and his anger seems to deflate like a balloon. "I'm going to smoke."

With the slam of the back door, the spat ends just as abruptly as it began. I risk a quick glance over at Isaac, who has his head down as he places a fresh garbage liner in the can. Everyone else quietly starts talking again, looking curiously over to where Isaac works and stews in anger.

He sighs, reaching down and grabbing the full bag, before slowly heading toward the back door. The same one Jameson just walked through. Meeting him halfway across the room, I hold out a hand for the bag. "Why don't I take it out for you. I'll go out and smooth things over with my brother."

Isaac closes his eyes for a moment and meets my stare. "You don't have to do that. I can handle your brother."

I flash him a smile. "I know you can, but when he's upset like this, it's best just to give him some space. I'll check on him and make sure he's not ripping apart the dumpster or dismantling the picnic table."

He holds my gaze for several long seconds before his shoulders sag. "Yeah, fine. I just...the worst part of this isn't the breakup. It's the fact I know he's right. They've been telling me for a while now, but I just keep taking her back. Every time." He clears his throat once more and averts his eyes. "Thank you for taking that out. And for checking on him."

I nod, reaching down and grabbing the bag of trash. "I'll be back."

I move to the exit my brother used and step outside. It's a brisk mid-March night, the air hitting me in the face and making my eyes sting. Spotting my brother sitting on a picnic table behind the restaurant next door, I make a quick stop at the dumpster before heading his way.

"I expected it to be Jasper who drew the short straw and had to come out here," Jameson says, inhaling deeply from the cigarette between his fingers.

"I volunteered," I confess, taking a seat across from him and reaching for the cigarette in his hand. He doesn't say a word as I take a drag, hating the way my body recognizes the nicotine and perks up, wanting more, even if the taste disgusts me now.

"I thought you gave this shit up," he mutters, flicking ash before he takes another drag.

"I did. Haven't smoked in almost five years."

He shakes his head in disbelief. "Then what the hell are you doing now?"

"Relax, Jameson. I'm not going to start smoking again just because I took one drag. Besides, you were the one who started me smoking in the first place."

His eyes narrow in that way only a big brother's can. "That's because you stole my pack of smokes."

I shrug, resting my elbows on the rough tabletop. "I was sixteen and wanted to be like my brother. Can you blame me?"

He exhales, blowing the smoke away from me as he puts the butt out in the ashtray. "No, I can't. I wasn't exactly the best role model for you."

"You were the perfect role model," I counter, both of us knowing damn well we didn't have much of a choice growing up. Not with our dad in and out of prison and our mom barely getting by, most of the time not even bothering to come home at the end of her day. My brother raised me, kept me grounded and out of trouble, even though he always seemed to have a knack for finding it himself.

He's also the one who cultivated my love of art and bought me my first tattoo gun. He sat at our kitchen table and let me draw a skull and crossbones on his arm when I was only fourteen years old. He helped me research cleaning and sterilizing practices, eventually getting me in touch with a guy he knew who ran a tattoo parlor. I've never had a bigger support person than I have in Jameson, and there's no way in hell I'm going to let him beat himself up on how we were raised.

"If it weren't for you, I probably wouldn't be this amazing woman you see before you," I state, giving him a wide smile.

Jameson laughs. "Amazing, yes. Also sarcastic and a pain in the ass."

"Some of my finest qualities," I state proudly with a chuckle. "You okay?"

"I'm fine." His answer is quick and flat, just as I expected.

"Of course you are, but fine doesn't exactly explain why you went off on Isaac that way."

My brother sighs deeply and shakes his head. "She's not good for him, Beej. She breaks his heart over and over again, and he just lets her. As his friend, I'm just tired of sitting back and watching it happen."

I meet his gaze, respecting him even more. My brother might be gruff and blunt, but he's a good friend. "I think he knows."

Jameson nods. "I should probably go in there and help them finish up. At the least, I probably owe Numbers an apology."

I shrug and squeeze his hand. "I'll go. You take a few more minutes to calm down. We don't need you coming back in there, fists blazing," I quip, knowing my brother wouldn't do that, at least not to one of his friends. He's been known to throw punches, but only when the guy really deserves it.

"Yeah." His light brown eyes meet mine. "Thanks."

"I didn't do anything."

He squeezes my hand. "You've done more than you know. You always do."

I jump up, brushing my hair over my shoulder. "I'm gonna go before you get all sappy and start crying on my shoulder."

Jameson barks out a laugh. "I don't think you have to worry about that."

Shrugging, I reply, "Probably not, but I better get back in there before they accuse me of not helping."

"If they do, you tell me. You've done just as much as everyone in there has tonight."

Bending down, I place a kiss on his scruffy cheek. "They wouldn't. Your friends are good guys."

He huffs in agreement, but doesn't say a word. "Tell them I'll be in shortly."

"Will do, big brother."

I return to the building, stealing one quick glance before I slip inside. Jameson's still seated at the picnic table, his shoulders drawn down as he lights another cigarette. My brother has many demons, ones he battles daily. Despite all of that, he's one of the good ones, and I'm not saying that because he is my brother. He's faced each one head-on and overcome them, refusing to let them win.

Inside, I jump back into the fold, helping clean up the mess from the celebration. Everyone is pleasant, almost overly so, probably trying to keep things light and happy. To not focus on the argument that happened just a short time ago. Fine by me, really. I'm not one to get in the middle of spats, especially between my brother and his friends. I haven't witnessed or been told of them happening often, but they've been friends long enough that the occasional disagreements arise.

Walker comes over and hands me an envelope, thanking me for all my hard work tonight. His wife, Jasper, Lyndee, Dustin, and a few other staff members all do the same. Eventually, my brother comes back inside and joins in, thanking all of the staff for working the open house celebration. He even takes his time to walk everyone out to their cars.

However, one person is noticeably absent at the end of the night.

Isaac.

Isaac

A knock sounds on my office door, and before I even look up, I know who it is. I've heard his boots on the stairs more times than I can count in the five plus years since we started this business together. When I look up, I find Jameson's brown eyes staring back at me.

Eyes that suddenly remind me of his sister.

"Hey," I say in way of greeting.

He lifts his chin and steps inside. "Mind if I sit for a minute."

"Of course not," I reply instantly. At the end of the day, he's still my friend, despite any disagreement we may have.

He sits down in one of the worn, wooden chairs and runs his hands through his hair. It's a lot longer on top than normal, a sign he's probably missed a haircut or two. Not surprising, considering how busy we've been these last few weeks. "Sorry about earlier."

I can't help but smile. Jameson is always direct and to the point. "Don't worry about it." Clearing my throat, I continue, "You're right anyway."

He just stares at me with an intensity I'm not sure I'll ever really get used to. When we first met in college, I was a bit intimidated by him. He was bigger and scarier than anyone I had ever associated with, in his combat boots, take no shit attitude, and tattoo-covered arms. Even now, he has a way of unnerving me. I'm not intimidated by him, per se, but he does make me squirm a little with his intensity.

"Maybe," he says, shrugging his shoulders, "but I shouldn't have said anything tonight."

I snort out a laugh. "Since when have you ever bit your tongue?" I ask, a grin flashing across my lips.

Jameson snorts in agreement. "Never."

"And I wouldn't expect you to bite it now. Listen, Jameson, we may not always agree, and I probably won't always like what you have to say about things, but I'd never want you to hold back to save my feelings. We've been through too much over the years for that."

"We have."

The heaviness I've felt lifts a little, and I quickly realize it wasn't because of what happened before the party with Savannah. It's because of the argument with Jameson and the fact I know he's right. He usually is, though I'd never tell him that. He has this way of looking at the world, from the outside in, without rose-colored glasses.

And I have always been accused of not seeing the real world around me.

"Why are you up here? This shit can wait until tomorrow," my friend demands, looking down at the rental contracts I was reviewing.

"Just double-checking everything before tomorrow. The rental company will be here at ten to pick up the tables and chairs."

Jameson stands, stretching his long arms above his head. "Go home, Numbers. It'll all be here waiting on us in the morning."

I nod, knowing he's right. The problem is, I don't really want to go home either. Not that Savannah has a lot of stuff at my house, but it's there. Her shampoo and conditioner, fancy bodywash she buys from New York, and some clothes. I was expecting her to come home with me after tonight's event too and went as far as to put a full box of condoms and some candles on the nightstand. It's been weeks since we've been intimate, her work schedule struggling to line up with mine, and now the thought of going home alone is a little depressing.

"See you in the morning?" Jameson asks, watching as I slip both my laptop and the stack of contracts in my bag with a snort. Clearly he knows I'll be just moving this operation to my house.

"I'll be here," I state, flipping off the light and locking my office. "Everyone else head home?" I ask as we descend the stairs.

"Yep. I was on my way out too when I saw your car still here. I knew there was only one place you could be."

Yeah, he knows me well.

Hell, they all do.

We've been through a lot together these last eleven years.

"Later, man," Jameson hollers, shoving his hands in his pockets and strolling to where his vintage Harley Davidson is parked. He fires it up, the heavy roar of the engine rumbling through the quiet, and takes off out of the parking lot.

Once I'm settled in my Maxima, I do the same, but driving in the opposite direction toward my condo. I live in a great little subdivision with white picket fenced houses and swing sets in the yards. Everyone has welcome mats on their porch and waves when you drive by.

But that's the story of Stewart Grove, really. It's a great little town of about eight thousand, where everyone knows your story. I wasn't from here, but they accepted me quickly when I relocated to join my friends in opening our business.

It's a much different pace than I had become accustomed to. Sure, my job keeps me busy, but when you work finance in Columbus, Ohio, it's an entirely different ball game. The corporate world was eating me alive, working me like a dog seventy hours a week, because I was the young guy in the office. Their idea to start our own restaurant and bar came at the perfect time, one that changed the course of my life forever.

It was the easiest decision I ever made.

As I approach the intersection of Main and Oak Street, movement registers out of the corner of my eye. I turn and find a disabled truck with the hood up, an older Ford with big tires and probably a loud exhaust. A total teenager truck, if you know what I mean.

When the person jumps down from the bumper, I'm surprised to see a woman. Not just any woman, but BJ. I'd know her anywhere.

I turn left at the light and pull up behind her truck, keeping my engine running as I hop out of my car. She looks back the moment she sees headlights, her body relaxing the moment she spots me. "Oh. Hey."

"Hi," I reply, shoving my hands in my pockets as I approach. "What seems to be the trouble?"

She throws her hands up in the air, strips of blonde and pink hair falling from the elastic band holding it back. "It's overheating," she says, climbing back up on the front bumper and working on something under the hood. "Blew a hose and now it's out of coolant."

"Sounds like you need a mechanic," I reply, trying not to look at the way her pants mold to her ass as she bends over the front end.

"A mechanic?" she snorts, rolling her eyes. "I don't need a mechanic. I can fix this."

"You?" The question comes out before I can stop it, and I know I've said the wrong thing the moment her gaze locks on mine.

"Yes, me. I'll have you know I've done most of the mechanical work on this baby, including the metal restoration. Rust from the shitty salt roads had chewed her up pretty good, but I was able to get it back into shape," she says, wiping her hands on a shop towel lying on the fender. She reaches up, unlatches the hood, and drops it back into place. "I can fix her, but not right now. I'll need a new hose and clamp, which I can't get until the auto store opens up in the morning."

I'm impressed with her automotive knowledge, but honestly, I shouldn't be. Jameson still loves to tinker with vehicles, even though he hasn't worked in a shop since we started our business. "What can I do to help?" I ask, knowing I can't offer much.

"I was just about to call Jameson to give me a ride home."

"I can do it."

She gives me a look, as if accepting help doesn't come easy to her. "I don't mind calling him."

"I'm sure you don't, and I'd be willing to bet he'd drop anything and everything to come help you, but I'm already here. Doesn't make much sense to call him when I'm perfectly capable of giving you a ride home."

BJ sighs and tosses the used towel into the cab of the truck. "Let me get my stuff," she says, stepping up on the running board and grabbing her keys from the ignition and a duffel bag from the passenger seat. She shuts the door, making sure it's locked, and says, "All right, let's go."

I walk her to the passenger door, reaching down to pull it open. She gives me a look, but doesn't call me out on my chivalry, and slides into the seat, holding her bag on her lap. "I can put that in the trunk," I say, reaching for the old, worn duffel.

BJ shrugs and doesn't hand over the bag. "It's okay. I don't mind holding it a few blocks."

"Actually, I need to put it in there. The open bottle of tequila your brother gave you is against the law to transport in Ohio," I state, grabbing her bag and ignoring her chuckle as I take it to the trunk of my car.

Once it's safely tucked inside, I return to the driver's side, glad I kept the car running. Not that it's super cold out for mid-March, but there's definitely a chill in the air. "Where to?" I ask, using my turn signal before pulling back out onto the road.

BJ catches it and snorts under her breath. "Up at the next light, turn left. I'm all the way at the end of Lincoln."

I do as instructed, noting it's way more than a few blocks to her house. When I finally get there, I'm a little surprised to find the cute little bungalow at the end of the road. "This place is nice," I state, putting the car in park.

"Thanks. I've been here about three years now," she replies, smiling as she looks up at the small porch with the wooden swing. She looks over, the moonlight filtering through the window giving her an angelic glow. "Wanna come inside for a drink? As a thank-you for driving me home?"

Yes.

"I probably shouldn't. It's been a long night," I end up replying, even though I'm interested.

She huffs out a deep breath. "You sure? That expensive tequila is calling my name. I'd be happy to share it. Besides, good tequila's way better than going home alone, right, and I think if anyone needs a drink, it's you."

The way she says alone makes me pause. It wasn't an insult, but she's clearly referring to my breakup tonight. She was not-so-subtly reminding me I have nothing waiting for me there. At least here, I have strong liquor to drown my sorrows in. "I suppose one drink wouldn't hurt. I do have to drive home, though."

She smiles perfectly white, straight teeth, and the gesture is like a kick to the solar plexus. How did I not notice how pretty she is before tonight? "Of course you do," she replies, pushing open the passenger door and jumping out, heading to the back of my car to retrieve her belongings.

I do the same, locking my car after grabbing her bag, as I meet her at the base of the steps and follow up to the front door. The inside of her house is exactly as I'd pictured it. Well, as best as I could picture it in the few minutes I've been here. Eclectic and fun. Splashes of color everywhere, unlike my own home with its bare, white walls. She has bright throw pillows and sunshine yellow walls. Hell, she has a purple chair.

A purple chair!

"Make yourself at home," she says, tossing her bag onto the couch. "I'm gonna run and change my clothes. No offense to this fancy polo or the business I was representing, but it's way too professional for my liking." She chuckles, heading down the small hallway and closing the door to the room at the end.

I can't help but glance down at my pressed button-down and black vest. She thinks her polo is too formal? What must she think of me?

Not that it matters what she thinks of me. She's just being nice, considering I was dumped mere minutes before one of the biggest nights of my professional life. Throw in the fact I gave her a ride home and she's just showing me her appreciation.

A grouping of three drawings catches my attention. They're positioned above the couch, each one hand drawn. It's a couple embracing and sharing a kiss as the sun drops below the horizon. The first one, they're just staring into each other's eyes, the sun just starting its descent. Even for a drawing, their intent and desire are evident. The second one is the first brush of their lips, the sun now barely visible behind the tree line. And the third drawing is the kiss. It's powerful, consuming, intoxicating. You can feel the emotion pouring from the paper, see it in the way they grip onto each other, holding on tight.

"These are beautiful," I state when I realize I'm not alone. I can feel her presence.

"Thank you."

I turn and almost swallow my tongue. BJ is definitely more comfortable now, her hair pulled up high on her head and wearing a loose-fitting crop top that hangs off her bare shoulder and a pair of black shorts that should probably be considered illegal in the state of Ohio. I can picture her wearing it to bed, and that image takes my mind right over the line I had been straddling between appropriate and inappropriate.

Now, my thoughts have landed me directly into the latter category, ones that would get my ass beat if my friend—her brother—knew about.

I return my gaze to the drawings, careful not to let it stray back to the stunning woman as she walks up beside me. "You drew them?"

She smiles. I catch it out of the corner of my eye. “I did. Right after I moved in here. I wanted something original to go on this wall, and when I sat down to draw, this first drawing was the result. The next night, I did the same, followed by a third. The fourth, well, I don’t have that drawing out here.”

A lump forms in my throat as I risk a look her way. “There’s a fourth in this series?”

She nods and meets my gaze. “It’s over my bed.”

I don’t reply. No, I can’t reply. Words fail me as blood rushes south of the border and pools in my groin. I really want to see that damn drawing, but I know I shouldn’t.

I can’t.

“Ready for that drink?” she asks, the faintest grin playing on the corner of her lips.

“Hell yes,” I reply through a dry throat.

She grabs the bottle of tequila out of her bag and heads for the kitchen. I lean against the counter, mesmerized by the way she moves. She’s so graceful, but not like a dancer. Like she’s comfortable in her skin.

And speaking of skin, there’s a lot of it on display. Yet, I don’t feel like she did it on purpose. I don’t feel like she’s slowly seducing me, even though my thoughts are headed in that direction. No, she’s relaxed, content in her space. As if she’s wearing what makes her happy in the presence of a friend.

A friend.

That’s what I am. Even though I might not necessarily be her friend, in a way, I am by extension. She’s Jameson’s sister, and it’d be best if I remember that.

Anything else, and I could be in serious trouble.

BJ

I can feel his eyes on me as I pour two shot glasses of the smooth liquid and try to ignore the way my body heats with anticipation and desire. Clearing my throat, I hold his glass up, extending it toward him. When his fingers brush mine, a bolt of lust shoots through my veins like lightning, and it takes everything I have not to groan.

Trying to clear my head, I hold the shot up. "To friendship."

Friends. You know, what Isaac and I are?

He flashes me an uneasy smile. "To friendship," he repeats, adding, "and to getting over breakups."

We each take the shot, the subtle burn of the alcohol sliding down my throat is a reminder not to get too comfortable here. As I set the glass back on the counter, I ask, "Do you want to talk about it?"

"Hell no," he says, licking his lips and carefully placing the glass in front of him. His eyes study me. He looks at my hair, my lips, my bare shoulder. He seems to be very focused on watching me, his eyes slowly dilating. Isaac clears his throat, looks away quickly, and reaches for the bottle. "Another?"

"Sure," I reply, watching the slight tremble of his hand as he pours the alcohol. I'm usually a pretty good judge of character—well, everyone except the guys I date—and there's no mistaking the desire I see reflecting in those hazel orbs.

This was a bad idea. I definitely shouldn't have invited him inside, but I felt like he didn't really want to be alone right now. The guy just went through a breakup only hours ago, and if I'm being honest with myself, I wasn't really that excited about coming inside alone either.

Maybe I should get a dog?

But that's not the answer either. Not when I work long, very late hours at the shop.

This time, when we hold up the shot, we don't toast. We clink glasses and down the liquid. This shot lacks the burn as it slides down my throat, already mixing with the previous one and starting to heat my gut. I place the empty glass on the counter and lick the moisture off my lips. Isaac watches my every move, his focus locked on my tongue, no doubt not missing the glint of metal there.

When he rips his gaze off my mouth, he closes his eyes. The way his lips barely move, it's like he's speaking to himself or counting. A part of me really wants to know what he's thinking right now. Yet, I can't find the will to ask. What if he's thinking about her? Not that I should care, I mean they did just break up, and according to him, he was in love with her.

Still is.

You don't just fall out of love with someone moments after you break up.

Isaac sets his glass down beside mine, and in a surprising twist, reaches for my arm. He carefully shifts it so my partial sleeve is in full view, and I'd be lying if I said I wasn't affected by his touch.

He just stares at the ink on my arm, gingerly pushing the sleeve of my shirt up and exposing more of the dark lines and brightly colored tattoo. "You're very talented," he says, tracing the outline of the large lily in the center of the design.

"Thank you," I whisper, trying to ignore the fire dancing across my skin.

Time stands still as he examines as much of the tattoo as he can. Well, without removing my shirt to see how it continues across my shoulder blade. When he finally meets my gaze, I realize how dangerously close we've become. I can feel the warmth of his body being so near, and it starts to mess with my head.

It makes me want...*things*.

Things I've never wanted before, at least not from one of my brother's friends.

My breathing hitches as he, almost absently, glides his finger down my forearm like a caress. His eyes dart to my open lips, and I swear I know what he's thinking. I can see it swirling in the depths of those hazel eyes, feel it in the way he touches me.

Isaac lowers his head, his lips hesitantly hovering over my own. His warm breath tickles my skin as I close my eyes, waiting. When he doesn't initiate the kiss, I make the move, lifting my chin ever so slightly and brushing my mouth against his. Electricity sores through my veins like a current, alive and reckless. It's so unexpected, so breathtaking, I want more.

Need more.

Unfortunately, though, like a bucket of ice-cold water being thrown on my head, I realize he's not kissing me back. No, Isaac is standing statue-still, his lips unmoving even the slightest.

I shouldn't be doing this.

Not with Isaac.

He's my brother's friend.

I rip my lips back, wishing the floor would open up and swallow me whole. Is it too much to ask for a magician to suddenly make me disappear? Or, if I keep my eyes closed, maybe he'll leave and we can forget this entire thing happened?

I'm not one to embarrass easily. I take what I want, and sometimes that includes men. Single, eligible men, mind you, but I'm not some shy, wilting flower who stands back and doesn't make her intentions known.

I don't think I've ever read a situation as wrong as I have right now, thinking a guy wants you, but really doesn't. I think that's the worst part. Yes, kissing one of my brother's best friends is bad, but thinking it was a warranted kiss is a whole new level. Confusing what I thought was desire in his eyes with what it probably really was is mortifying.

Sadness.

Anger.

Everything else that goes along with breaking up with someone you love.

God, I'm the stupidest woman in the world.

"I'm so—" I start but am cut off abruptly.

By. His. Lips.

Hard, demanding lips that slam against my own with force, knocking our teeth together slightly. Big hands gently grab the sides of my head as he tilts my face to the side and coaxes my mouth open with his tongue. Desire slams into me with the force of a thousand semis, and all I can do is grip the sides of his vest and hang on for dear life.

A loud groan fills the room as his tongue delves deep into my mouth, sliding along my tongue piercing, and causing wetness to flood my shorts. This kiss is carnal, erotic, powerful. It consumes me like a wildfire, destroying everything in its path.

Destroying *me.*

Isaac uses his body to move me, pressing me against the counter. I can feel his very hard cock against the very spot I need him most, the dull ache growing into an intense craving. He releases my head only to reach my sides and lift, setting me on top of the counter. My legs instantly wrap around his waist, my body rocking against his, creating glorious friction.

When he finally rips his lips from my own, he drops them to my neck, licking and sucking on my overly sensitive skin. My head falls back as a groan of pleasure flies from my mouth. His lips continue to move, skimming across my shoulder, his tongue blazing a trail of need with every swirl it makes.

He pulls down my shirt, the wide neckline making it super easy to gain access to my body. Specifically, my chest. His eyes are wide as he shifts the top forward farther, completely exposing one breast. He meets my gaze, licks his lips and descends, covering my hard little nipple, sucking it deeply into the hot, wet recesses of his mouth.

The groan that fills my kitchen sounds foreign, even to my own ears. The sensations slamming into me have me closing my eyes, my head falling back against the upper cabinets, as I thrust my chest forward, seeking more.

A big hand slides up my side and cups my other breast, gently pinching my nipple as he licks the other. Suddenly, he pauses, and I realize why. Isaac meets my gaze, a hot, yet questioning look in his eyes. Slowly, he lifts my shirt, pushing it up and over my head and tossing it on the floor. I sit on the counter, my boobs on full display, as he stares at my nipple piercing.

"Jesus Christ," he mutters, scrubbing his hand over his face and locking his sights back on the silver hoop. "I want to suck on that piercing more than I want my next breath."

Oxygen swooshes from my lungs and my thighs clench as best they can, considering they're still wrapped around him. "Yes, please. That's what it's for. They heighten the sensitivity and pleasure."

"Fuck," he grumbles, licking his lips before moving to my other side. He hesitates, but only for a second before swiping his tongue over the silver hoop. The best feeling sweeps in as he continues to lick and gently suck on the piercing, reaching over and pinching the unpierced one he had in his mouth a minute ago.

My fingers slide through his hair, gripping and pulling on the silky strands. I can feel my body tightening, the orgasm starting to build. "You're going to make me come."

He groans.

And uses his teeth.

"You can orgasm from this?" he whispers, nipping at the tip.

I close my eyes, letting the pleasure course through me. "Yes. God, that feels so good," I moan, rocking my pelvis and rubbing along his cock.

Isaac seems to double down on his efforts, sucking the hoop deep into his hot mouth and swirling his tongue around my nipple. I cry out, pulling on his hair and practically pressing his face into my chest. He moves his own hips, pushing his erection into the apex of my legs. One more bite down on my nipple floods my body with pleasure and pushes me over the edge. I come hard—harder than I ever remember—and ride the waves of euphoria while gyrating against his cock.

"That was so fucking beautiful," he whispers, continuing to lightly lick my very hard nipple.

I open my eyes and find his still flowing with desire. Throwing my arms around his shoulder, I lick the shell of his ear and whisper, "If you think that's sexy, you should see me come while I'm riding your cock."

Subtle has never been my strong suit.

Why start now?

His mouth is urgent as he takes my lips in another bruising kiss. Warmth continues to flood my pussy as he grinds against me. His hand moves to where I ache, his big fingers easily slipping inside my shorts. "You're not wearing panties either?" he asks, his voice almost sounding pained.

"I never do. In fact, I don't think I own a single pair anymore," I state, clenching down on the first finger he pushes inside of me.

He groans. "You mean every time I've seen you, you haven't been wearing underwear?"

I nip at his earlobe. "Every single time, Isaac. In fact, tonight was the first time I've worn a bra in weeks. Perks of having tiny boobs."

"Fuck that. Your breasts are perfect," he insists, bending down and licking the piercing once more. He presses a second finger into my body and twists his wrist, his palm grazing across my clit. "I think I found another piercing."

A wide smile spreads across my face. "Like my nipple, it really loves getting some tongue attention."

He closes his eyes, his control clearly slipping quickly. "Fuck, you're going to kill me," he whispers, almost absently, like he didn't mean to say it aloud.

I dig my teeth into his clean-shaven jaw. "But what a way to go."

He pushes my shorts aside and lowers his mouth. The first flick of his hot, wet tongue across the curved bar has me rocking my hips. "Tell me about this piece," he says, the vibrations of the words rocking through my core.

"It's called a VCH piercing, or vertical clitoral hood. It's through the hood above my clit, not the actual clit itself," I reply, gasping as he toys with the bar with his tongue.

"And it stimulates you during sexual activity?" he asks, lightly sucking on the bottom jewel.

I groan loudly and fist his hair in my hand once more. "Fuck, yes."

After only a few minutes of licking my clit, he stands up and places his hands on the counter beside my hips. His gaze is dark, slightly hooded, and speaks volumes about how badly he wants to fuck me.

Reaching up, I place my hands flat on his chest before slowly moving them down the vest, carefully releasing the buttons. "You're wearing too much clothing."

The hesitation I witnessed earlier is gone. All I see now is desire and intent, and it makes me even wetter.

Once I have the vest open, he starts to release the smaller ones on his blue button-down. His eyes fall to my askew shorts, and he abandons the removal of his own clothes to relieve me of mine. "Lift," he demands, grabbing the hem and sliding them down my legs. After tossing them on the floor, his eyes drop down to where I glisten with moisture for him. Isaac lifts my legs, spreading them wide on the counter, my ass automatically scooting back, my palm pressed against the countertop to make myself a little more comfortable.

I can't get over the way he watches me. I'm sure he's taking everything in. My tattoos I hide behind my clothes, the piercings he's already explored with his mouth, and my general nakedness on full display.

He continues releasing the small buttons on his shirt, his voice low and husky as he instructs, "Play with yourself."

Fire spreads through my veins at his demand, mostly because it feels so out of character for this man. I've always considered Isaac the safe, conservative friend. The one who only has sex in the missionary position on certain days of the week.

But the actual man before me is a stark contradiction to the version I had in my head.

This one is bolder, sexier, dirtier than I ever expected, and I can't wait for more.

I reach between my legs and glide my fingers across my jewelry. A bolt of desire races through me as I keep my eyes locked on him. He's watching me, slowly unfastening the rest of the buttons, and licking his lips, as if recalling the exact taste of me.

When his shirt falls open, I'm a little surprise at what I see. Behind the stuffy dress clothes is a lean frame. Isaac isn't as broad and muscular as the others, but his body is still a work of art. Hard pecs and abs that make my mouth water. If it weren't for my hands already being a little occupied, I'd have them on his chest in an instant.

He releases the smaller buttons at his wrists before dropping down to his belt. It takes all the strength I possess not to tell him to hurry up, but the sight of Isaac undressing is something I don't want to miss.

When he has his trousers open, he grabs his wallet and pulls out a condom, tossing it on the counter beside me. Then, he pushes his pants and boxers down, his very hard, long dick bobbing free for the first time. My mouth waters and my hands itch to wrap around that smooth, steely shaft.

The moment he kicks off his shoes, pants, and boxers, his gaze finally meets mine. I can see the question in his eyes. He's wanting to make sure I want to do this. Oh, hell yes, I want to do this. I need him to fuck me more than I need food or water, more than I need air. I need him so badly, I may never remember what it was like before this moment.

To answer his unspoken question, I reach for the condom and rip the package open with my teeth. I set one leg down so I can reach his cock and carefully position the protection over the head. Meeting his gaze, I slide it into place, palming his hardness as I go, and watch as his eyes practically glaze over.

The moment it's set, he grabs my legs and places them on top of his shoulders. His cock sits heavy against my piercing as he reaches down and slides it over the metal. Another zap of electricity rocks through my body as I lean back and watch. It's erotic, seeing him slide through my folds before gently pressing the tip into my body.

"Ready?" he asks, the smallest beads of sweat already forming on his brow. He looks like he's barely in control at the moment.

A smile spreads across my lips.

Time for Isaac Thompson to lose that precious control.

"Oh, I'm ready. Fuck me, Numbers."

Isaac

Fuck me, Numbers.

I may never get the sound of those words coming from her lips out of my head. Hell, I pray I never do, but as I slowly push inside, I quickly realize it's not just her words I'll never forget.

It's this.

Jesus, I've never felt anything so amazing in my life.

When I'm halfway in, I lift her hips, changing up the position and allowing myself to push all the way inside. "Oh my God," she groans when I stop moving, completely filling her tight pussy.

I pull back and thrust forward, hard. I continue pistoning my hips, setting a fast, rough pace. Over and over, I pump, slamming my hips into her thighs. I'm not really sure what has come over me, but I like it. And by the glassy, euphoric look in her eyes, I'd say she does too.

"Touch yourself again," I instruct, mesmerized as she reaches between her legs and flicks her finger across her clit.

Her moans of pleasure fill the space, as does the sound of my body slapping against hers. She starts to work herself over harder, faster, and I find my body completely taking over and following suit. She angles and lies back completely, her head awkwardly positioned against the backsplash. I open my mouth to ask if she wants to change positions, but she stops me with a demanding, “Don’t stop.”

So I don’t.

Hell, I couldn’t if I wanted to. I’m too close to the edge, chasing the release looming in the shadows. It’s right there, just within my grasp.

BJ places her other hand on her breast and squeezes the pierced nipple. I can feel her internal muscles squeeze my cock, which causes me to groan and my spine to tingle. My release is coming hard and fast, and all I can hope is I take her over the edge with me.

“Fuck, fuck, fuck,” she chants as I rocket forward, my grip on her hips tightens as I move. “Yes, right there!” she yells, her hands frantically rubbing her most sensitive places. She tightens around me, her orgasm squeezing me so hard, it’s difficult to move.

My own release is triggered immediately, my body bucking against her, as I come with an intensity I’ve never felt before. It’s almost impossible to breathe, let alone think. All I can do is feel as my orgasm barrels through me, and I let go completely.

I fall forward, my forehead resting between her breasts. BJ’s heart pounds ferociously in her chest, no doubt matching my own beat. She reaches up and slides her delicate fingers into my hair, something I’ve noticed she does a lot. At least this time she’s not pulling it. Not that I minded.

Not really.

When I open my eyes, I’m staring straight at that nipple piercing. My tongue darts out and licks over the hard, swollen bud, and the result causes her body to squeeze mine once more. My cock responds, jumping with anticipation. "I think…I think I'm a fan of your piercings," I whisper, mesmerized by that little piece of metal through her rosebud nipple.

BJ wiggles, digging her nails into my scalp. "If you think those are nice, wait until you see what the one in my tongue does to your cock."

I wake with a start, my body draped in warmth. When I open my eyes, nothing immediately looks familiar except the sunshine spilling through the cracks in the curtains. The warmth against my side moves, making me realize it's skin.

Hot, soft skin.

BJ.

Memories of last night flood my mind. Everything from her showing me the fourth, more erotic image she drew, to the discovery of her piercings, sex on the counter, and the trip to her bed, which resulted in her swallowing my dick just to show me how amazing that metal in her tongue really felt. Yeah, it felt as spectacular as she insinuated as I came down her throat with my hands gripping her hair so tightly, I thought I'd pull it from her scalp.

Even then, we weren't done. I played with her hood jewelry until she came a third time on my fingers. Finally, she proved exactly how gorgeous she looks while riding my cock. How I can even move today is beyond me.

But as I let the pictures of last night—and very early this morning—play through my mind, a wave of guilt crashes down, snuffing out any joy I once experienced.

Jesus, I slept with one of my best friends' sister.

Shame doesn't even describe what I feel right now.

I close my eyes, ignoring how good her body feels against mine, as well as my eager, hard cock, which is clearly ready to play once more. Instead, I focus on the fact I'm in BJ's bed, when I should be anywhere else. Like at home. I should be home, in my own bed—alone. Not cuddled up to an incredibly sexy, desirable woman who seemed to turn my world upside down in a few hours' time.

She shifts against my side, her arm draped over my chest and her palm resting against my pec. I'm very much aware of how naked she is, her leg thrown over my own. I can feel the heat of her bare pussy pressed against my thigh, and it gives me ideas.

Ideas I have no business thinking about.

Not now.

Not ever again.

I have to get out of this bed, put a little distance between us, before I ignore that little angel perched on my shoulder. He's the reminder of who this woman is, or more importantly, who she's related to.

Plus, there's the fact I just got out of a relationship mere hours before I fell into bed with another woman. In all the years, after all the breakups, I've never rebounded by sleeping with someone else. No, usually I'd go home and sulk, trying to figure out how it went wrong that particular time.

Hell, I haven't even slept with a woman I wasn't in a relationship with. Never. In high school, there was only one woman I had dated most of our senior year, and in college, there were two more over the course of four years. Then Savannah. Off and on, we've dated for the last few years.

We met not too long after Burgers and Brew opened. She was sitting in the dining room with a client, pitching them her ideas for their kitchen and dining room redesign. I was walking through the room when she dropped her folder on the floor. When I stopped and picked it up, she gave me the biggest, most grateful smile, and end up slipping me her phone number.

She's the only woman I've ever wanted. No, she isn't the only woman I've loved, but is the one I saw myself spending the rest of my life with.

Now, I'm naked in a stranger's bed the morning after we broke up.

What kind of man does that make me?

I scrub my hand over my face and know I have to get out of here. Even if my dick is strongly protesting that thought.

Carefully, I pull my arm, trying to extract it from beneath her body. Of course, as soon as I start to move, BJ wakes up. Those whiskey brown eyes lock on mine, making my heart lurch in my chest. The feeling is both startling and settling.

"Morning," she says through a yawn, as she lifts her arms over her head and stretches. The action does two things: It presses her body harder against my own and it tugs the sheet down and exposes her nipples.

My cock jumps in appreciation.

"Hi," I reply, holding completely still and trying not to think about how soft her skin feels against mine.

"So," BJ starts, yet not finishing her sentence.

"So…" I parrot, unsure what to say.

What *do* you say to the woman you barely know, yet spent the entire night memorizing the curves of her body and making her come so hard she saw stars?

It's in that moment I see her brother.

No, not lying beside me, naked, but I see his angry face, the disappointment in his eyes when he realizes I slept with his sister.

Dammit, I royally messed this up.

"I, uh, should go."

BJ doesn't reveal any emotions on her face, doesn't say a word. She just stares at me with those intoxicating eyes, the very ones that I've learned are usually so expressive, so vibrant.

"This thing…what happened last night…it, uh, shouldn't have happened."

I feel like the world's biggest asshole. I'm lying right beside her, my dick so hard it could cut glass, and I'm telling her our time together was a mistake. No, it doesn't feel like one, but it shouldn't have happened in the first place.

"Right," she confirms, grabbing the sheet and covering her chest. "It was probably just the alcohol."

It wasn't.

"Yeah," I reply, nodding. I sit up myself, making sure the blanket is also covering my groin, and glance around for my pants, only to realize they're probably in the same spot I took them off. "Definitely, the alcohol," I add, absently and unnecessarily.

When I glance back over at her, she looks so unaffected, so casual. Like this is nothing new to her, which, perhaps it isn't. I don't really know BJ, not like that anyway. She could be the type that partakes in casual hookups all the time. Jameson hasn't mentioned a boyfriend in a long time—hell, if ever. There might have been a guy he didn't like a few years ago, but I don't remember any other details.

Now, I feel like the world's biggest heel because, as much as I've enjoyed my time with BJ, it needs to end.

Stat.

"I'll let you gather your things," she replies, her tone completely aloof once more, as she slips from the bed and walks naked to the en suite bathroom. My eyes fall to her body, to the gorgeous ink on her back and the subtle sway of her narrow hips.

God, she's fucking sexy.

I scrub my hands over my face and look away as she closes the door, the click of the lock as loud as a gunshot through the room. Plopping down on her bed, I lower my head and close my eyes. The worst case of remorse nips at my chest, making it hard to breathe. I shouldn't have done this.

I shouldn't have been this weak.

Yet, here I am.

The weakest man alive.

I have to be, right? I keep taking Savannah back, even though, deep down, I know it'll end the same way. Over and over again. So I run into the arms of another woman, only to have that woman be one of my best friends' little sister.

And not just any friend, either.

Jameson.

The man who could probably kill me, dispose of the body, and then help everyone look for me like he didn't have a hand in my demise.

Ignoring the condom wrappers on the nightstand, I get up and swallow the lump in my throat. Then, I set out to find my clothes.

They're still in the kitchen where I discarded them, and after a few minutes of dressing, I head for the front door.

Except, I don't want to go.

Not really.

The problem is, I know it's for the best. No way would anything between BJ and me work. Even if the sex was off the damn charts.

That's all this was.

Sex.

Clearly she thought so too. She seemed completely unaffected and couldn't get away from me quick enough, couldn't wash me off her skin any faster.

I stop and listen, the sound of the shower running the confirmation I need. Our time is most definitely over, and in no way will be repeated again. This was a mistake, that's for sure.

One I'd best forget about.

Even if it was the most amazing mistake I've ever made.

After making it home, I run through the shower myself. I can still smell her on my skin, taste her on my lips. She's like a drug I crave. One I can't seem to stop wanting, even though it's not what's best for me.

Once I'm dressed in a pair of tan trousers and a dark green button-down, I head to the kitchen to make a pot of coffee. My head is heavy, but I'm certain it has nothing to do with the alcohol. I didn't drink enough of it to cause a hangover. Unless you consider BJ the hangover. We didn't exactly get a lot of sleep last night, if you know what I mean.

I growl in frustration, pouring rich, black coffee into a travel mug. As I take my first sip, I realize I sort of left her isolated. Her truck is broken down. "Jesus, you asshole," I mumble to myself, reaching for my phone.

I can't call BJ. I don't have her number.

I can't exactly call Jameson, because then he's going to wonder how I knew about her truck. I suppose I could always say I gave her a ride home, and that's it. No details are needed. Not that I'd give them to him anyway, but you get my drift.

Decision made, I click on Jameson's name and bring the phone to my ear. It rings three times before he answers. "Hey."

Trying to sound way more casual than I feel, I reply, "Hey, man. How's it going?"

He sighs. "Just helping my sister out. Her truck broke down last night, and I had to run and get her a new hose to connect the radiator to the water pump."

Relief washes through me, knowing she's getting help with her truck. "That sucks."

"Yeah," he continues, "she's fixin' it now. I guess she had to walk home last night. It was only a handful of blocks, but still. I hate knowing my sister was broken down and had to walk home."

I swallow over the sudden lump in my throat. So she didn't tell him I drove her home. That hurts way more than I expected it to. "That sucks. Do you need my help?" I offer, and I really have no clue why. I know as much about cars as I do about military strategies pertaining to war.

Zero.

"Naw, it's all good, man. She's almost got 'er fixed up. Won't let me help, stubborn woman," he replies, the hint of humor in his voice evident.

"I can fix my own truck," BJ declares in the background. A moment later, I hear the heavy sound of a truck hood shutting. "Done."

"Fire it up so we can make sure," Jameson says absently. The moment the big beast is running he says, "Watch it for a few days to make sure it doesn't overheat again."

"Yeah, yeah, yeah. Thanks for grabbing the hose," she says, her voice much closer than it was a few moments ago.

"Next time don't walk home. Call me."

She replies, but I don't hear what she says. Instead, I hear a door shut and the truck take off, leaving me with only Jameson on the other end of the line.

"Sorry 'bout that. She's good to go now."

"I'm glad," I state honestly. Relief washes through me, a combination of knowing her truck is back up and running and the fact she didn't tell her brother about us spending the night together. No way would he be this pleasant to me if he knew all the places on her body I had my tongue. "You working today?"

Jameson clears his throat, the door of his car shutting in the background. "Yeah. Gonna run home and shower, since I didn't get one before Beej called me."

"I'm headed in too. The rental company will be there soon to get their stuff. I'll grab coffee at the deli since Sugar Rush isn't open," I say, referring to Lyndee's bakery across the street. Sundays are the worst day of the week, since I'm unable to get my caffeine craving handled at her place. It's the best.

"Sounds good. Grab some of those bear claw things too."

Again, they're not nearly as good as Lyndee's treats, but they'll do in a pinch. I can't help but smile. Jameson has the biggest sweet tooth of anyone I know. "You got it."

"Later," he replies before signing off.

I set my phone down, both reassured and disappointed. On one hand, I'm grateful BJ didn't say anything to her brother, yet I still can't help but feel a little disheartened that it was easy for her to forget about our night together. How quickly she was able to move on.

Because if I know anything, it's that I'll never forget it.

The feel of her skin against mine is branded in my mind like a tattoo.

No, I'll never disregard our time together.

Even if I wanted to, it's impossible.

I'll carry her memory with me forever.

BJ

I'm exhausted.

And deliciously sore in all the right places.

But I refuse to think about the reason why.

Not when I can still see the confusion and regret written on his face, hear it in his voice.

To be fair, I can see where he'd be a little worried about what happened. However, as close as I am to my brother, I don't share details of who I sleep with and when. It's none of his business, frankly, and that includes if the person I'm sleeping with is Isaac Thompson.

But that's one of the main differences between Isaac and me. He's straitlaced and by the book. He only sleeps with girls he's taken out a respectable three to five dates before taking them to bed, and even then, I'm sure it's not his best friend's little sister. I know his type, and it isn't me.

Me? Sex is a release. A biological need everyone has. An urge, if you will. One I enjoy. Not as often as I'd like—at least not in the last few years. I've been busy, building my clientele and working.

Okay, fine. Seven months. It's been seven months since my last...release.

I'm sure that's why last night was so amazing. It was timing, not compatibility. It had nothing to do with the mind-blowing orgasms he administered, one right after the other like a principal hands out detentions to the bad kids smoking by the dumpster. Or the way he made me feel. Wild, free, and desirable. As if I was the only woman in the world, or at least the only one he wanted.

See? This is me not thinking about it.

I grab my keys and head for the front door of my house. The light March breeze blows my hair into my face and slices through my sweater. I ignore the way my nipples draw tight beneath my top, because images of Isaac licking said nipples invades my mind, causing my core to clench with desire.

Nope, not going there...

Hopping into my truck, I head toward the studio where I work. Xpress Urself is located a block off the main road through Stewart Grove, about four blocks away from my brother's restaurant and brewery. We're not open on Sundays but often I still go in. It's a great time to catch up on paperwork and to work on my designs in peace and quiet.

I park my truck behind the shop, and instead of going inside, I walk the block up to the main artery through downtown and make my way to the deli two blocks over. Since I'm more of a night owl, coffee usually isn't my thing, but when it's still early enough on a Sunday, a little jolt of caffeine won't hurt.

Especially with my lack of sleep and last night's late-night mattress acrobatics.

I step inside the small restaurant with the best spicy mustard turkey paninis in the world and head straight for the counter. There's only a small line, since most people are probably still at church. Closer to noon, this place will fill to capacity, every table full with small families in their Sunday best.

"Hi, BJ. What can I get you today?" Agnes asks when it's my turn to order.

"I'll have a large coffee with hazelnut creamer and two bear claws, please," I reply, reaching into my pocket for cash.

"Four fifty," Agnes announces as she sets the cup and small white bag on the counter.

The door behind me chimes as I hand over the cash, tip included. "Thanks, Agnes. See you soon."

Just as I turn around, bag and coffee in hand, I almost slam into a wall directly behind me. Big hands reach out to steady me and bolts of electricity sweep through my arms. "Careful."

I glance up into the same spellbinding hazel eyes I stared into last night. And this morning. "Oh. Hey."

He flashes me a quick smile, but it lacks warmth. In its place is uncertainty and discomfort, much like I saw earlier this morning after we woke together in my bed. "Hi. How are you?"

Deliciously sore and ready to go again.

Of course, that's not what I say. I'm not a desperate or needy woman, and the last thing I want is to make it appear like I am. "Good. Just heading into work for a bit."

Isaac nods. "Me too."

"Hey, Isaac. You want your usual?" Agnes asks, pulling our attention to the front counter.

"Yes, please. Oh, and throw in a handful of those bear claws. I promised I'd bring some for Jameson." Agnes chuckles as she goes about gathering his order, and I don't miss the way Isaac blanches ever so slightly when he says my brother's name.

"Him and his sweets," I add, bringing a more natural smile to his face. His very handsome face.

"I've always been amazed at how he can eat so much crap, yet still be as fit as he is."

I chuckle. "It's not fair, is it. He's always had a sweet tooth. When he'd hide food from our mom, to make sure we always had it, there was always cookies or something in there too."

Isaac's face sobers. Even though he's not from here, I'm sure he knows all about our past. Jameson's like a vault when it comes to information, but he's never shied away from speaking his truth, and our childhood was part of that. At least to his friends. "Yeah."

"Anyway, I'm heading to the studio," I reply lamely, not really knowing what to say.

Isaac pays for his order and walks with me to the door. "I didn't think it was open on Sunday."

"It's not," I reply when we hit the sidewalk out front. "I like to go in and get caught up on things I left during the week."

He nods, as if understanding completely what I mean, and considering he's on his way in to work already too, I'm sure he understands more than anyone. "Me too."

Awkward silence fills the space around us, and I hate it. Mostly because I'm not used to it.

"Listen, about last night," he starts, clearing his throat and rocking back on his heels.

"Don't," I quickly interrupt, shaking my head. "What happened, happened. There's no use apologizing or rehashing it. We're both adults, right?"

He holds my gaze for a few moments before nodding. "You're right."

"Then, let's just move on, okay? I don't want it to be weird or uncomfortable when we're around each other. I think Jameson is likely to pick up on tension, you know?"

His Adam's apple bobs as he swallows. "Yes."

"Great. All right, well, I'm gonna head to the shop. Have a good one," I reply, quickly turning and heading in the opposite direction as him before he can reply. Especially because I took a strong notice of what he's wearing. Tan trousers and a button-down in a gorgeous shade of green, which only brings out the gold color of his eyes.

Apparently, stuffy businessman is my new *thing*.

I walk against the breeze back to the shop, grateful for the hot cup of coffee in my hand. I sip on it the entire way and try not to think about how uncomfortable it was to be around Isaac. I've never been that way post-sex. I'm usually the one walking away. Is that why I'm so unsettled by Isaac's hasty retreat this morning?

The moment I set foot inside the studio and relock the front door, all the tension and uncertainty just seems to melt away. This is where I belong. My home. Ignoring the front waiting area lights, I head back to my room and flip the switch, bathing my space in artificial lighting.

My eyes take in the room. It's exactly how I left it yesterday afternoon, but I wouldn't expect it any other way. Jax doesn't mess with my stuff, and I don't touch his. Our rooms are our own. The only places we share are the piercing room and the office, though I don't touch anything on the desk. There's a couch in there where I've been known to take a few naps and relax between clients, but the rest of the room I leave alone.

I set the little white bag down on my cart and pull out one of the two bear claws. While I eat, I look through the photos stapled to my walls. The tattoos I've completed in the eight years I've been providing professional ink to my clients. There's one framed photo in the middle of them all, the one that always makes me smile.

My very first tattoo in this shop, and it's my brother sitting in the chair.

We're both smiling widely as I lean over his arm. I remember that moment like it happened yesterday. It was actually the fourth or fifth one I'd given Jameson, but on this day, he insisted he be the first to officially sit in this chair, his name scheduled as my very first appointment. I added barbed wire with drips of blood to his arm and did some fill-in work to the clock already drawn on his left bicep, and the moment is documented as a reminder of how far I've come.

And who has been by my side the entire time.

I log in to our computer system and check my upcoming appointments for tomorrow. There's one particular memorial piece I'm doing for a woman that I still have to finish up. She was very specific in what she wanted on her arm. A combination of a palm tree, orchids, and sheet of music with the words "Always my little girl" is being drawn together in memory of this woman's mother. The best part is the words are in her mother's own handwriting, which is something I've done more and more of recently. It's a special tribute to someone you love.

Sixty minutes later, the design is almost complete when I hear the back door open, followed by Jax's heavy boots on the old tile. "Hey," he hollers moments before filling the doorframe with his large, imposing body.

"What's up?" I ask, blowing the pencil dust off my paper.

"That the one for tomorrow?" he asks, glancing down at the image.

"Yep. What do you think?" I hold it up so he can see the full detail because I value his opinion as my mentor and friend.

"Fuckin' sweet. She's gonna love it," he responds after stepping closer to inspect the piece.

"You're late," I say when he's done looking and set the drawing back down on my cart. "Hot date last night?"

Jax shrugs his broad shoulders, grabs the white bag with his bear claw, and drops down into the chair in the corner of my room. "Maybe."

"Do I know her?" I ask, dropping my pencils back into the holder on the counter.

He takes a huge bite, devouring half of the treat in one single motion. "Probably." He kicks his feet out in front of him and leans back in the chair. "How'd your thing go last night? I wanted to drop by after I closed, but, well, got busy."

I almost snort. He got busy all right. "It went fine," I reply, just as memories of Isaac discovering my nipple piercing flash through my mind.

"You sure? You got all weird when you said that," he says, then promptly shoves the other half of the bear claw into his mouth.

"I'm sure. Truck broke down. Had to fix it before I could come in."

He glances at the clock. "And you're still here before noon? How did that happen?"

I shrug, averting my gaze. "Just got up early to get it fixed, since I had to leave it on the street. Didn't want anyone to touch my baby," I reply, knowing Jax will buy my reasoning immediately. He knows I love that truck and wouldn't willingly leave it anywhere but in my own driveway at night. Which is true, for the most part. It also keeps the focus off the fact I'm probably blushing a little now that my mind is replaying everything that happened after my truck broke down.

Jax balls up the wrapper from his donut and tosses it in the trash. He's a good-looking guy, with his dark hair and even darker eyes. He has gauges in both of his ears and more ink than any man I've ever met. Considering my line of business, that's saying something. He's also the proud owner of the very first frenum piercing I ever did, which was quickly followed by a Prince Albert piercing. His nipples are both pierced too, but he had those done before I started at the shop.

"I'll make sure to stop by one of these days and congratulate your brother. Pretty fucking cool we have a brewery right here in Stewart Grove."

Jax and Jameson actually go way back. Jax is a few years older than my brother, but they hung in the same circles. In fact, Jax is the only other person who has tattooed my brother, besides me. Jameson showed my designs and work to his friend when he first opened this shop and convinced him to give me a shot. When I was twenty, Jax brought me on as an apprentice, teaching me everything he knew about the business. Two years later, I had my own chair, and I've been here ever since.

"I'm sure he'll appreciate it," I reply honestly. Jameson has put in a lot of work in the brewery and deserves all the accolades he can get.

Jax nods, slaps his hands on his knees, and gets up. "Well, I'm headed to the office. Holler if ya need me."

I wave as he leaves and turn my attention back to my work. I spend a little more time getting ready for tomorrow, making sure my designs are ready for approval. As soon as I get the go-ahead, I'll make the stencils, but never beforehand. Too many clients make last minute changes to their tattoo, and the last thing you want is to have to toss out a stencil.

Once I'm set for tomorrow, I head to the piercing room. This room has a door that locks, unlike our tattoo spaces, which just has a closeable curtain. When a customer is exposing their most intimate areas, the last thing you want is everyone walking down the hallway to see. Since I have two piercings on the books tomorrow as well, I make sure the room has everything I'll need ready.

Only then do I shut off the lights and make my way toward the back exit where I left my truck. Since Jax is still in the office, I stop in the doorway. "I'm outta here. See you tomorrow."

He looks up and gives me a smile. Such a nice smile, one that used to make my heart flutter and my body react. Now, it just reminds me of a friend. A good friend, actually. Besides Amanda and my brother, he's one of few I know I can trust with anything. "All right. Take 'er easy."

With another wave, I head out the door, making sure it's securely locked before I go. The moment I hop up into my truck, I grab my phone and fire off a quick message to my best friend.

Me: Dinner plans?

She responds almost immediately.

Amanda: Unless Jason Momoa calls, no plans.

Me: Jason Momoa, huh?

Amanda: It's the hair. I want to wrap my hands around it like reins while I'm riding him to next Sunday.

I snort out a laugh. Amanda has never been shy about what she wants, which might actually be why we're best friends.

Me: Noted. If *Aquaman* calls, I'll respectfully bow out for the night.

Amanda: My vagina appreciates it. How about Mexican? I feel like eating my weight in chips and salsa.

Me: Meet you there at six?

Amanda: Sounds good. Smooches!

I set my phone in the cupholder and start the engine. My girl purrs like a kitten, and thanks to a new hose, isn't overheating and threatening to destroy my motor. That would have really pissed me off.

As I head for home, I can't help but wonder what Isaac's doing. Is he still at work? I'm well aware of the crazy amount of hours he puts in. Jameson has mentioned it on more than one occasion. The fact I'm wondering about him now is pretty telling, considering I've known him for years.

But now I know how he feels inside of me. How his mouth feels on my nipples and between my legs. What sounds he makes when he comes. How as much as I wanted him to hurry up and get me off, he took his time, as if savoring my taste, my scent, the feel of our bodies together. How surprised he was when he discovered my piercings, and how awestruck he looked as he gazed down at my tattoos.

No, I'll never forget our time together, even if I wanted to. There's no forgetting my night with Isaac Thompson.

Isaac

I can't stop thinking about how hard she came when I sucked on that piercing above her clit.

Closing my eyes, I try to vanquish the memory, but it just won't leave. It replays over and over again, making me so damn hard, I've had to contemplate going into the bathroom and taking care of my little problem no less than five times.

Five.

The only thing that effectively kills my hard-on is Jameson. He walks into the room and a fresh wave of guilt sweeps in, essentially squelching any desire I feel for his sister. The problem is it's short lived. My dick doesn't forget, and the moment I'm alone, he gets hard all over again.

Traitorous bastard.

I've spent the last few hours trying to get work done, but it's useless. My mind isn't here, which means I'm more likely to make mistakes. What's crazier yet, I haven't once picked up my phone to text Savannah.

Not once.

When I think about our breakup last night, sure I feel sad and a little angry, but it's what I don't feel that catches my attention. Usually, I'm wallowing in self-pity and doubt by this point. What went wrong this time? What could I have done differently? Why wasn't I good enough? The questions that usually plague my mind aren't there.

Instead, I'm wondering what BJ is doing, if she's eaten lunch yet, and worse, is she thinking about me as much as I'm thinking about her? Chances are slim there. Not after the way we ended it early this morning, and then again on the sidewalk outside the deli. She made it clear it was a one-time thing and that's all.

Which I'm grateful for, don't get me wrong.

I just wish I monopolized her mind as much as she's monopolizing mine.

Sighing, I realize I need a change of scenery. Considering this is the place I usually run to when I need a break from something, that's telling. Maybe something in me broke last night, when Savannah stood in the hallway just down the stairs and said goodbye. Maybe I'm just exhausted and so fucking tired of the bullshit. Either way, I need to get out of here.

I grab my phone, noticing the mid-afternoon time. Jasper and Lyndee spend Sundays together, since that's the only day they both have off, and the last thing I want to do is be a third wheel there. Jameson's downstairs or next door at the brewery. That leaves Walker, and I'm pretty sure I know where he is.

Me: What are you doing?

Walker: Watching Mal eat her second dessert of the afternoon.

Me: Ha! Leave her alone. She's cooking your baby.

Walker: Oh, don't you worry. She can eat as much as she wants. Hell, I'm the one who went and got her the second plate. Seeing that little baby bump only fuels my need to take care of her.

Walker: You working?

Me: Just leaving. Need a break.

There's a long pause, and I wonder if maybe he got distracted and isn't going to reply. But after a few moments, the bubbles finally appear.

Walker: I'm sorry, did you say you need a break? Is this really Numbers or did someone get a hold of his phone?

Me: It's really me, asshole.

Walker: Wow, never thought I'd hear those words come out of your mouth. Or your fingers, I guess. Anyway, come on out to Aunt Edna's. You can have some apple pie. I'd offer you some peach cobbler, but unless you get out here in the next few minutes, Mal will probably have already eaten the rest of it.

I smile at the invitation, even though I know I don't really need one. Walker's family would welcome me—or anyone, for that matter—at any time without complaint. They're the type to have you sitting on their porch, drinking lemonade, and eating the best fried chicken this side of the Mississippi before you even knew what hit you.

Me: Thanks

I slip my phone into my pocket and lock everything up. Once I reach the hallway downstairs, I run into Jameson. "Hey, man. Headed out?" he asks, a flash of confusion on his face.

"Yeah, I'm gonna head out to Aunt Edna's for a while," I reply. "Dessert was just served."

"Dessert?" His entire face lights up.

"You know the invite is always there, unless you have to stay here for anything." It wasn't that long ago, there was always a partner on duty. Jasper, with his need to dominate the kitchen, worked seven days a week, and me just as eager and focused in the office. I'd practically get off on creating financial graphs, ones I knew made my friends' heads spin. Each one, I'd make better than the last, perfecting the display of information, and making sure the details I was giving were accurate.

It's a sickness, really. One I've always loved, thrived on.

"Maybe later. I was headed next door to make sure everything's as it should be. Save me a piece of whatever Aunt Edna made?"

I snort as I push through the exit. "Good luck with that, buddy. Walker says Mal is on her second plate, eyeing the last bit of peach cobbler as if it were going to get up and run away."

He blows out a breath. "Dammit, I fucking love peach cobbler," he mumbles.

"I'll save you what I can," I holler, waving as I hit the pavement outside and walk toward my car.

The moment I slip inside my Maxima, I can't help but recall BJ's comments about my car. The *safe* choice. I've always done that, my entire life. I've chosen the safest routes I could take. When I was a child, when I went off to school, hell, even when I got my first adult job after college. They were all the safe bets, thanks to a shitty childhood and my fear of getting hurt.

BJ is anything but safe.

Shit, she's so far out of my comfort zone, I can't even see the line anymore. Yet, something calls to me, beckons me toward her, like a siren in the night.

I drive out to Walker's aunt's house and find the driveway full of vehicles. Edna has always welcomed family after Sunday church, a tradition she started well before I moved to Stewart Grove.

Just as I exit the vehicle, a figure appears at the front porch. Aunt Edna is wearing a long, floral dress with a white apron over the front. Her gray hair is pulled back in a tight bun and she's wearing the biggest smile on her pretty face. "I was wondering when you were gonna come see me." She holds out her arms and adds, "Come give me some suga."

I'm already smiling as I head for the front entrance to her home. Aunt Edna is much shorter than my six one and her head hits at my chest. "Hi, Aunt Edna," I state the moment she wraps her arms around my waist.

She steps back and gazes up at me with a critical eye. "You've been working too hard. I can see it in your eyes."

I nod, knowing there's no reason to lie to her. "I have been, yes. But the brewery is now officially open, so I'm hoping to take a little extra time off."

Funny, that thought never really crossed my mind, but now that I've said it, I realize I really do need a little time away.

"You make sure you do." She searches my face once more. I swear this woman can read my thoughts and stare straight into my soul. "How's your young woman?"

I swallow over the sudden lump in my throat. "Oh, uh, Savannah and I broke up."

Her eyes narrow. "I wasn't talking about that woman. The other one. The one who has relit the fire in your eyes."

My mouth opens, but nothing comes out. I'm saved from having to reply when my attention is drawn behind her, to the slamming of the screen door and Walker joining us on the porch. "Leave him alone, Aunt Edna. We all know Numbers here spent the night home alone, weeping in his ice cream."

Another flashback enters my mind in bright Technicolor, one of BJ naked and laid out on the counter like some delicious all-you-can-eat buffet.

No, I was most definitely not alone last night.

I just can't tell anyone that.

She raises a single eyebrow, as if challenging me to dispute the claim. I don't, however. Instead, I head for the front door. "I hear there's pie."

Edna just rolls her eyes. "Of course there's pie. I should have made a pecan pie so you can take it to that Jasper. The poor boy still thinks his is better than mine," she quips, slipping through the door I pull open for her. "Everyone, Isaac is here!" she announces before my feet even hit the foyer.

Aunt Edna's house is on the smaller side, and when it's brimming with family, it's even smaller. There are people everywhere. Walker's cousins, aunts, and uncles all offer me greetings and waves. I spot his mom, Marie, over on the couch, reading a book to Lizzie. And then there's Mallory, sitting at the dining room table with a cookie in her hand.

The moment she spots me, she jumps up and gives me a hug. I've always liked Mallory. From the second she stepped into my office for an interview, I liked her. Not like that. Sure, she's pretty, but my eyes don't see anything but an amazing woman and friend. In fact, she's perfect for my friend. They have one of those relationships I've longed to have. The one I pretended my parents had when I was little. Well, up until the day my father walked out the front door and never came back, leaving my mom, me, and my two sisters behind.

"I saved you some cobbler," Mallory announces, the swell of her small baby bump pressing into me as she squeezes me tight.

"Jameson is gonna be pissed," I declare with a chuckle.

"He should have come himself. We'll send him home a slice of pumpkin and apple pie," she says, reclaiming her seat and pushing the near-empty pan of cobbler my way.

"You sure you don't want this? I'd be happy with a piece of apple pie."

She exhales a deep breath. "No, I couldn't eat another bite," she proclaims, picking a piece off her cookie and popping it in her mouth. "Well, after this cookie. Those don't count."

"Of course not," I reply, trying to hide my smile.

"Anyway, I don't think the baby wants any more peaches. He's going to turn into one."

I pause from scooping the last bit of dessert from the pan onto a paper plate. "He?"

She rolls her eyes and takes another bite of cookie. "No, we don't know yet. *Someone* has decided we should wait and be surprised," she mutters, sarcasm dripping off every word.

Walker takes the seat beside her and kisses the side of her head. "I voted to not find out."

"And I voted to find out, so I can shop and be prepared," Mallory interjects.

"Sounds like a tie to me," I reply, taking a hearty bite of Aunt Edna's homemade peach cobbler and almost groaning in pure sugary delight.

"It was. Lizzie was the tie-breaker," Mallory states.

"And she voted to be surprised too," Walker declares, giving her a proud grin.

"That's because you bribed her with a new *Curious George* movie." Mallory gives him a pointed look, which only makes Walker laugh.

"You're just mad you didn't think of it first," he declares, kissing her on the lips and making me shovel my dessert into my mouth faster.

"Isaac!" Lizzie hollers, running into the dining room and making a leap to where I sit.

I catch her easily, giving her sides a little tickle as I bring her to my chest. "Lizard! How's my favorite little girl?"

"Dood! I gotted a new movie to watch. You wanna come watch it wiff me?" she asks, those hopeful emerald green eyes staring back at me with eagerness and anticipation.

I already know what my answer will be. "I'd love to. What's it about?"

"A monkey! Like what mommy's gonna have."

Her statement catches me completely off guard. “Mommy’s having a monkey?”

She nods enthusiastically. “A baby monkey, like George!” Someone hollers for the little girl, and she quickly jumps down and runs into the kitchen. “Be white back!”

“She’s going to be so disappointed when her brother gets here and he’s not a monkey.”

“You mean sister,” Walker interjects, reaching for a brownie, splitting it in half, and handing one part to his wife.

“So, how are you doing?” Mallory asks with pity in her green eyes as she bites into the chocolatey treat.

“Fine.” I scoop up another bite of dessert.

“Listen, if you want to talk about Sa—”

“I don’t,” I interrupt. Clearing my throat and setting down my fork, I add, “I appreciate it, really, but I’m fine. It hurts, but I guess…well, I guess I’m just more disappointed at myself than I am at her. She’s the same person she was before, right? So it’s on me. I let her back in to hurt me all over again. It’s been like six times. You don’t do that if you truly love someone, do you.” It’s not a question, because I already know the answer.

They both give me a sad smile as Mallory reaches out and squeezes my hand. “I think you’re right.” She glances over at Walker. “No, you don’t keep doing that if you really love someone.”

I pick my fork back up and inhale the rest of my peach cobbler. “Thanks.”

“You’re going to find someone, Isaac. Someone who sees how absolutely amazing you truly are. Of course, you’re probably going to have to leave the office upstairs every now and again to find her, but she’s out there, waiting.”

Another image of BJ creeps into my mind. Look what happened last night when I stepped away from the office. I slept with one of my closest friends' sister. But as amazing as it was, I can't help this dull ache of confusion and guilt I feel. I knew it was wrong, yet did it anyway.

"Can I ask you guys something?"

"Sure," they both reply in unison.

"When you guys first started seeing each other, how did you get over the whole employee slash employer hang-up, Walker?"

He snorts. "Well, I believe you were the one who told me to man-up or I was liable to let a good woman pass me by."

I flash him a smile, mostly because I remember how conflicted my friend was when he was attracted to Mallory and fighting it tooth and nail.

"Why? Do you like someone?" Mallory asks, leaning in closer. "Like, an employee?"

Now it's my turn to roll my eyes. "No. Nothing like that."

"But there's someone," she derives, the corners of her lips turning upward. I can practically see her devil horns popping out of her head. "Who?"

"Stop it," I insist, tossing my used napkin down on my empty plate.

"Who?" she sings, refusing to let this go.

I glance at Walker and can practically see his wheels spinning. "You going to get a hold of your woman, Meyer?"

He snorts out a laugh. "You kidding me? There's no controlling my woman."

"That's right! Now, spill, Numbers. Who is she?"

I push the chair back and stand up. "There's no one, Mal, now drop it."

She stares up at me, probably trying to figure out if she believes me or not, before finally nodding. “Okay, sorry. Just know if there *is* someone, that’s okay. You deserve to be happy.”

Another giant lump forms in my throat. “Thanks.”

After spending an hour with Walker and his family and making sure I watch part of the movie with Lizzie, Aunt Edna wraps up a to-go platter for me, as well as one for Jameson. I make a promise to drop it off at his house on my way home, give everyone hugs and handshakes, and am the recipient of at least four hugs and kisses from Lizzie before I’m able to walk out the door to head home. But when I do, I feel recharged. Being around everyone helped me to relax and let go of the tension I was holding onto where BJ was concerned.

What’s done is done.

But it doesn’t mean it needs to happen again.

I drive over to Jameson’s place and head for the door. I sent him a text before I left letting him know I was dropping off some goodies. He responded immediately with a thumbs-up emoji.

“Was there peach cobbler left?” he asks as I approach his front steps.

“Nope, sorry.”

“Mal got the last of it?” Guilt stains my cheeks pink, and there’s no way he would miss it. “Really, dude? I thought you were my friend!” he declares, though there’s no bite behind his bark.

“Sorry,” I reply, following him into the house. “She pushed the pan in front of me. What was I to do?”

He crosses his arms and glares. “Not eat it, that’s what you were supposed to do.”

I can’t help but laugh. “Aunt Edna says next time you need to come yourself.”

The big guy flashes a rare smile. "Yeah, yeah. Maybe next Sunday. It's been a while since I've been to Sunday lunch. Ever since we decided to open this brewery, my time's been preoccupied with that."

"You don't have to explain it to me," I insist. "If anyone understands the hectic schedule, it's me."

Jameson nods and peeks inside the foil-covered dish. "Two slices of pie?"

I slide a bowl across the counter. "She even sent some of her homemade caramel sauce for the apple pie."

Jameson groans. "Hell yes." He quickly covers up the container. "But first, I need meat. Let's go eat."

He doesn't even wait for me to respond, just grabs his worn beat-up leather jacket off the chair and slips it on. "What if I have plans already?"

Jameson stares at me, in both question and a dare. After a few long seconds, he adds, "That's what I thought. Let's go. I'll even buy."

"Fine, but I'm getting an appetizer too." I won't. There's no way I could eat an appetizer, as well as an entrée after all the desserts I had this afternoon.

"Deal. I'm craving tacos," he says, heading for the door.

I tap my wallet in my back pocket and follow him out without asking where we're going. There are three places that serve Mexican, but only one Jameson regularly goes to. Looks like we're headed uptown, but that's all right. They have the best queso in the state of Ohio. Plus, they serve cold beer.

I have a feeling I'm going to need it.

BJ

"What's going on?" Amanda asks the moment our waiter delivers two strawberry margaritas to the table and leaves to put our food order in. "You seem all twitchy."

I take a long, hearty sip before releasing the straw. "So much, it's not even funny."

"Spill it. Is it about Jax?"

Her question catches me off guard. "No, of course not. Why would it be?"

She shrugs, taking a much smaller drink from her glass. "You know, there's just a lot of history there."

"*Ancient* history," I reiterate.

"History is history," she says, waving off my comment. "Anyway, if it's not about him, then what's going on?" Then suddenly, like a lightbulb clicking on, she leans forward and adds, "Your brother's event was last night. Did something happen?"

I close my eyes and swear I can still feel his hands on my body. I'm usually a vault when it comes to personal details, much like my brother, but there are certain things a girl must share with her best friend. “Something happened.”

Her eyes widen. “Tell me.”

“I might have...well, I kinda slept with one of my brother’s friends.”

Amanda gasps. “Seriously? Which one? The hot bartender?”

I instantly shake my head. “No, not him. He’s married anyway.” She opens her mouth, but I quickly interject, “And not the broody chef either.” I swallow over the lump in my throat. “I slept with Isaac.”

My dearest friend gasps once more. “Shut up! Really?”

“Really,” I reply through a groan.

“And...”

I glance around, making sure no one is listening. “And it was really, *really* good. Like mind-blowing and life-changing. The kind of sex they write about in *Cosmo* or in romance novels.”

She flops back against the bench, her eyes still holding shock. “I can’t believe it.”

After taking another big drink, I ask, “Which part? The part about sleeping with him?”

She shakes her head. “No, the part that he was that good. Isaac Thompson? Really?”

I nod in confirmation. “Yes. The man has...skills with his tongue,” I murmur, a shiver sweeping down my spine in recollection.

“Damn. I never would have guessed. He’s Mr. Straight and Narrow.”

“Believe me, I know,” I reply, looking around once more.

“Tell me all about it,” she demands, dipping fresh tortilla chips into homemade salsa.

I recount everything—leaving out the super intimate details—starting with his breakup, and work my way through his departure this morning. Amanda is hanging on my every word.

"I don't know what to say. I mean, you think you know someone, but then they turn out to be a ravenous animal with super tongue skills and a cock made of steel. They don't make many men like that, BJ. Most don't understand what multiple orgasms even mean, let alone how to administer them. Those are things guys don't learn from watching porn."

The woman at the table beside us snickers, letting us know her comment wasn't as quiet as she intended.

Amanda shrugs. "Anyway, so what happens next?"

"Nothing. It was a one-time thing."

"No!" she declares. "You owe it to women everywhere—and your *vagina*—to be the lucky recipient of multiple O's!"

"Stop being dramatic. One and done. I'm pretty sure I won't be seeing him for a while," I state, recalling how guilty and uncomfortable he looked earlier.

"Oh, I doubt that," Amanda mutters, looking over my shoulder when the door to the restaurant opens.

"Why?"

She meets my gaze and gives me a wide smile. "Because he's right behind you, coming this way. With your brother."

Panic sets in the moment her words register, but before I'm able to do anything crazy, like excuse myself to go to the bathroom, or better yet, fly to China, a large shadow falls across our table. "Hey, ladies."

"Hi!" I squeak out in reply to my brother.

"Didn't know we'd see you here," Jameson says, standing squarely between myself and Amanda. That means when Isaac finally appears, he's left right next to where I sit.

The moment he stops, I catch the subtle hint of his cologne. My lady parts instantly take notice, perking up like the hussies they are. Even my nipples draw into tight little buds, as if they know Isaac's mouth is nearby.

"Why don't you guys join us?"

Her invitation registers, and my eyes practically pop out of my head. My best friend is sitting across from me, smiling sweetly. Yet, I know she's the devil. Why on earth would she invite them to join us? After what I just told her?

"You don't mind?" Jameson asks, giving me a quick glance, which has me immediately shaking my head.

"Of course not."

I slide over, as does Amanda, giving my brother room to share my bench. Except, Jameson slips onto the one across from me, directly beside my friend.

That means...

Isaac takes a seat beside me, careful not to get too close.

"So, how's it going?" Jameson asks, glancing across the table at me.

Before I can reply, Amanda jumps in, "Oh, you know, just girl talk. Work and sex..."

My mouth drops open as I stare at my best friend. She sips on her drink, the corners of her mouth curling upward as she tries to hide her smile. Isaac beside me suddenly seems to choke on air, coughing and sputtering.

Jameson pulls a face. "Gross, I don't want to hear a word about that."

"You sure? It's quite the sto—"

"So," I start, interrupting my former best friend and desperately looking for a redirect, "what are you two out doing this evening?"

"Numbers brought me some Aunt Edna dessert, but I needed food first. Here we are," my brother replies, reaching for a chip and dipping it in salsa. "Where's the queso?"

"I didn't order any," I reply, sticking out my tongue.

"Bullshit," he mutters, flagging down our waiter and ordering a large bowl with queso, extra basket of chips, and two beers.

While we're waiting for their drinks to be delivered, I shift in my seat, only to brush my leg against Isaac's. It's like a jolt of electricity every time we touch, and apparently, that includes the times we're fully clothed. Even after I rip my leg away from his, I can feel the heat from his body, and that only makes me think about the heat we created last night.

And in the early morning hours.

"Jesus," I grumble while rubbing my forehead, forgetting for a brief moment I'm not alone.

"Everything okay?" Jameson asks.

Amanda grins.

"Oh, yeah, fine. Just the start of a headache. Too much tequila in this drink," I reply, even though it's complete bullshit. I'm actually really good at holding my liquor. Half a margarita isn't enough to give me a headache.

"And this tequila tastes like shit compared to the Don Julio last night," Jameson states, and now I'm the one choking on the air I breathe.

Idle chitchat happens around me as the guys order their food and it's delivered a short time later with our order. Isaac and my brother tell Amanda all about the brewery, which, despite the sexual tension I felt near Isaac last night, seems to be neutral ground. They boast about all their hard work, describing their first few varieties of beer brewed.

"Right now, we're selling it at the bar and restaurant, but hopefully soon, we'll have the approval we need to sell it directly from the brewery, like its own store," Isaac says between bites of his chicken burrito.

"Then we can add a couple more beer options too. I've been toying with the recipes and should have a few fall flavored beers ready by September," Jameson adds, finishing off his steak enchiladas. "Those damn apple beers are huge right now."

"They are so good. I'd love for you guys to start brewing it. Then I can support a local business instead of a national corporation only out to grow their bottom line," Amanda replies.

"Well, that's our plan too, but on a much smaller scale," Isaac says, pushing his plate forward. "We want Crüe Brewery to be profitable, otherwise, what's the point? But we also want to create a brand locally, maybe even regionally someday. We want good quality beer that keeps the customers coming back for more."

Coming back for more.

Yes, please!

Why did my mind just go straight into unnecessary dirty territory?

I finish off my own food, anxious to put a little distance between myself and my bench mate. These accidental brushes of our arms or legs are slowly driving me insane. For a woman who spends a lot of energy controlling her life and as much as she can around her, I find myself completely out of character where Isaac is concerned.

Finally, our waiter returns to take our plates and deliver our checks. "I'll take them all," Isaac says, reaching for the black folder.

"You don't have to do that," I quickly insist, reaching across him for the checks.

He pulls it back, just out of my reach, but that doesn't stop me from trying. I lean into him, making a grab at the folder he's keeping from me. "I said I got it," he insists, making me pause.

I wait a few beats before one last attempt to steal the checks, except when I do, I basically press my chest against his arm. I swear my body knows it's him and responds accordingly. My nipples pebble against my sweater, the material grazing across the metal ring and sending shock waves of lust through my body. All I can think about is how it felt to have his tongue licking and sucking on that very spot.

Isaac must feel how much I'm affected by his proximity and glances down at my chest. All I can do is pray my nipples aren't protruding through the sweater like a sailor saluting an officer. There's fire in his gaze, as if he's remembering the exact same bits and pieces from our night together. My core clenches in excitement.

We're both completely sidetracked, with my boobs pressed against his arm and all, and neither of us see my brother's big hand reach across the table and snatch the black folder from Isaac's hand without warning. "I told you I was buying," he states, setting it on the table in front of him and digging his credit card out of his wallet.

I huff. "You didn't even know we were going to be here. I can buy my own dinner," I insist.

My brother just stares at me as he slips his card inside the folder. "You're funny."

I narrow my eyes at the man who came from the same gene pool as I did, ready to throw a few verbal jabs his way, except I realize I'm still practically lying across Isaac's arm.

"You two are so cute," Amanda coos with a lazy grin on her face, her chin resting on her hands as she watches the show.

Clearing my throat, I rip myself back as if I were burned by his touch and sit up straight, making sure my top isn't revealing too much. "Whatever," I mutter, making my best friend giggle.

Jameson looks between his friend and me before shaking his head. "I'm gonna go pay and head outside. I need a cigarette." He slides out of the booth, his big boots thumping across the floor as he walks toward the front register.

I glance over at my friend and give her the stink-eye. Of course, my horrible best friend just laughs as she slips from the bench and makes her way toward the front door.

"Ready?" Isaac says, getting up and stepping back to give me room to exit.

Nodding, I follow suit with my back straight and my head held high, even though my legs are a little wobbly. As we move through the restaurant, I feel the warmth of a hand placed gently at my lower back.

Does he do this on purpose? Is he just trying to remind me of how much he affects me?

No, something tells me that's not it at all. Isaac is the epitome of a gentleman. Opening doors, being polite, escorting women through a restaurant. It's in his DNA. I'm sure that's all he's doing now, and the fact I even considered the reasoning as being anything but just pisses me off.

Because. I'm. Not. This. Woman.

I'm not the one who fawns over a guy. I don't get all flushed and tongue-tied whenever a cute guy is near. Hell, I didn't even do that in junior high, when all the other girls turned into annoying, giggly piles of hormones who stuffed their bras with tissues to get boys' attention.

Yet, here I am, swaying toward his touch just so I can feel more of his hand.

And it pisses me the fuck off!

I pick up the pace and head straight out the front door, knowing my brother has the bill and tip covered. I could try to slip him some money, but I've been around him enough over the years to know he'll never take it. I've discovered it's best just to let him have his moment, and I'll try to get the check the next time we eat together, or I'll make food and deliver it to his refrigerator. I've done that a lot over the years.

As soon as my boots hit the concrete sidewalk, I stop and turn. Isaac's hand falls from my back and he stuffs both of them in the pockets of his trousers. "What are you doing?" I ask.

His eyes fill with confusion as he meets my gaze. "What do you mean?"

"The hand," I state.

He seems genuinely puzzled by my question. "I guess I didn't even realize I was touching you. I'm sorry."

I hate that I'm reacting this way, but I truly don't understand why I'm being so moody. It's like a defense mechanism where he's concerned. Because I'm attracted to him, even though I shouldn't be, and I don't like it.

"No, it's fine," I mutter, rubbing my forehead and feeling guilty for jumping all over him, especially when he was just being polite.

Isaac takes a step back, as if putting extra distance between us, and I'm grateful. As much as I want him to step away, I want to pull him against me and kiss him even more.

Before we're forced to make more awkward conversation, Amanda and my brother walk out the door. She's smiling widely again, eyeing us suspiciously as she pops a sucker in her mouth. "Ready?" she sings, her eyes volleying between me and Isaac.

"Yes." To my brother, I give him a big hug and whisper," Thank you for dinner."

He returns the gesture, never one to shy away from hugging me. I'm probably the only one he actually let's touch him freely, thanks to our asshole of a father before he walked away. Jameson doesn't like people being in his space and hates being touched even more, but thanks to his tattooed, badass appearance and surly attitude, most don't even try. "No problem. Love you, kid," he mutters quietly.

The moment I step away, Amanda swats at Jameson's arm. "Thanks for dinner. You can buy anytime," she teases my older brother. She's been my best friend for years, which means she's accustomed to his moodiness, and as my best friend, she's also a huge fan of pushing his buttons just for the sake of getting him all worked up.

They very much have a big brother, little sister relationship. Maybe a few years ago, for like five minutes, I entertained the idea of my brother and best friend dating, but I know it would never have worked out. There's no spark, no chemistry there, and that's okay. This way I can keep my friend and my brother without there being any awkwardness.

Like there is with myself and Isaac, now that I've seen him naked.

And felt him inside of me.

"Isaac, good to see you again," Amanda hollers, throwing him a quick wave.

Isaac nods, but doesn't take his hands out of his pockets. "You as well, Amanda. BJ," he replies with a second nod before taking a few steps backward and falling into step with my brother as they walk to his car.

"Ummm, girl, that was hot."

I startle, not realizing my friend had moved to stand directly beside me. "What?"

"Those 'have sex with me again' vibes you two were sending off like fireworks on the Fourth of July."

Rolling my eyes, we walk toward the parking lot, making sure to not get too close to the men ahead of us so they can't overhear. "You're nuts."

"No, but I am a little turned on. Seriously, you two are hot. I can see why the sex was so amazing."

I stop in my tracks and just look at my friend. "Seriously, Amanda, did you smoke something in the bathroom?"

She snorts. "I wish. But no, I didn't smoke anything. All I'm saying is I could feel the sexual tension between you two, and I think you deserve to explore it a little. I mean, I may not see what you see when he's wearing those khaki pants and button-down, but he was definitely putting off some 'I want to sex her again' vibes. Hard."

"Just stop. It's not happening again," I insist as I reach where my truck is parked. I notice my brother's car down the row, and while he's sitting in the driver's seat, smoking, he's not moving either, which means he's waiting for me to leave before he does.

She blows out a deep breath. "That's dumb. Your vagina's sad now."

I almost agree because my vagina *is* sad. She's definitely a hussy in heat when it comes to Isaac.

But it's for the best. He's not interested in the complicated mess it would become if he took his friend's sister out on a date, if he was even interested in that. He's also nursing some pretty big heartbreak, and that's not something I want to get myself tangled in.

"See you at work tomorrow," I state, giving my friend a quick hug.

"Yeah, yeah, yeah. If you find yourself driving over to his condo and banging out your frustration, you better call me! Not during though. I'm not into that, even for you." Amanda gives me a kiss on the cheek and slips into her car.

All I can do is shake my head, because as appealing as that image might be, it's not happening. Not ever again. The quicker my vagina listens to my head, the better off she'll be. Until then, she'll have to settle for my vibrator.

Because I'm not sleeping with Isaac Thompson again.

Isaac

I swear Jameson is gonna call me out on the ride home for lusting after his sister, but he remains blissfully silent. In fact, he's almost too calm, and that's almost just as worrisome as if he were sitting there stewing. At least then I'd know what he's thinking, but the guy's like a vault when it comes to his emotions.

Unless he's pissed.

Then you'll know it.

"I was thinking…" he says, breaking through the silence and making my heart jump in my chest. "When we hired George, it was with the understanding of promoting him as soon as we got ourselves established and hiring an assistant brewer. I think that'll happen faster than we expected."

My mind goes to the place that usually helps settle me: work.

When Jameson brought the idea of a brewery to our attention, he had done a lot of research prior to our initial meeting, but I spent weeks agonizing over details and data. I called breweries of different sizes across the continent, soaking up any information they would share. Most were receptive to talking to me; a few were not. Like many businesses, they viewed their data as a closely guarded trade secret, and I couldn't fault them for it.

We agreed to have Jameson manage and run the brewery, and while he was instrumental in the start-up of the business, he's not exactly a master brewer, so we sought out the assistance of George Vargo, a brewer from Cincinnati, who agreed to move to Stewart Grove for a minimum of two years to oversee our operation. He came with the experience and knowledge we needed, and he's been a godsend ever since, teaching Jameson everything he knows. At the end of the two years, the partners and George have the option to extend his contract or allow him to move on.

"I can run some numbers and report back tomorrow," I tell him, referring to our partners' meeting. We meet every Monday afternoon to discuss the business at the restaurant. It's probably one of the only work-related moments we're all sitting down at the same time.

"Sounds good. I just think it would help him out a few days a week, but also keep the operation running over the weekend too."

I nod, completely understanding what he's saying. Even though our business really just started, it took off right away. We started serving our beer in the bar a few weeks back, as soon as we were given our approval. The reception was huge, especially with our American pale ale. It was instantly being compared to some of the biggest names in beer on the market, and we're damn proud of that.

Jameson should be damn proud.

"Okay. Let me know if you need anything from me," he says, taking one last drag from his cigarette before putting it out in the ashtray.

"Will do. I'll run some figures and let you know."

"Appreciate it."

We pull into Jameson's driveway, and he instantly pulls his Nova into his garage. "Won't be long and you'll be able to take the Harley out more regularly," I say, spotting his motorcycle parked along the wall. Even though he'll bundle up and ride it, it was definitely on the colder side this winter, and I know everyone is ready for some consistent warmer weather.

He shoves his hands in the pockets of his jeans and leans back against the door of his car. "I've had it out a few times for quick rides during the day, but it's still too fucking cold once the sun goes down. I'm ready though. Summer can't get here quick enough."

We visit for a few more minutes, but before long, I'm back in my car and heading for home. To be honest with you, I'm not exactly looking forward to it. I still haven't dealt with the stuff in my bedroom. You know, the roses, candles, and wine I expected to surprise my then-girlfriend with after last night's open house?

Sighing, I pull into my driveway and park in my garage. I drag up the steps and enter my laundry room, tossing my jacket onto the washing machine. I completely ignore the voice in my head chastising me for not hanging it in the front closet. My feet carry me straight to the refrigerator to grab a beer. I only had one at dinner, and that was before I even ate my food, so I'm definitely ready.

My bedroom door looms down the hallway. Sure, I was home earlier, showered, and got ready to head into the office, but I was able to ignore everything left from the day before. Now, I know it'll need to be cleared out before I go to bed. Yet, instead of grabbing a garbage bag and doing the job, I move to my back patio door and gaze out into the yard. The first thing I notice is my neighbor sitting on his half of the patio, legs kicked up on a chair and drinking a beer.

Smiling, I unlock the French door and step outside. "Awfully chilly for you to be out here, isn't it?"

Jeb gives me a wide grin and holds up his beer bottle. "I'm plenty warm, thank you very much."

We share one massive backyard, with our own concrete patios off the doors. My space has nothing but a few chairs and a grill, but Jeb's has a nice little firepit he uses often, comfortable padded chairs, and some plants. He loves his outdoor space, and I often find the seventy-year-old widower out back relaxing. Ever since his wife passed a few years back, I think he opts to be outside, as opposed to inside, surrounded by their memories.

"Mind if I join you?" I ask, already heading for the empty chair.

"I'd be offended if you didn't." He takes another drink of his beer. "How's work going? You got any more of that new beer of yours?"

"I can get you some," I reply, stretching my legs out in front of me. "The pale ale or the dark lager?"

"Surprise me," he replies, saluting me with his bottle. "Where's your young lady tonight?" I must pull a face at the mention of Savannah because he quickly adds, "Uh oh. Trouble in paradise?"

"You could say that, Jeb. She broke things off again." No reason not to tell him the truth. Jeb has met Savannah many times, though I'm pretty sure she usually found some excuse to be on her phone the whole time.

He whistles and shakes his head. "Sounds like someone needs to get their head out of their ass."

I can't help but snort a laugh. "You talking about me or her?"

"Her," he states, pointing his finger my way. "Definitely her. I hate to hear it not work out again, but I think it's a sign. My Margie believed in all those signs and fate and shit. She'd probably have some great words of wisdom for you right now, but me? I'm not as good with the words as she was. I believe you're either a good person or you're not. I hate to say it, boy, but that girl wasn't right for you. You deserve better."

BJ flashes through my mind once more, just like she has off and on all day.

"I know." We sit in silence for a few minutes, both sipping our drinks and watching the stars fill the cool night sky. "I wasn't even that torn up about it afterward. Don't get me wrong, I was pissed off, but now, I don't know. I'm just...over it. What does that mean?"

"It means the relationship had run its course, probably a long time ago, but you were comfortable, content. Now, you can move forward without looking back. They say the past is behind you for a reason."

I glance over at the man I've lived beside for almost three years now. In the time we've been neighbors, we've become friends. He's a damn good man, if not a tad bit lonely every now and again. "And you said you weren't good with words."

He lets out a boisterous laugh. "I get lucky every now and again."

"Thanks, Jeb."

"You're welcome, boy. Oh, before I forget, Jerran and his kids are coming for a visit next month. If you're not working, you'll have to stop by."

"I'll make sure to say hello," I reply. Jerran is married with three late teen/early twenties kids. Back when he was younger, he went to college in Indiana, met a woman there, and ended up staying. He's an eye doctor near Indy and doesn't get back to his hometown but about twice a year. I always enjoy visiting with him and his wife when they are here, and the fact that it sounds like all three of his kids are coming too makes me happy for Jeb. He needs his family, especially since his wife passed.

"Sounds good. Well, I'm gonna head back inside. It's getting close to my bedtime."

Jeb stands up and reaches for my empty. "I got it, but thanks."

He nods and shuffles toward his door. "Don't be too hard on yourself, boy. Sometimes the best things in life happen when you least expect them."

Again, a mirage of images parade through my mind, all featuring one woman.

"Thanks," I reply, my throat thick.

"Night."

I wave at my neighbor and wait until he's inside and his condo is secure before I head next door to mine. Once inside, I toss my empty in the trash and lock my own door. As I turn around and survey my empty, quiet house, his words replay in my head.

Sometimes the best things in life happen when you least expect them.

He's absolutely right. Reaching into the cabinet, I grab a trash bag and set off toward my bedroom. The room smells fragrant, thanks to the roses on the nightstand and the petals on top of the comforter. I quickly scoop them up and start dropping them in the bag. Next, I move on to the candles. The new one I purchased at the bed and bath store in her favorite scent comes in handy on the rare occasion the power goes out.

Finally, I grab the bottle of expensive wine she likes and the two glasses and take it all to the kitchen. The glasses are placed in the cabinet, while the wine goes on the rack above my fridge. I'm not a big wine drinker, but if I do, it's not the sweet stuff she prefers. I guess I could give it to Lyndee to drink or maybe save it for when Jeb's daughter-in-law is here. She might like the wine.

Once everything is cleaned up, I'm able to finally relax. Kicking off my loafers, I set them on the rack inside my closet, completely ignoring the few things hanging there that don't belong to me, and remove my belt. My slacks and button-down go into the laundry, and I reach for a pair of flannel lounge pants.

Only, when I have them in my hands, they don't feel right. Tossing them back on the shelf, I rip off my white undershirt and socks before returning to my bedroom in my boxers. I slip into the bathroom and brush my teeth, making sure I do a little extra flossing, since I didn't get it done last night.

That's because you were doing *something else.*

Excuse me, someone.

Once I've completed my nightly routine, I slip into bed and turn on CNN. For several minutes, I watch the latest news headlines parade across the screen, but it's hard to concentrate. My mind isn't on the stories or the latest stock numbers.

No, my mind is across town.

I can't help but wonder what BJ's doing right now.

"What the hell is this?" Jameson asks the moment four plates are set down on the table.

"Lyndee and I came up with something new this weekend," Jasper declares, matching his friend's grumpy tone.

Walker bends down and sniffs the burger. “Is that…peanut butter?”

Jasper smiles proudly. “It is. Try it.”

“You want us to eat a burger with peanut butter?” I ask, a little hesitant. Our friend is a wizard in the kitchen and rarely leads us astray, but I’m not sure peanut butter is the best choice of condiments for a cheeseburger.

Jasper lets out a frustrated growl. “Just take a bite.”

I lift the burger and give it a sniff. Yeah, I definitely smell peanut butter too, but there’s also something else there. It’s tangy, like a rich tomato. Carefully, I take a small bite, not really sure what to expect. The result is a little shocking, actually.

“Well?” Jasper asks, all eyes on me.

“It’s not…horrible,” I reply, chewing the surprisingly familiar flavors.

“It’s a PB and J burger,” Jasper states proudly, finally taking a seat on the fourth chair. He looks at the other two. “Try it.”

Walker gives him a skeptical look before bringing it to his mouth and taking a bite. “Tell me about the jelly,” he finally says after he swallows.

“It’s a sun-dried tomato and basil spread, with a hint of red wine vinegar. Lyndee made the buns last night at the bakery with a light peanut butter swirl. The maple bacon is caramelized, which gives it that sweet flavor you expect from the jelly.”

“It’s actually not bad,” I report, taking a second bite of my sandwich. I glance over at Jameson, who has yet to try it. He’s just staring at the burger, as if it were a snake about to bite him. “You gonna try it?”

He glances over, an uneasy look on his face that makes my heart stutter a beat. “No, I’m good,” he states, pushing the plate away. He stands up and reaches into his shirt pocket for his cigarettes. "I'm gonna have a quick smoke. I'll be back in a few." And then he's gone, leaving the three of us sitting at the table.

"What's that about?" I ask, glancing at my friends.

Walker sighs and shakes his head. "He's not a fan of PB and Js. Won't eat them. When he was little, he had to hide bread and peanut butter under his bed so he had food for himself and BJ."

Jasper closes his eyes. "Fuck. I didn't know."

Walker waves off his comment. "No one really does. You know him. It's not something he talks about."

"I should go out there," Jasper replies, pushing back from the table.

"No, don't. It's just going to piss him off more if you draw attention to it. Give him a few minutes, and he'll be back in."

But Jasper doesn't sit down. Instead, he reaches for the plate with the burger and returns to the kitchen. Walker and I both eat, but my food sits heavy in my stomach. We all know Jameson's had a rough life. Worse than my own, which wasn't easy being raised by a single mom.

In fact, out of the four of us, Jasper's parents were the only ones married and together during his childhood. Walker never knew his father, and Jameson's was in and out of his life when he was young, thanks to stints in jail.

As for me, my dad left when I was seven. Apparently, he decided he wanted a different family more than the one he already had. We only saw him for major holidays, and only because it was court ordered. My sisters and I weren't included in their family pictures, Christmas cards, or birthday celebrations. Her kids got it all, while we were left trying to figure out how to help Mom out while she was working three jobs just to keep a roof over our heads.

The invitations to holiday meals dried up the day my younger sister turned eighteen, but that's okay. We didn't need him. *I* don't need him. I haven't spoken to the man in several years, and definitely not since I moved to Stewart Grove. He doesn't care enough to reach out and say hi, so I don't care enough to try either. No love lost there. The only thing he showed me was how to work hard for what you want in this life.

Not because I saw it from him, but because I saw it in my mom. Because of what she was forced to do in the situation we were left in.

My drive to succeed stems solely from watching Mom work her ass off, sometimes failing in the process. The tears she cried late at night when she thought we were all sleeping, the bags under her eyes from getting four to five hours of sleep a night, the missed ball games and club events. My mom is the strongest person I know, and it's what fueled my desire to stand on my own two feet at a young age.

Because that's all I had then.

It's what I have now.

Jasper returns a few minutes later with a fresh burger and fries, and shortly after that, Jameson comes back from his smoke break. No one says anything about the burger, or the fact that a new one appeared in its place. We just continue on with our meeting, trying to push aside the baggage we all carry.

I pull out a stack of reports I ran for today and slide them in front of each of my partners. "All right, let's get started. Jameson thinks we're getting close to hiring a part-timer at the brewery. Here's what I got."

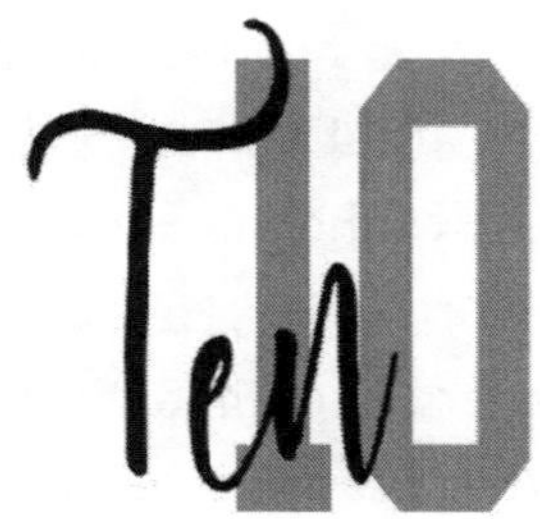

Ten

BJ

"What do you think?" I ask after wiping off the tattoo and handing the client a mirror.

"Oh my God, BJ, I love it!" she bellows, tears forming in the corners of her eyes. "I can't believe how gorgeous it is. I mean, I knew it'd be amazing, but this…" she trails off, staring down at the butterfly spreading its wings I just tattooed on her side.

"It's a great piece. I'm glad you like it," I state, standing up and stretching my back. "Here's information on caring for your new ink, as well as a list of our frequently asked questions. Do you have any right now?"

She shakes her head, handing over the mirror. "Nope, I'm good."

I lead her down the hall to where Amanda sits at the front counter. "She's all set," I inform my best friend, handing her the paper I filled out with the total charge for the work. Amanda has worked with me for the last two years, answering the phones, scheduling appointments, and taking payments. She's been a godsend to have here, and I'm so grateful Jax finally brought on the extra help.

To the client, I add, "She'll take care of your payment, and if you approve, a photo for our social media pages. Good to see you again." I throw a wave and turn to head back to my room. I'll have a thirty-minute break before my next client, and I could really use a drink.

I head to the break room and grab a bottle of water from the fridge. Then I move to the office, since Jax is busy with an appointment. Lying back on the couch, I take a few drinks before closing my eyes and just relaxing.

I wish I could say I was sleeping well, but that would be a lie. It's been just over two weeks since I spent a wild and crazy night with Isaac, and I can't stop thinking about him. He invades my thoughts constantly, day and night. It's been forever since I've had a crush, and this one is slowly killing me.

Frankly, it's frustrating as hell.

"You okay?" Jax says, drawing my eyes open.

"Fine."

He draws his eyebrows together, letting me know he doesn't believe me, before heading over and plopping down on his desk chair. "You look like shit."

I snort out a laugh. Leave it to Jax to not hold any punches. "Thanks for the compliment."

He just holds my gaze. "I give you plenty of compliments when they're warranted. So," he says, kicking his big boots up on the desk, "what's up?"

I sigh, not really wanting to get into it with Jax. Not that I know he won't give me sound advice, but because it's both complicated and a tad juvenile. "Just not sleeping well is all."

"You know, I have a cure for that," he replies, waggling his eyebrows suggestively and flashing me a wolfish grin.

I bark out another laugh. "Yes, I recall your remedy quite well."

He lets out a low, slow chuckle. "Well, I wasn't referring to me particularly, but who am I to deny a beautiful woman in need of medical assistance?"

I shake my head and plop back down on the couch. There was a time I enjoyed his assistance quite often, but over time, we realized that's all it was—sex. Very good sex, but sex nonetheless, and it hit us that we were better friends than we were at trying to navigate the minefield of bullshit that came with a relationship. So we ended it, and have been close ever since.

"Have you ever met someone who's not your type? Someone who doesn't typically check off any of your usual boxes, yet somehow has wormed their way into your head and monopolizes all of your thoughts? So much so you can't stop thinking about them, even when you really want to?" I'm almost out of breath when I finish talking, probably because I didn't actually expect myself to open up to Jax like that.

"Yes."

I open my eyes and roll to my side, staring at my boss and friend from across the room. When he doesn't say anything else, I ask, "Are you going to elaborate?"

"If you want me to," he replies, sitting up a little straighter in his chair. "Her name is Amanda, and I find her fascinating."

I slowly blink. Then again. My thoughts are a jumbled mess in my head, like a one-thousand-piece puzzle just dumped on the floor. "Amanda?" I finally ask, my throat dry and hoarse.

Jax doesn't say anything for several thundering heartbeats, just stares at me with those soulful chocolate eyes that seem to make women lose their minds—and their panties. "Forget I said anything," he quickly replies, clearing his throat and reaching for a stack of papers on his desk.

"Wait," I insist, jumping up and heading for his desk. I take a seat on the old wooden chair in front of him and search his gaze, looking for answers to the dozens of questions I suddenly have. "So...how long?"

Jax shrugs and sighs. "A few months. But I'd never do anything with her, BJ. I swear."

My heart is pounding a heavy beat in my chest, but I quickly realize it's not for the reason I thought it'd be. "You like her," I state, and quickly add, "Does she like you?"

He lifts his shoulders. "I don't know. Probably not."

I'm instantly offended. "Why wouldn't she? You're amazing, Jax. You're sweet and charming when you want to be. You have a great job and stable income. And you have great friends," I reply, throwing him a wink and a grin.

"Ha," he says, before sobering. "Isn't that the problem? I do have great friends. One friend in particular. One I used to date long ago, who just so happens to be best friends with the woman I'm crushing on."

I lean back, resting my arms on the rests. "Well, I can see how that might be a little confusing and slightly frowned upon in modern society, but lucky for you, your ex-slash-now friend doesn't get hung up on what society thinks is appropriate or not. Listen, Jax, if you want to ask Amanda out, I'm fine with it. Honestly. In fact, now that I think about it, you two would be pretty cool together."

One lone eyebrow arches heavenward as he just stares at me. “Really?”

“Really,” I reassure him. “You and I have history, but as someone recently reminded me, your past is behind you for a reason, right?”

“Your friend sounds brilliant,” he states, flashing me a blinding smile.

“He’s okay,” I state, waving off his modesty. “If you like her, I’m not going to stand in your way, but I will warn you that if you hurt her, I’m going to have to rip off your balls and have them made into earrings.”

He pulls a face of horror, which makes me laugh. “Damn, BJ, you don’t have to get so fucking violent on me.”

“Well, you just remember that when you’re taking my friend out on a date.”

He sobers instantly. “I don’t know if I’ll ask, but I do appreciate you givin’ me the green light.”

I stand up and move behind the desk, throwing my arms around his big, tattooed shoulders. “She’d be lucky to have you, Jax, and I swear I’m okay with it.”

He rests his hand on my arm and lightly squeezes. “You sure? You’re not just doing that thing chicks always do, like saying you’re fine even when you’re not?”

I snort. “When have you ever known me not to say what I think or feel?”

“Good point.”

I release the hug and head toward the door. “I’m serious, Jax. Go for it.”

The corner of his mouth tips upward. “I’ll think about it.”

I swipe my bottle of water off the table before I add, "Yeah, well, don't wait too long or someone better looking with more tattoos is liable to swoop in and steal your girl." I throw him a wink and head for my space.

Before I even cross the threshold, he hollers, "You're a pain in the ass, you know that?"

"Yep! You remind me often," I reply with a huge smile on my face as his laughter follows me to my room.

Once I'm alone, I work on making sure my chair is prepped and ready to go for my next appointment. I have two more tattoos and a piercing today, then I'm heading home for the evening. Maybe I'll make a big pot of chili or a casserole. Cooking sometimes helps me relax. I can take the leftovers to my brother's house, since I'll never be able to eat it all by myself.

Or I could take Jax's advice and let off a little steam the *other* way.

Of course, my first thought is to hit up Isaac, but we both know that's a stupid idea. Hell, he's probably back with his girlfriend by now. His perfectly dressed, stable, boring girlfriend, without a single tattoo or piercing.

A shiver sweeps through my body as I remember how pleasantly surprised he was to discover all of my piercings.

But, it's time to move past that.

It's not going to happen again, and the quicker I get that thought through my head, the better off I'll be.

Now, if only my vagina could get on board with this no-more-sex-with-Isaac plan.

"Hey!" I holler, stepping inside the main brewing room, where I was told my brother would be.

He steps out from behind a large piece of equipment with valves and gauges, and I instantly know something's wrong. "Hey," he mutters, averting his gaze.

"What the hell is up with you?" I ask, making my way quickly to my brother. I notice the grayish tint of his skin and the thin layer of sweat across his forehead and upper lip. "Are you sick?"

He scoffs. "Of course not. I haven't been sick since I was ten," he argues, refusing to acknowledge what is so evident to me.

"You're fucking sick, Jameson," I demand, placing the back of my hand against his forehead. He swipes it away, but not before I can feel how hot he is. "You have a fever."

"I'm almost done here. Once I take all these readings and get this batch ready to process, I'll head home and take a shower."

"You need some Tylenol and a bed, you big dummy. Get out of here," I argue, crossing my arms over my chest and shooting him eye-daggers.

"I can't. Have to finish," he grumbles.

"No, I'll do it. Go home and rest."

"You don't know what you're doing," he retorts, even though I don't take offense. He's right. I don't know anything about brewing beer.

"I might not, but someone does. I'll call someone. Who? Walker? George?" I ask, reaching for my phone.

"No," he insists, rubbing his temples with his hands. "I'll make a call. There's about an hour's worth of work left. If you can hang out until reinforcements get here, I'd appreciate it."

"Of course! Just tell me what you need."

With his eyes closed, he pulls his phone from his pocket and squints down at the screen. "Hey, I need help. I'm a little under the weather, and BJ's insisting I head home." He coughs, proving my point. "Yeah, that'd be great."

Hanging up the phone, he glances my way and yawns. "He's on his way."

"George?"

"No, Numbers." My heart skips a beat. "He's the one who knows enough to get through this batch so we don't have to dump it. George went home sick yesterday and wasn't in today."

"Sounds like he gave you whatever it is he has," I reply.

"I guess." He shows me what I need to do, which really isn't much of anything, but there's another step coming up in just over thirty minutes, and then I can head home. "I got this," I reassure my brother as he gathers up his leather jacket.

"Call me if you have any problems," he mumbles before heading out the door to go home for the night.

I watch the gauges for several minutes, making sure all the readings are where they should be. No, I may not know what I'm doing, per se, but I can make sure I don't screw this up for my brother. I fire off a text message, making sure he made it home okay. He doesn't live too far from here, so he should be there by now.

Jameson: Fine. Took drugs. Going to bed.

Me: I'll bring soup over later and put it in the fridge. You can eat when you get up.

Jameson: You're the best.

I can't help but smile as I slip my phone back into my pocket and step out of the brewing room. A few minutes later, the back door opens and slams with a loud bang. I glance over and see Isaac walking toward me.

"Hey," I greet, throwing him a little wave.

"Hi. How's Jameson?"

"He's got a fever and sounds like shit. He just took some Tylenol and is going to bed."

Isaac nods. "George came down with it yesterday. I hope the virus doesn't make its way through the staff. Fortunately, there's really only two of them over here together."

"So, I watched those gauges and made sure the numbers stayed where Jameson told me they should be," I start, pointing into the large room. "There's not too much time left on this cycle."

"Okay," he says, rocking back on his heels.

I get my first good look at him in over two weeks. He's in dark gray slacks and a light green button-down that only seems to bring out the gold in his eyes. He's wearing a striped tie, and his face is a little scruffy, like he might have forgotten to shave this morning. Then there's his hair, which is sticking up in a few places, as if he has constantly run his fingers through it. The total picture is of a gorgeous man, one who sparks a fire inside me I've never felt.

At least not on this level.

"Do you want to help me?" he asks, somewhat hesitantly. When I gaze at him in question, he adds, "With this batch. I can show you the final step in today's process."

There's something that looks a lot like hope reflecting in his eyes, which might be why I reply, "Sure." That and the fact I'm not ready to head home yet.

For the next thirty minutes, he shows me the brewery, explaining each step in the beer-making process. It's fascinating, really, to see it come to life. For months, I've been listening to my brother share the details, but now that I can see it—to really visualize his dream—it's truly remarkable.

We work through the final step together, and before I know it, we're done for the day. "Thanks for forcing your brother to go home and rest. If I know Jameson, it wasn't an easy feat."

"He didn't put up too much of a fight, which tells me he knew he was sick too. He just fought it."

"Well, I still appreciate it," he says, flipping off the lights as we make our way toward the back exit. "You're gonna go check on him?"

"Yeah," I say, glancing at my watch, "but not yet. I'm sure he's asleep, so I'll let him rest for a bit."

He nods, setting the alarm on the back door before pushing it open for us to exit. I glance over at my truck parked in the employee lot and turn to head that way.

"Hey, do you want to grab something to eat?"

I stop in my tracks and look over my shoulder. "What?"

"I can have Jasper whip up a few burgers for us. As a thank-you," he quickly adds, "for all your help tonight."

"I didn't really do anything," I insist.

He stuffs his hands in his pockets and shrugs. "Yeah, but I appreciate it nonetheless."

To be honest, I'm not really looking forward to going home alone. I've never minded the peace and quiet home offers, but these last couple of weeks, the silence has been almost deafening.

"Okay," I reply, bringing a wide smile to his handsome face. It lights up his eyes, even under the dark sky, and brings a warm sensation to life within me.

One burger won't hurt any, right?

Eleven 11

Isaac

"Do you prefer in here or the restaurant?" I ask, leading her through the bar entrance. Even for a Tuesday night, we're busy, which makes me damn proud of what we've accomplished in five short years.

"In here is good," she replies.

Honestly, I expected it. She doesn't seem like one who needs the fancy restaurant or crowded room. BJ prefers the quiet, more intimate setting, which is definitely more my speed.

I lead her to a pub table toward the back, the one Mallory and Lizzie always sit in when they come for dinner and to see Walker. I wait until she's seated before I take the chair across from her.

"Hey, Isaac, how's it going?" Kellen asks when he approaches our table. "Whatcha drinking tonight?"

I nod to BJ, allowing her to select her drink first. "Actually, are you serving your new beers?" she asks, glancing between me and the bartender.

"We are," I confirm before he has a chance. "We have five on tap right now."

"My brother has been talking about the American Lager lately, so I guess I'll try that."

"One All American Crüe coming right up," he says, flashing her a quick grin. "And for you, boss man?"

"I'll have the same," I reply, reaching out and grabbing the bifold pamphlet in the middle of the table. "These are the beers we have right now. Your brother was instrumental in getting the recipes and tastes down. He worked with George, our brewmaster, to fine-tune it until we had it the way we wanted it."

She takes the informational piece and starts to look it over. There's the slightest grin playing on her lips as she reads. "He talked a lot about the process, including all the taste testing."

I can't help but laugh. "There were a lot of late nights tasting batch after batch after batch. A few months ago, I swore I'd never drink beer again," I confess as Kellen delivers our mugs of beer.

"You guys eating dinner too?"

"Yeah, but we may need a few minutes on that," I start, but she quickly jumps in.

"I'm ready now. I know what I'm having." To me she adds, "I get the same thing every time." I wave my hand, indicating for her to go ahead and order. "I'll have Between the Sheets, please, with a side of ranch for the fries."

Between the Sheets?

I almost can't stop the groan threatening to fly from my mouth. Clearing my throat, I add, "I'll take the Morning BJ, Kellen."

He snorts as he writes, smiling like the cat that ate the canary. "Won't we all," he mutters, closing his notepad and taking a step back. "I'll get these in right away."

"Morning BJ?" she asks, a wide smile on her gorgeous face. "Who came up with these names?"

My mind flashes back to the discussions we had during the planning phase of Burgers and Brew. There were a lot of talks about the menu, the atmosphere, the brand we wanted to create. "Actually, that was Jasper. He wanted clever, slightly inappropriate names for the burgers so that they weren't like every other burger joint in the country."

She brings her beer to her lips and takes a small sip. "Wow, this is good," she states, drinking a little more before setting it back down on the table. "And Jasper's right. It's your niche, your thing. From a marketing standpoint, it's brilliant."

"Yeah, we all agreed too. I was probably the hardest sell at first, if you can imagine," I inform, taking a healthy drink of my own beer.

BJ snorts out a laugh. "Oh, I can just imagine you were. I bet a man who wears loafers and ties every day had a hard time agreeing to call a cheeseburger Strip and Go Naked."

I shrug but don't dispute her statement. Mostly because she's spot-on. I was the hard sell on naming our gourmet hamburgers after dirty innuendoes, but I was quickly outvoted. And to be honest, I'm glad I was. Turns out, the names are part of the restaurant's charm and keeps everyone talking.

"So, speaking of BJ," I start, redirecting the conversation away from the food.

Her eyes widen with surprise, and her mouth falls open in the cutest little O. I'd be a little turned on if it weren't for the realization of what she assumed I meant.

"No! That's not...I wasn't meaning...shit, that came out wrong. I wasn't referring to you and me and...God, I'm really bad at this," I mutter, rubbing my forehead with my hand. "I wasn't asking for one," I add, but my dick twitches in disagreement. "I was referring to your name."

"Oh. Well, for a minute there, I thought we were jumping right past the dinner portion of the evening and going right to dessert," she teases, the softest giggle spilling from her lips. Lips I'd love to touch and kiss again, even though I shouldn't.

"No, I'm sorry. I was just commenting on your nickname."

She rolls her eyes and sighs. "Yeah, my mom was a huge fan of Michael Jackson, apparently. She named me Billie Jean, which in turn got shortened to BJ along the way. Do you know how hard it is to go through school with the nickname BJ?"

I can't imagine, honestly. I recall exactly how juvenile and horrible kids can be in junior high and high school, and I'm sure she was teased mercilessly.

"Anyway, as I got older, I started to not care, you know? I was able to tune them out. But, one time, freshman year, a senior boy asked me if I got my nickname because I gave good head and my brother overheard. That kid was practically drinking out of a straw for the rest of the school year. Jameson got suspended for two weeks his junior year, but he didn't care. He said punching that kid in the jaw was worth it. After that, they didn't tease me near as much."

"High school is definitely rough, isn't it?" I ask, almost absently.

"You too?"

I gaze over at her and nod my head, fighting off the memories. "It's not easy being the smart kid sometimes."

"Nor the dumb one." My mouth falls open, so she quickly continues, "It's not that I was dumb, but I didn't care about school. I liked art, and everything else was just a waste of time to me. I got horrible grades to the point I almost failed my eighth-grade year, but

Jameson wouldn't let me. He helped me with my geography, English, and math until I got my grades above failing."

"He's a good guy."

She nods solemnly. "He is. If only he would actually believe it."

I know my friend has a lot of baggage, and I'm not one to pry, but over the years of our friendship, I've picked up on things. Most look at my rough around the edges friend and refuse to see any deeper than the tattoos and pissed-off scowl he wears like a suit of armor, but I see him.

And so does his sister.

Our food arrives, and there's no missing the way Kellen smirks at me. I know what he's thinking, and while I might have invited her to join me for dinner, it's not a date. Not that I would mind if it were, but I know we're not at that place. That's evident by the awkwardness in our last couple of encounters.

Though, tonight is way less uncomfortable, if I do say so myself.

"How's your food?" I ask after she's several bites into her burger.

"Delicious," she confirms, dipping a French fry in the glob of ranch. "I could live here and die a happy woman."

I swallow my food before I reply, "I have it on good authority it gets old after a while."

BJ glances over at me and smiles. "Dedication to your business isn't a bad thing, Isaac."

I snort in disagreement. "Tell that to Savannah." Suddenly, I sober, realizing what I just said. "Sorry, I shouldn't have said that."

The smile falls from her face. "You know, she doesn't deserve you, right?"

A lump forms in my throat the size of Rhode Island, making it difficult to swallow. "I know." And I do. The more I think about it, the more I realize she's correct. Actually, I probably should have realized it long before these last couple of weeks since she walked away and hasn't so much as looked back.

We finish our meal, and when Kellen brings the check to the table, I grab it before BJ is able to. "My treat."

"You don't have to buy mine," she insists, reaching into her pocket and grabbing cash.

"I invited you in as a thank-you for helping at the brewery earlier. I insist," I state, slipping cash into the black folder.

"Well, let me get the tip then," she replies, setting a few bills onto table before hopping off her pub chair.

Placing my hand on her lower back, I lead her toward the back exit where her truck is parked. As soon as we hit the hallway, it hits me. "Hey, do you mind if we run up to my office before we leave? I left in a hurry earlier and didn't grab a few things I wanted to take home with me."

I wait for her to tell me I don't need to walk her out but am pleasantly surprised when she doesn't. "Sure."

We take the stairs up to my office, the warmth of her skin seeping through her clothes and burning my hand. I don't release my hold on her though. It's as if I need the connection to breathe.

I unlock the door and push it open. BJ steps in first and takes a look around my space. "Wow, this is exactly as I pictured it," she states, the corner of her lip turned upward in a grin.

"How so?" I ask, glancing around to try to see what she sees.

"Well, it's neat and very orderly. Everything has a place, and I bet, if I open those filing cabinets, all of the folders are in alphabetical order and color coded."

I blink across the room, surprised by the accuracy of her assumption. "That bottom drawer there," I start, pointing to the cabinet, "is in date order, actually."

Her smile is big and makes my heart flutter in my chest. "I stand corrected."

I hurry to my desk and gather up the files I was wanting to review regarding the brewery. I slip them into my satchel bag, along with my laptop, and zip it closed. As I turn, I realize BJ is standing directly beside me, so close I can smell the clean shampoo scent in her hair. She's looking at the two photos I have framed on my desk. The first one is my mom, two sisters, and myself on my college graduation day, and the other is of my friends and me the day we purchased this building.

"You all look so young," she observes.

"Hard to believe that was almost six years ago now," I reply.

She stands up to her full height, which puts her head at my shoulders, and suddenly, we're very close. Very, *very* close. The room crackles with electricity and heat. We both turn at the same time, and before I even realize what's happening, she's in my arms and our mouths are crashing together.

The kiss is pure fire. Our tongues dance, as I pull her flush against my chest and grip her ass in my hands. She's wearing leggings, and all I can think about is what she's *not* wearing beneath them. I turn her, pinning her against the desk. BJ sits back, lifting her legs and wrapping them around my waist. My cock throbs in my pants, begging to be let out from its confinement and slide into the one place he thinks about day and night.

I release her mouth, only to trail my lips down the long, slender column of her neck. The sweetest sigh spills from those luscious lips, spurring me on. My hand slips beneath her sweater and slowly moves up the soft skin of her side until it covers her small, perky breast. The ring through her nipple makes my cock jump for joy and my mouth water to taste.

Suddenly, there's a heavy beat pounding in my brain. It's loud and drawing closer with each passing second. Realization settles in with the fact the noise isn't coming from my brain or my heart. It's coming from the stairs.

I rip my mouth off BJ's neck, my hand out of her top, and jump back as if I were being burned. Her eyes grow wide, and she hops off the desk and rights her sweater just as Jasper comes into view at the top of the steps. "Hey, glad I caught you. Oh, hey, BJ," he says, entering my office, carrying a bag.

"Hi, Jasper. What's up?" I ask, my voice sounding a little pitchy, even to my own ears.

He stares at me for a few seconds before looking over to BJ. Besides the slight flush to her cheeks, she looks cool and calm, while I probably have guilty written across my forehead in permanent marker. "I heard Jameson went home sick," he starts, stepping farther into my office and setting the bag on top of my desk. "I whipped up some of his favorites, as well as some soup."

My eyes narrow at the bag. "You made soup? In the last hour?"

He shrugs. "I still had the base in the freezer from when Lizard wasn't feeling well last month. I just threw some chicken and whatever vegetables I had on hand into it and let it simmer for a bit."

"No onions though, right?" BJ asks.

Jasper shakes his head. "Hell no. I learned that lesson the hard way a long time ago, when I tried to chop them up so fine no one would find them."

"He did, right?"

"Bastard found every little sliver," Jasper confirms with a grin.

"Yeah, he hates them with a passion. Thanks for this. I'm getting ready to head over there," she replies, grabbing the bag.

"I'm heading out for the night too. BJ helped me close up the brewery so Jameson could go home and rest. I just came up here to grab a few things before leaving."

Jasper nods. "Well, I better get back down there. Pretty busy for a Tuesday night. Thanks for running that to your brother, BJ."

"No problem. Thanks for making it," she replies, following behind him as he heads for the stairs. I grab my satchel bag and do the same, making sure the door is secured on my way.

We throw Jasper a wave as he continues down the hallway to the kitchen, while we slip out the back exit. The cool air hits us square in the face as we make our way to her truck. "If you want, I could take that over for you. It's on my way home."

BJ pauses and turns to face me. "No, I don't mind. I'd like to check on him. If I don't, I'll just worry about him."

I shove my hands into my pockets and rock back on my heels. "I get it. Would you mind if I follow you over there?" When shock crosses her features, I quickly add, "Just to make sure he's doing what he's supposed to. You know how he is, and I'd feel more comfortable checking on him too."

The truth is, I just want to see her again. Even if it's from across the room, and the room happens to include her brother.

"Uh, sure. I don't mind."

"Okay, great. I'll be right behind you," I reply, waiting until she climbs into her truck before I walk to my car.

Once inside, uncertainty crosses my mind. This probably wasn't my brightest idea. It wasn't five minutes ago I had my hand up her top and was fondling her breast while sucking on her neck.

Now, I'm about to head over to her brother's house with her to check on him. Probably not my smartest move, but there's no changing it now.

We're headed into the lion's den together.

Let's just hope Jameson's out of it enough not to pick up on anything.

Like the fact I really want to take his sister to bed.

Again.

BJ

I tighten my grip on the white bag and my keys, praying it's enough to keep me from grabbing Isaac. As I step onto Jameson's front porch, Isaac reaches out and opens the old, heavy screened door so I can let us in.

"Jame, it's me," I announce as I step inside my brother's house.

The first thing I notice is the silence. The only thing I can hear is what sounds like a lumberjack sawing logs off in the distance. I follow the sound to the living room and find my brother passed out on the couch.

In his underwear.

"That's something you can't unsee," Isaac mutters, making me smile.

"You get used to it. He sleeps that way, but I'm gonna assume it also has something to do with the fever. He looks awfully sweaty," I say, walking over to where my brother lies on his stomach on the couch. He has a blanket wrapped around his legs, but there's no missing the fact he's in only his black boxer briefs, the dark lines and muted colors of his tattoos on his back on full display.

I bend down and place my hand on his forehead. Jameson mumbles something incoherent before settling back into a deep sleep. "He's warm, but not burning up the way he was earlier."

"Maybe his fever is trying to break," Isaac states, glancing around the small living room. "I'm going to grab a fresh bottle of water and some more fever reducer."

When he disappears down the hallway toward the bathroom, I take the bag of soup to the kitchen and slip it into the fridge. Of course, I notice it's practically empty, which makes me sigh.

"What's the matter?" Isaac asks, joining me in the kitchen with the bottle of medicine in his hand. He looks over my shoulder and adds, "He barely has any food."

When Jameson was younger and starting off on his own, he used to overspend on food. So much so, most of the meat and fresh produce went to waste. When I asked him about it, he just shrugged and changed the subject, but I knew the reason. He never wanted to be without food again. Over the years he's gotten a little better, only buying what he plans to use or eat, but I know the urge to stock up is still something he deals with regularly.

"Actually," I start, opening the freezer above the fridge and finding it completely packed. "I figured."

He has a chest freezer in the garage too. It's probably just as full.

"Wow, he's stocked up well."

I just shrug and close the door. I'm not quite as traumatized as Jameson, mostly because he did everything he could to always make sure I ate food. Even if that meant he went without. Looking back now, I can see his sacrifices. I know what he did. He'll always be my big brother, my biggest protector, even if I was too young to truly understand then.

Perhaps I did on some level. I always shared my sandwich with him, which was usually peanut butter. It was easy to shove a jar of generic peanut butter under his bed or hide it in his closet. The bread was a little more of a challenge, but we didn't care. Food was food and we weren't picky.

I grab an envelope off the counter and jot down a note, letting him know there's soup in the fridge and to call me when he's feeling better. I take the note into the living room, smiling when the sounds of his snoring fill the room, and set it on the coffee table. Isaac places the water bottle and the bottle of fever reducer beside it, in hopes he'll see it as soon as he wakes.

Another thought hits me. Knowing he needs to stay on top of the fever, I go in search of his phone. The least I can do is have it close by and set an alarm to make sure he wakes up to take the medicine.

After locating it in his room, I input his passcode and pull up the alarm app. There are a dozen times pre-set, but none are what I'm looking for. I add the time of two hours from now and set the phone down beside the note. Then, I quickly add a PS on the bottom, so he knows when the alarm goes off to take more meds.

Finally, I place a kiss on his clammy forehead and make my way to the front door, Isaac hot on my heels the whole way. Outside, I suck in a deep breath of cool air. After making sure the door is securely locked, I turn to face Isaac.

"Do you think I should stay?" he asks, running his hands through his hair. "In all the years we've been friends, I've never seen him sick. Maybe he shouldn't be alone."

I consider his words, mostly because I've already thought of it. I don't know if I've ever seen my brother sick besides the occasional cold, and even those are rare. But I also know he'd hate it if we were here and made a fuss. Unless he's on stage playing guitar, he hates attention. Doesn't want any extra focus on him when it doesn't need to be. But mostly, he doesn't like appearing weak.

"No, I don't think he'd like that. I'll check on him in the morning before I head to work and see how he's doing."

Isaac nods. "You're probably right," he says, shoving his hands into his trousers. After a few long seconds of awkward silence, he asks, "Would you like to come back to my place and hang for a bit?"

A smile spreads across my lips at his sudden nervousness. "I'm not so sure that's a good idea. Last time one of us went to the other's home, things got…heated."

He meets my gaze, his pupils dilate. Isaac's mouth falls open into this cute little O, and all I can think about is all the naughty things he can do with that mouth. It's like that Bill Murray movie, *Groundhog Day*. Day and night, over and over again, on instant replay in my mind.

It's exhausting.

But so is trying to fight my attraction to him. Obviously, he feels something too, otherwise he wouldn't have kissed me in his office earlier tonight—or me; I'm not really sure who initiated it. He also wouldn't be inviting me over now, and even though I should probably decline his invitation for obvious reasons, I won't.

I can't.

Like a moth to a flame…

Isaac's face blushes, and when he drops his eyes to stare at the crack in the concrete, there's no missing the way he smiles. "Yeah, probably not the smartest."

Deciding to stop fighting the pull, I step forward and place my hand on his chest. I can feel the pounding of his heart against my palm. "You know what, I'd love to hang out."

Naked.

But I don't say that.

Mostly because it's already insinuated.

"Okay," he replies, clearing his throat. "You can follow me to my place, if that works for you."

"Sounds great."

He walks me to my truck and waits until I climb up before heading to his perfectly safe, perfectly boring mid-sized car.

Huh. Perhaps a little back seat sex will liven up that car.

We head to a great subdivision on the opposite side of town. This is an area full of families, with white picket fences around the front lawns and minivans in the driveway. I'm not surprised to find Isaac smackdab in the middle of suburbia, USA.

He pulls into the left side of a two-unit condo and parks in the garage. I stop my truck behind him and jump out, meeting him inside the garage. Isaac closes the door and leads me to the entry, one that opens to a laundry room. It's bright, spacious, and white.

Very white.

"Come on in," he says, closing the door behind me and escorting me to the kitchen and dining room. "Can I get you something to drink?" he asks, a hint of nervousness in his question.

"Just water." While he grabs two glasses and fills them with filtered water, I take a look around his place. All of the walls are white, the space roomy, and the furniture a touch on the formal side.

The only color is in the painting above a buffet table, and it looks like something you'd see in a catalog promoting fancy, formal living spaces.

However, it lacks pizzazz. It lacks warmth and color and life.

His dining room is boring, honestly.

"Here you go," he says, handing over a glass of cold water.

"Thanks," I reply, taking a sip and meeting his gaze. The iced liquid does nothing to squelch the heat flooding my veins.

Isaac takes a drink of his water before setting his glass down on the placemat and reaching for me. I move willingly, stepping forward and into his body so naturally, I can't help but think how perfectly we align. The desire swirling in his eyes tells me he's about to kiss me. I've been ready for more since we broke apart back in his office, even if I haven't been willing to admit it to myself.

An admission is a complication neither of us need.

Suddenly, there's a knock on the back door. Isaac jumps back and turns to face the French doors. On the opposite side is an older man wearing a warm flannel and a wide grin. Isaac clears his throat and moves to unlock the door, his motions a little hurried and shaky. "Hey, Jeb. Nice to see you this evening."

"Isaac, my friend," he starts, glancing around the man I was seconds away from mauling and offering me the kindest smile I've ever seen. "Good evening, miss. I'm sorry for interrupting your evening."

"You're fine, Jeb," Isaac quickly interjects. "This is my…friend, BJ."

The older man steps inside the condo, walking around Isaac and heading my way. "BJ is it?" A curious look on his face, as he offers me his hand.

I nod. “It’s short for Billie Jean,” I inform, shaking his outstretched hand and finding something comforting in his warm eyes.

“What a beautiful name. Can I call you Billie?”

I shrug, feeling a little off-kilter. “No one really calls me by my birth name,” I state.

“They should. It’s unique and beautiful, just like you,” he says, turning to face Isaac. “Don’t you agree?”

Something flashes across Isaac’s face, but it’s pushed away before I can dissect what it was. “I agree completely,” he replies, his voice a touch raspy.

“Well,” Jeb starts, turning back to face me, “It is lovely to meet you, Billie. I didn’t realize my neighbor here had company, or I wouldn’t have intruded.”

Isaac laughs. “I highly doubt that. I’m sure you were looking out the front window when I got home.”

The old man feigns innocence before leaning in and whispering, “I can’t help it if my television faces Isaac’s driveway.”

I smile widely, appreciating Jeb’s candor more than he’ll ever know. “I’m glad he has a friend to watch out for him.”

“That’s right,” he says, taking a step back. “She appreciates my efforts to make sure my neighbors are safe.”

“It’s called nosiness,” Isaac replies, the corner of his mouth tipped upward.

“Whatever you want to call it,” he teases, waving off the comment. “I’ll head back home and leave you two. Alone.” Jeb winks at Isaac, making him roll his eyes.

“Thanks for stopping by,” Isaac states, holding the door open for his neighbor.

"Miss Billie, it was wonderful meeting you. I hope to see you again soon." Then he walks outside and disappears into the night, leaving Isaac and me alone again.

"Well, that was subtle," he says, shutting the door and making sure it's locked before sliding vertical blinds across the door and cutting off the outside world.

I chuckle. "He's sweet."

"He's a great man. I've enjoyed living next to him." Isaac shoves his hands in his pockets and walks my way.

"So..."

"So..." he mirrors, stopping in front of me. "Where were we?"

"You were about to kiss me," I remind him, bringing the faintest of smiles to his lips.

"Ahh, yes. Now I remember."

He reaches out, running his knuckles down my cheek. A shiver sweeps through me at the touch, one I'm sure he feels. "He's right, you know."

My eyebrows draw up in confusion. "Who?"

"Jeb. He's right. You're beautiful."

I feel my skin heating at the compliment, not because of the words, but because I can see it in his eyes. Those hazel eyes are so truthful, so honest, and frankly, it scares me a little. I've never felt so scared and so safe with someone in my entire life, but that's how he makes me feel.

Needing to redirect this to something I can handle, I whisper, "Are you going to kiss me already?"

He flashes a quick grin. "Oh, I'm definitely going to kiss you," he says, brushing his lips across my neck and down to my collarbone, "all over."

And he does. Isaac starts at my neck and works his way down, removing articles of clothing as he goes. When my sweater hits the floor, I've never been so grateful for not wearing a bra as I am right now. My breasts ache for his touch, for his mouth, and he doesn't disappoint in reminding me how amazing he feels.

Next thing you know, I'm positioned on his very formal dining room table, my pants being thrown over his shoulder and his eyes devouring my naked body as if I were a Thanksgiving Day feast. "Fuck, I can't stop thinking about you. I close my eyes, and I see you. Like this," he murmurs, sliding his big hands up my thighs and holding me open for him.

He crouches down and takes a long, leisurely swipe with his tongue, swirling it around my piercing as if it were an ice cream cone on a hot summer day. Pleasure barrels through me at Mach speed, drawing a loud moan of pleasure from my lips. "God, that feels so good."

"You know, I really like this," he mutters right before sucking the piercing into his mouth.

I shout out, rocking my hips against his face. "Yes, yes, yes, I really like that too," I gasp, my head rolls to the side as I close my eyes, letting the sensations carry me.

"Maybe I should consider a piercing," he says, startling me. The thought of Isaac getting his dick or balls pierced shocks me, mostly because it would be so out of character for him.

"Dick piercings are more for the woman," I state, rolling my hips against his mouth. "If you really want something for you, you need a woman with a tongue piercing."

He glances up, curiosity written all over his face, yet he doesn't stop administering pleasure with his mouth. "Yeah?"

My eyes cross. "Oh yeah. I've been told the tongue ring and a blow job make a better combination than macaroni and cheese."

"Interesting," he hums, flooding my core with delicious vibrations.

"Do that again," I beg.

"What? This?" he asks right before he hums long and loud against my clit.

"Yes, that," I groan, my hips moving all on their own now.

It takes him approximately four seconds of humming, sucking, and licking to send me over the edge and about twice that time for Isaac to lose his pants. When he reaches up and starts unbuttoning his shirt, I sit up and decide to help. Guys I've been with in the past weren't exactly button-down shirt kinda guys, and I've discovered there's something wildly erotic about releasing those little buttons and exposing the body he hides away from the rest of the world.

While Isaac works to unfasten the smaller buttons at his wrists, I run my hands up his chest. I don't have long nails—they get in the way at work—but I have enough to dig into his flesh. My fingers tangle in his dark chest hair, something else I find incredibly sexy, before moving up to his nipples. "You know, maybe we should put some hardware here," I say, pinching his small, dark nipples before leaning forward and swiping my tongue across each one.

His head falls back and his Adam's apple bobs. "I'm pretty sure, right here, in this moment, I'd let you pierce whatever the hell you want."

"Good to know," I whisper, right before I bite down on the left one.

He groans before pushing me back, somewhat roughly. He reaches down for his pants, rips a condom from his wallet, and sheathes his erection. When he meets my gaze, there's fire dancing in those hazel orbs, and it's electric.

Isaac lifts me from the table and runs his thumb over my lips. "Turn around and hang on tight. This is going to be a rough, hard ride."

Isaac

I watch in pure rapture as she maintains eye contact and slowly turns around, wiggling her little ass against my groin in a teasing manner.

So I slap it.

Not super hard, but enough to cause a slight sting and the pink imprint of my hand. Fear grips my chest instantly. I've never struck a woman, even during sex. But when BJ groans deeply and presses back against my cock, I realize she liked it.

I run my hand over the spot to help soothe the sting. "Please tell me that was okay," I whisper, my voice hoarse.

"God yes. Do it again," she demands, rolling her hips.

I lift my other hand and give that ass cheek a small whack, immediately running my palm across the smarted skin. Then, I quickly line myself up with her body and press inside. She's wet—soaked, really—and the moment I'm fully seated, she clenches down on me—hard—and moans.

So, I do what feels natural to me and give her already pink ass another little swat. The moment I make contact, her muscles squeeze the life out of my cock and my hips jolt forward once more.

BJ cries out and presses back against me, even though I'm already buried as deeply as possible.

I pull out before pistoning forward again and again, my eyes glued to the way my groin slams against her glorious ass. It's a sight I will never forget, but now's not the time to think about that. Tingles spread up my spine and I know I'm too close to stop my release.

With her hands placed on the table, she arches her back and moves with me. I reach around and pinch her pierced nipple, recalling exactly how sensitive it is. The result is a loud moan and her head falling forward, exposing her ass once more. I pause my movements, but only long enough to give the globe of her rear one final smack.

The result is an explosion. She rocks back and comes so hard I'm pretty sure Jeb can hear. Hell, the entire neighborhood could probably hear. Her pussy squeezes me so tightly I have no choice but to follow her over the edge. I grip her hips and slam forward one final time, emptying myself into the condom.

When my body stops shaking, I lean forward, placing open-mouthed kisses across her sweaty back. She reaches her arm up and over the back of my neck, holding her back to my front tightly. BJ turns her head, giving me slight access to her mouth. "Wow," she mumbles as soon as I finish kissing her soundly.

"Yeah." I dislodge myself from her body and glance down at her smarted skin. My hands instantly rub the pink area, another pang of guilt settling in my chest. "I'm sorry I did this."

She looks over her shoulder and down to my hands. "Please don't be. I really liked it."

I sigh in relief. My hands work their way up her sides and wrap around her front. "I did too. I never thought I'd enjoy spanking as much as I did."

She turns in my arms and wraps her arms around my shoulders. Her small breasts press firmly against my chest. "When you did that and slammed into me the way you did? Best. Orgasm. Ever," she informs, kissing my neck. The combination of her words and her mouth against me is like a bolt of lust straight to my cock.

I kiss her everywhere. Over flower and butterfly tattoos, across bright colors and gray hues. Each piece is unique and gorgeous and looks striking in contrast to her fair skin. She's a beautiful work of art, one I can't seem to get enough of. "You're stunning."

She meets my gaze, her eyes shining with gratitude. "Thank you."

"Come on," I say, helping her stand up. I remove the condom and toss it in the garbage can before reaching for her hand. "Let's get you cleaned up."

We walk around the corner, through the living room, and down the short hallway. Together, we pass the guest room that doubles as my home office and a full bathroom. There's a hall closet too, full of linens and extra toiletries, and then finally, my bedroom.

I hadn't planned to have anyone in here, but thankfully, it's in neat and tidy order. My bed is made, like it is every day, and my dirty clothes are in the hamper in the closet. There are even vacuum lines on the carpet from my early morning cleaning spree when I couldn't sleep.

"Shocker," BJ says, fighting a smile.

"What?" I ask, glancing around my room.

"Blue. I pretty much already knew what your room would look like without even walking in here. Blue bedding with beige carpet and white walls. Natural oak furniture and landscape prints on the wall. Your towels are probably taupe, aren't they?"

I run my hand over my face, ignoring the fact I'm completely naked, and look around. When my gaze meets her happy one, I blurt out, "Yes, they're taupe," making her laugh.

Suddenly, I realize there's a nude woman in my room, making the space feel smaller than it is. "You know," she murmurs, walking toward me. "I could probably use a shower."

I swallow over the lump in my throat. "You're welcome to use mine. It's in there," I state, pointing to the open bathroom door.

She glances down to my cock, which is now standing at attention once more. "I think I'm going to need help with my back." BJ reaches down and wraps her delicate fingers around me and leads me to the shower.

I'm pretty sure I'd follow her anywhere, anytime.

Especially when her hands are where they are.

"We probably need to talk about this," I mutter, BJ tucked into the crook of my arm.

The clock on my nightstand reads after midnight, but I'm surprisingly not tired. In fact, I'm more energized and alive than ever before, despite two rounds of great sex.

"Okay."

Taking a deep breath, I decide to just speak what's on my mind. "I don't know what the future holds, but I like you, BJ. The thing is, I don't think I'm ready for a relationship yet. It hasn't been that long since Savannah and I ended ours for the fifth, hell, maybe even sixth time. I hope that doesn't make me sound like an asshole."

She looks up and holds my gaze. "You're honest. I appreciate that. And to be honest, I'm not looking for a relationship either. I work crazy hours, and in my experience, they just don't work out. Someone's always left wanting more than the other can give."

Savannah flashes through my mind, but not because I wish she were here. She wanted more, said I was never available, even though I felt like I was giving her everything. "So where does that leave us?"

"Well, we're really good together in bed, right?" she asks. "What if that's it? What if we just hang out for a bit, have more great sex, and then move on when this has run its course?"

I've always been a relationship guy. The thought of having a friend with benefits doesn't exactly sit well with me, but walking away from her doesn't either. So I'm torn between wanting to do the right thing and wanting to do what I need to keep spending time with her.

But let's be honest, we're both busy. Our jobs keep us occupied day and night. I have little time for a social life outside of work and my friends, so maybe this idea isn't so bad. Perhaps it's the best idea I've heard in a long time. Phenomenal sex without all the relationship stuff to go along with it?

Sounds like a winner to me.

But there's still one tiny problem…

"What about Jameson? I won't lie to him."

She shrugs her shoulders and runs her hand across my chest. "I'm not usually in the habit of talking to my brother about the guys I'm screwing."

"Guys? As in plural?" I ask, the humor evident in my voice.

BJ snickers and kisses my shoulder. "No, not plural. I'm not in a habit of sleeping with more than one guy at a time."

"So, this is an exclusive screwing then, huh?" I ask, my heartbeat calming a little with that realization.

"It is." She looks up and meets my gaze once more. "I'm only sleeping with you."

"And I'm only sleeping with you," I tell her, turning us so she's beneath me.

"Just promise me you'll tell me when this has run its course?"

I stare at those intoxicating eyes and feel my heart lurch. Why does the thought of this ending cause an ache deep in my chest? "I will, and you do the same."

She nods, and I bring my lips down to hers. Once I've kissed her soundly, and my dick is anxious for another round of sex, I release her mouth and take a deep breath. "We'll just keep this simple and casual, all right? Hang out when we can, no expectations, no rules."

"I like that," I state, running my lips down her neck and across her collarbone. I keep going, my mouth blazing a hot trail to her breasts and down her stomach. Her skin is so smooth and soft, so delicate in comparison to the tough exterior she puts out there. "Tell me about this," I whisper, tracing the words surrounded by black and gray-scale flowers across her side.

"Whisper words of wisdom, let it be," she sings quietly. She clears her throat before continuing, "When we were growing up and Jameson was learning to play guitar, that was the first song he learned. Late at night, when we were home alone because our mom was at work or off with her friends, he used to play that song over and over again and sing it until I fell asleep. Now that I'm older, I realized it was my brother I went to for advice as I was growing up, not my mom. He was my constant."

A smile plays on my lips as I stare at the song lyrics of the classic Beatles tune. "He's a good brother."

"The best. Now, when that song comes on, I only want to hear his version."

I continue to study the intricate work on her side. "He doesn't sing it often, but I've heard it a few times," I state, referring to the weekly Friday and Saturday nights he plays at the bar.

"His voice is a lot deeper than John Lennon's, so when he sings it, it's like a whole new take on the song."

"I would agree with that," I murmur against her skin. I move her leg until I'm between them, the bar piercing glistening with wetness in the moonlight filtering through the window. "Now, let's not talk about your brother."

BJ hadn't meant to spend the night, but after another round of sex, we both passed out from exhaustion. When my alarm went off at six, there was none of that uncomfortable vibe like the first morning after. Today, we had an understanding, and even though she got up and left as I got ready for work, there was a contentment in having her there.

Now, I'm in my office, and I can't help but wonder what she's doing. Did she go home and back to sleep, knowing she has to work at the shop until close tonight? Maybe she went to Jameson's to check on him, to see if his fever is gone.

Speaking of, it's almost noon, and I haven't heard from him yet. I grab my phone and fire off a text.

Me: How are you feeling today?

His reply comes only a few seconds later.

Jameson: Like I was hit by a truck.

Me: Do you need anything?

Jameson: No, BJ just brought over more meds. I ate some of the soup from Jasper.

I instantly grin at the thought of BJ visiting her brother and making sure he has everything he needs.

Me: Do I need to do anything at the brewery?

Jameson: No, talked to George. He's better today so he's there. Let's hope mine is only 24hrs too.

Me: OK, let me know if I can help.

Jameson: Will do. Gonna take a nap.

I set my phone down on my desk, finding no reason to reply anymore. Hopefully he gets more rest and is back to his surly self in no time.

I spend the better part of the afternoon and early evening working on quarterly tax and projection reports for the restaurant and bar before switching over to the brewery. I compare our estimates with actual sales, and even though we've only been selling our own beer a short time, the numbers are staggering.

My stomach growls, reminding me I haven't eaten anything since the muffin I bought from Lyndee's bakery across the street. It's definitely time to eat. Just as I'm shutting down my laptop, I hear footsteps on the stairs. Only these footsteps are much smaller and hitting the steps at a much higher rate of speed. Immediately, I smile.

"Isaac!" Lizzie hollers the moment her feet hit the landing outside my office.

"Lizard!" I bellow, already taking a knee as she barrels into the room and straight into my arms.

I hug the small girl and place a kiss on her forehead. "How's my favorite preschooler?"

"I gets to be weader again soon! I'm dunna bwing mommy for show and tell so I tan show my fwends!" Her eyes light with excitement when she talks about the baby.

"You're going to show your friends your mommy?"

She nods enthusiastically. "Her belly," she states with those sweet little giggles I've come to love.

"Speaking of mommy, where is she?" I ask, glancing over her shoulder and finding the stairwell empty.

"Down eating with Daddy Walk. You come too?"

I stand up and take her outstretched hand, grateful for the distraction. "I'd love to join you."

Once I lock up my office, we head down the stairs and to the bar, where I find Walker and Mallory sitting at their usual pub table, the one BJ and I sat in last night.

"There they are. We figured if anyone could get you to come out of the office, it was Lou," Walker says, referring to his stepdaughter by the nickname he gave her very early on in his relationship with Mal.

I help the little girl onto her booster seat before taking the remaining available seat. "You talk to Jameson today?"

"Tank sick," Lizzie says, referring to Jameson. She's called him Tank, like many of the employees do since his last name is Tankersley, because she had a hard time saying his first name.

"He is, but I talked to him earlier. He'll be back to normal soon."

Her bottom lip juts out as she whines, "I miss him."

"As soon as he's feeling better, we'll go over and see him, okay?" Mallory says, which appeases her daughter.

"Otay! We'll take him cookies!"

I can't help but snort because this little girl has his number. She knows Jameson has a sweet tooth and loves to share treats with him. "I'm sure he'd love that. Make sure they're chocolate chip," I add, knowing that's Lizzie's favorite kind.

"Is there any other kind?" Walker asks sarcastically.

Their food comes out a few moments later, delivered by Jasper himself. "Cheeseburger and fries for my Lizard," he says, setting the first plate in front of the child, and kissing her forehead. "One Strip and Go Naked for Mama, minus the bacon and with extra mayo. Also a container on the side for the fries," he adds, placing her food down and placing a kiss on Mal's forehead too. "And the Panty

Melter for the bastard who told my girlfriend this morning she could do better."

Walker bursts out into laughter as his plate is practically dropped in front of him without fanfare. "Don't be mad, sweetheart. I can't help that I speak the truth."

Jasper's face is void of emotion. "I dropped your patty on the floor...after I cooked it."

Even though I'm smiling because I know Jasper's lying, I can't help but glance around to make sure no one around us heard the comment. "Please don't say that too loud. The last thing we want is for someone to hear a comment like that."

Jasper glances around too but realizes no one is nearby. "Maybe your friend should keep his unsolicited comments to himself. If he doesn't someone is liable to tell his wife about the time he passed out in the bathroom at some chick's place and peed in the little garbage can because he was too drunk to get off the floor to use the toilet."

Walker narrows his eyes at Jasper. "I hate you."

I fight my grin. "Gentlemen, let's not get into that here. Poor Lizard doesn't need her childhood tarnished because her dad and her uncle are jackasses."

"Jackasses!" Lizzie bellows, loud enough to draw the attention of the rest of the bar.

Mallory turns her glare on me. "Thanks."

Jasper sets the fourth and final plate in front of me, which is shocking, considering I just came down to the table. "I don't even know what's on this one. I just threw stuff together," he announces.

I glance down at the burger in question. "Uhh, thanks?"

Jasper shrugs. "I'm off to the kitchen. One of you want to run some food over to Jameson? He said he's starving for something other than soup, and I'm here until close."

"We can do it on our way home," Mallory announces, dipping two fries in the cup of mayo before taking a bite.

"Great. I'll have it packed up and ready for when you're done."

"Thanks," Walker replies, adding a quick "asshole" in a whisper so little ears don't hear it. The moment Jasper leaves, Walker looks over at Mallory and says, "It wasn't *some chick*. I was seeing her, and it was a long time ago."

She gazes over at him, her eyes dancing with laughter, as she takes a huge bite of her burger. "How long ago?"

"College. Right after we met Jasper, and suddenly, I'm wishing we would have just kept on walking before we got to talking to him at that party."

I lift the bun off the top of my burger and discover a variety of toppings. I guess he's right. He just threw a bunch of stuff on there, but since my stomach is growling once more, there's nothing on it to keep me from eating it.

As I take a bite, I can't help but admire the couple at the table. Even though they haven't known each other a year yet, they have an amazing relationship. Mallory was just what Walker needed, and I think he was exactly what she needed too. If I'm being honest, their relationship is one any couple would strive to have. No, it's not easy, and they have to work at it every day, but when push comes to shove, they're a team and they make it work.

Together.

I admire them.

And, just maybe, I'm a little jealous too.

Probably because I had been in a relationship with a woman off and on for years, and at the end of the day, I don't think I really knew her, and vice versa. All that wasted time.

It's sad, really.

And a little pathetic.

But now isn't the time to dwell on the past. No reason to bring up things I can't change, and that includes my time with Savannah. All I can do now is learn from my mistakes and move forward.

That thought makes me grin, because there's only one woman I'd even consider dating, and we just agreed last night neither of us are ready for that. But that's okay. I'm in no hurry. For now, I'm content with my friends and my work. They'll help me get to the point where I'm ready to move on.

Someday.

"Mommy? What's a jackass?"

BJ

"Your eight o'clock is here," Amanda announces, waiting for me to give the nod to escort her back. As soon as I do, she returns to the front to retrieve my next client.

It's been a crazy Wednesday, with back-to-back appointments, but fortunately, this is my final one for the day. Courtney Day is getting her new husband's name on her abdomen, despite me trying to talk her out of it. Names are always a bad idea, unless it's in memory of someone. If I had ten bucks for every name of an ex Jax and I have covered up, I could make a down payment on a new truck.

"Hey!" Courtney greets the moment she steps into my room.

"Hi, Courtney. You ready?" I ask, waving her to my chair. It's laid back flat, ready for her to lie on.

"I'm so excited," she says, setting her purse down on the side chair.

"You're absolutely sure you still want to do this?" I hold up the stencil of the design we settled on, the cursive name across a double heart.

Courtney grins widely as she looks at the design. "Yep. Let's do it."

"Okay." I sigh, wishing I could change her mind on this tattoo, but knowing it's not going to happen. "All right, lie back and we'll roll your shirt up."

Courtney gets comfortable, popping in earbuds and taking a deep, calming breath. Once I have the skin prepared, the design transferred to her skin, and clean gloves on, I give her a hand mirror to make sure it's in the right position.

"What do you think of the placement?"

She studies the design and nods. "Yes, it's good."

I set the mirror aside and grab my gun, situating my tray for easy access. "Here we go."

It's not a big piece, nor one too complicated and intricate. It should only take about forty-five minutes to complete, and then we're moving to the piercing room for a belly ring.

Once the black outline is complete, I sit up and stretch my back, allowing Courtney to do the same. "Doing okay?"

She pops out her earbuds and nods, looking down at the outline. "I'm doing good. Just a little sting."

After a few minutes, I'm ready to start the color when Amanda pops her head around the corner, a cat that ate the canary grin on her face. "You have a visitor?"

My eyebrows arch up, but I keep my focus on my work as I turn on the gun. "Who is it?"

"An incredibly sexy man wearing a tie," she whisper-yells.

I pause my work and glance up, instantly knowing who she's referring to. "He's here?"

She nods. "Want me to send him back?"

I look around the room, unsure what to do. We've allowed onlookers into our rooms while tattooing, but they're usually a friend or family member of the one in the chair. "Uhh, I guess that's not my decision."

Courtney lifts her head. "There's a hot guy here? I want to see him."

Amanda smirks. "I'll bring him back." And then she disappears to retrieve Isaac.

I'm a little out of sorts as I look around my room. "You sure you don't mind? He can wait until we're finished here."

My client waves off my comment. "I'm fine. Maybe the eye candy will help take my mind off the pain."

I don't have time to reply before Isaac appears in the doorway, an unsure look on his face. "Hey, sorry to interrupt."

"It's okay, you can come in. Take a seat on the chair," I reply, motioning to the only available seat in the room.

Isaac does as instructed, throwing Courtney a smile. "Hi, how are you?"

Courtney grins widely. "I'm good. Getting my first tattoo."

He looks down at her abdomen and nods. "You don't mind if I watch?"

She shakes her head and looks at me, mouthing, "Oh my God!"

I don't say anything, just get back to work. One heart is blue, representing her husband, Carter, and the other heart is pink. She chose those colors because they are their favorites. Where the hearts overlap, I'm blending the colors, swirling the blues and the pinks and creating a gorgeous purple. Instead of just using the purple ink, I decided to add texture and design as I create my own.

When the piece is complete, I wipe it down and move my tray out of the way. "Well, what do you think?"

Courtney stands up and looks at her new tattoo in the full-length mirror. "Wow, it's stunning! I just thought you'd color in the hearts. I wasn't expecting so much detail," she states, her eyes filling with tears. "It's a work of art."

I smile at the compliment. "I'm glad you like it. Let's get it covered, and then we'll head into the next room for your piercing."

Once I've finished the process I've completed what feels like a million times, we set to head to the next room. "You coming?" Courtney asks Isaac.

He seems a little surprised by the question and glances at me. "It's just a belly piercing."

"It's not like you haven't seen my stomach anyway," Courtney adds with a chuckle.

"Okay," he says, standing up and following us down the hallway.

The hum of Jax's gun follows us as we step inside the room and I pull the curtain closed. "Go ahead and lie on the table."

I slip fresh gloves on my hands and get ready to pierce her belly button. After making the mark on her skin, I sanitize the area and grab the clamp. "This is the worst part," I tell her, using the device to flatten the area I'm about to stick. The whole thing takes less than thirty seconds, and when I'm all done, Courtney has a silver hoop with a small pink ball in the center. "Finished."

My client exhales loudly and glances down at her new hardware. "I love it. Thank you!"

I go over the cleaning instructions, as well as those for the tattoo, and once she says she understands, I escort her to the front counter for final payment. "If you have any questions on care, give us a call or stop by," I say, making sure everything's set before going in search of Isaac.

I find him still in the piercing room, examining the many photos on the wall. "This one looks like it hurt," he says, as if sensing my arrival in the room.

"Jacob's ladder. That one had six bars," I reply, taking in his appearance. He looks completely out of place standing in this room in a charcoal gray suit and bright red tie. I think the last time we had a suit in the studio was when a lawyer showed up three years ago to talk to Jax about a supposed paternity claim.

"Ouch," he says, pulling a face as he looks closer. "How does that even work?"

I step up beside him, the familiar woodsy scent of his cologne filling my nostrils. "Well, this particular one took three sessions. We did them two at a time, two months apart. The quantity we do is determined by the size of the penis and their ability to withstand the discomfort in getting their piercings."

He snorts. "Discomfort. Something tells me getting your dick pierced is a little more painful than discomfort."

I shrug, letting my arm brush against his. "Pain is subjective. It's all about how badly you want the pleasure that follows."

Isaac turns to face me, his hungry eyes dilated as he sucks in a deep breath. Heat radiates off him like a furnace, and I can feel the way my body reacts to his presence. I lean toward him, like there's some magnetic pull, and my core floods with wetness in anticipation of whatever dirty promises I see in those sexy hazel eyes.

Just as I go to throw myself at him like a cat in heat, a large figure steps into the doorway. "Hey, BJ," Jax says, giving Isaac a hard look. It's part curious, part hostile. "Who's this?"

I clear my throat and before I can introduce them, Isaac steps forward and holds out his hand. "Isaac Thompson."

"Jax Forrester," he replies, taking the outstretched hand.

"Isaac is one of my brother's friends and partners," I quickly add, drawing Jax's attention my way.

"Ahh, yes. I've heard of him. Nice to meet you, Isaac. What brings you to our shop on a Wednesday night?" he asks, leaning his large frame against the wall.

"Just stopped by to say hi. I was driving past and saw your lights still on," Isaac states casually, looking anything but.

"Hmm," Jax practically sings, the corner of his mouth turned upward as he meets my gaze. "Well, I can let you two catch up. Amanda's ready to head out. I'm gonna walk her to her car and then lock up."

As if on cue, I hear my best friend holler, "Night, BJ! I tossed your tips in your drawer."

"Thank you," I reply, stepping around Jax and into the hallway. Amanda is there, slipping her jacket on. The moment she sees me, she winks and brings her hand to her face, making the universal blowjob sign with her mouth.

I snicker and shake my head as Jax steps out behind me. Amanda clears her throat and drops her hand, guiltily. "All right, I'll talk to you tomorrow," Amanda says, heading for the back exit of the shop with Jax hot on her heels. I can't help but wonder if and when he's going to tell my friend how he feels.

But there's no time to think about that right now, because Isaac steps up behind me. Even though he doesn't touch me, I can feel him *everywhere*. "I need to clean up my room. Care to join me?" I ask, glancing over my shoulder.

Isaac flashes me a grin and follows me to my room. I jump right in, gathering up my tools for sanitization and throwing away the trash. The moment I scrub down the chair and raise the back, I wave for him to have a seat. He takes off his suit jacket and tosses it onto the other chair before climbing onto the one I use for tattooing.

I hear the back door close and expect Jax to make an appearance any second. I'm sure he's connecting the dots after our previous conversation about being attracted to someone you shouldn't be attracted to, but I don't expect him to drill me tonight. No, he'll wait until tomorrow when there's nowhere to get out of the uncomfortable conversation.

"You need anything before I go?" Jax asks the second he steps into the doorway.

"No, I'm good. I'm finishing up and will be heading home."

A single eyebrow shoots upward. "You want me to stay to walk you out?"

"No, I'm good, but thanks."

Jax nods but hesitates before walking away. "It was nice to officially meet you, Isaac."

"You too," Isaac replies.

Finally, I hear the front door lock and know he'll make sure everything but the hallway light is shut off before he leaves. I hear him tinker around in his office, whistling while he does it so casually, before eventually, hollering a quick good night and leaving out the back door.

When we're alone, I study the man in my chair. He's impeccably dressed, something I'm not used to seeing. Sure I've seen guys in nice polos or name brand T-shirts and girls dressed up for a night out, but usually, in this chair, there's more skin exposed.

Suddenly, I know what I need to do.

"Unbutton your shirt." It's not a question, but a demand.

Isaac seems uncertain for the briefest moment, but then curiosity settles in. He reaches up and loosens his tie, a movement that seems to turn me on even more. Then, he shifts his weight and tugs his white button-down from his pants. Once it's free, he slowly starts unfastening the buttons on the front of his shirt, exposing that delicious chest I've become quite fond of.

I make an appreciative hum, which pulls a chuckle out of Isaac. When the last button is released, I move the shirt, exposing his bare chest. It's like a glorious blank canvas. My mind reels as ideas pop into my head.

"What are you thinking about?" he asks, sitting completely still while I ogle his chest.

"You're a blank canvas, and all I want to do is mark you."

"Something tells me you're not talking about biting."

My core clenches. "No, I wasn't talking about biting, but we can circle back around to that one," I reply all breathlessly.

His eyes widen and his jaw clenches. "I'm all ears."

I can't help but smile. "I bet you are. No, what I was actually thinking about was how great you'd look with a little ink." I place my palms against the hard planes of his chest and run my fingers through the dark hair.

"Yeah?"

I use my fingertip like a pencil and start drawing imaginary lines and designs. "Definitely. Your skin is the perfect shade for some gray-scaled designs," I tell him, letting my creativity run wild across his chest.

"Do it."

His words almost startle me. "What?"

He holds my gaze and shrugs. “I’m just saying if I were ever to get a tattoo, I’d want you to do it.”

Words seem to evade me, and I’m pretty certain that’s never happened before. I hold his gaze, seeing the honesty in his eyes.

An idea hits me, and I retrieve the markers in one of my cabinets. Isaac doesn’t say anything as I lay them out on my tray and position it at my side. I reach for the black and remove the cover. “Ready for your first tattoo?” I ask, one side of my mouth curling upward.

“Do your worst,” he says, getting comfortable in the chair.

I lean over him and rest my arms on his body, the warmth of his skin seeping into my pores. I ignore the desire swirling inside me and focus on drawing. With my left hand holding his upper pec, I move the marker across his skin, watching as my thoughts come to life.

Once the outline is complete, I grab the gray marker to aid in shading. I sneak a quick peek at the man in the chair and find his eyes cast down. He’s not watching what I’m doing, however. He’s watching me.

Intently.

Ignoring the pull I feel toward him, I shade the design before grabbing the blue marker. Why? I’m not sure. The darker shade of blue isn’t enough of a contrast to really stand out against the black and gray but more of a subtle color change. More of the style I’d associate with Isaac.

Plus, the color reminds me of that dark blue shirt the night of the open house.

I fill in the main focal point of the design with the blue, making long lines with the color until his skin is completely covered. Then, I grab the fine black marker and add the final touches. When it's all done, I sit back and study the finished piece, loving the way it turned out. "What do you think?"

"Gorgeous."

A smile spreads across my face, and when I look up, I meet his hungry gaze. He's not looking at what I just drew on his upper chest.

He's looking at me.

My throat is thick. "I was talking about your tattoo."

The corners of his mouth turn upward ever so slightly. "I know. I was talking about you."

I move the tray to the side and climb onto his lap, straddling him as best I can, considering the armrests are down. Isaac's hands grip my ass, pressing my core firmly into his erection. With my chest smashed against his, I nip at his scruffy jaw, letting the coarse hair tickle my tongue.

Letting my palms splay across his chest, I curl my fingers and dig my nails into his flesh. The result is an animalistic growl that erupts from his lungs. He grips my ass so hard; I swear I'll have finger marks.

But I don't care.

He meets my gaze, desire swirling in the depths of those hazel eyes. "You know, I think I really like this whole tattoo thing."

Isaac

"What's got you so smiley?" Jasper asks, stepping up beside me at the bar.

"Excuse me?" I ask, even though I heard him over the low strum of Jameson's guitar.

"You. You've been all…happy for the last week or so. What's up?" my friend inquires, those dark brown eyes lasered in on me.

I shrug, trying to shake off the feeling of nervousness.

The truth is, I have felt a little lighter the last week or so. Ever since BJ drew that Pi sign on my chest and then we did all kinds of dirty things in that room. It's crazy, you know? I feel more connected to her than any other woman who's shared my bed.

Though, there hasn't been a lot of bedroom time since we started hanging out. The great thing about BJ is her desire and willingness to get naked *outside* of that particular room. It's been an adventure.

"See? That right there. What are you thinking about?" Jasper demands as Walker stops by our side of the bar.

"What's going on?" he asks, refilling my Coke.

"Nothing," I reply, leaning against the bar and watching our friend up on stage as he begins a Lennon song.

"I was commenting on his smile," Jasper says to Walker, sipping his water with a smug grin on his face.

"Ahh, yes. The smile. It's the same kind you had when you finally started getting naked with Lyndee," Walker states.

I can feel two pairs of eyes on me and hear their speculation about the reason for my smiles, but I refuse to look at them. Instead, I keep my gaze locked on our friend at the front as he sings "Imagine." I catch movement out of the corner of my eye.

"Shit, is that Savannah?" Jasper asks, standing up straight.

"What's she doing here?" Walker inquires, tossing the towel on the bar and resting his hands on the marred top.

Before I can answer either of their questions, my ex-girlfriend spots me across the bar and heads my way. "Fuck," I grumble, taking a long sip of my Coke and wishing it had a bit of Jack in it.

Savannah wiggles her fingers in a wave, her red nails glistening beneath the dim lights as she slips through the crowd until she's standing directly in front of me. "Isaac."

"Savannah," I reply with a nod. "What can I do for you?"

She gives me a blinding smile, one that not too long ago used to turn me into putty in her hands. Now, I want to roll my eyes at her blatant attempt to manipulate me with just a smile. "I wanted to say hi. I stopped by with friends," she purrs, flipping her long, blonde hair over her shoulder.

"Well, you said it. Now you can return to your group."

She seems positively stunned by my brush-off, which makes Jasper snicker behind me. "Yes, well, I wanted to say hello, but also see when I could stop by and retrieve my things." She seems a little more businesslike now, standing straight and holding my gaze.

I shrug casually and lean on the bar. "I have it all boxed up. I can drop it by your office one day next week."

Her nostrils flare, which does make me smile. It's obvious to her she's not in control of the conversation like normal, and I don't think she likes it. Not one bit. "I need my things before next week," she states, crossing her arms over her chest.

"Huh, you haven't needed them the last couple of weeks. What's the rush now?" I ask, popping a few kernels of popcorn into my mouth that we keep behind the bar for bartenders and staff.

Her green eyes narrow into little slits. "Well, I need one of my nighties from the dresser."

I can tell she thinks her words are going to upset me, but I'm pleasantly surprised when they don't. Not even a little. There's no jealousy, no outrage, no sadness. Not like there usually is after one of our breakups. Instead, I feel impassive and unaffected by the implementation. "It's in the box. I guess if you need it before next week, you'll just have to stop by. I can set it out on the porch."

Someone chuckles behind me—probably Walker—but I don't turn around. Savannah looks like she wants to explode with rage as she glares daggers at my friends. "I'll be by tomorrow sometime. Don't you even think about putting my stuff on the porch. The clothes alone cost more than you make in a month," she says through gritted teeth.

Again, I shrug. "Perhaps."

Finally, she straightens her spine and delivers one final message. "You know, I was trying to be civil to you, but it appears you're too immature for that."

"No, you were trying to manipulate me to get what you want, and it's not going to work. Not this time. Not ever again."

She makes a tsking noise in her throat and arches a perfectly manicured eyebrow. “I suppose we’ll see about that.” With one final toss of her hair over her shoulder, she adds, “I’ll see you soon.”

And then she’s gone, disappearing into the crowd to return to her party on the opposite side of the room.

“She’s so pleasant. I don’t understand why you’re not still together,” Jasper says, deadpan, making me laugh.

“She’s something,” I reply, reaching for my Coke and taking another sip.

I thought my first interaction with Savannah post-breakup would be uncomfortable and upsetting, but it wasn’t. Not even a little. Maybe I’ve finally realized how wrong we truly were for each other. Sure, we have our similarities, like our lust for nice clothes and good grooming habits, but the difference outweighs any of those now.

We watch Jameson’s set end, and I know what’s coming next. The crowd starts to liven as Walker makes his way toward the jukebox for our Saturday night eleven o’clock tradition. He tosses the money into the unit and picks tonight’s song. The moment the tune pumps through the speakers, the entire room erupts into cheers. Glasses are raised as people start singing along, waiting for the man behind the bar to make his grand appearance on top of the hard wood.

The heavy beat of “Same Ol’ Situation” echoes through the room, electricity humming through my veins. I’ve always loved this song, but now that I listen, the words seem to resonate on a whole new level.

I watch with a huge smile on my face as my friend jumps up on the bar and does his thing. Every weekend, it’s the same, and the crowd loves it. It’s our ode to not only our favorite band, but to us as a group too. It's how we started, and a tradition we plan to continue. At least, I hope we do.

Jasper hands him the shot, and Walker downs it easily before turning his hat around and dancing until the song ends. We watch until he hops down and heads our way, downing a glass of ice water.

"How long is Mal going to let you do that?" Jasper asks, his eyes dancing with humor.

"What?" Walker questions, confusion on his face.

"The dancing," he replies.

"Why would I stop?"

"There's panties on the floor behind you," I add, nodding to the hot pink lacy scrap of material lying near where Walker stands.

Walker turns and shakes his head. "Classy. Mal knows I have no interest in anyone but her. She has nothing to worry about," he insists, and we all know that's true. Walker would never cheat on Mallory, especially not with someone from the bar. He'd never risk his new life as a family man for anyone or anything.

"We know, but I guess things are slowly changing. You're married with a kid on the way, and I'm in a serious relationship," Jasper says, watching as bar patrons grab drink refills from the other bartender on duty.

"Speaking of, you ever going to put a ring on it?" I ask Jasper.

He smiles ever so slightly. "Yeah, someday. We're not ready yet, but we'll get there."

"We're not there yet, or *you're* not there yet?" Walker asks, reaching for an empty beer mug and refilling it with one of our tap brews.

Jasper snorts and leans on the counter. "Actually, I'd do it tomorrow if I thought she'd agree."

That causes both Walker and me to pause and slowly turn to face our friend. "Really?" I inquire. Of all our friends, Jasper is the one I'd least expect to be ready to walk down the aisle so quickly after meeting the woman he's with. It's only been a few months, but maybe that doesn't matter. It didn't with Walker and Mallory, and apparently, it doesn't with Jasper and Lyndee. When you know, you know.

Suddenly, my own life flashes before me. For years, I thought Savannah was the woman who completed that picture, but now I know she's not. I want someone with a thirst for life, who makes me smile, and who challenges me to be better.

I always pictured that person as someone with a college degree, designer clothes, and a thriving savings plan. But what if she's not?

What if she's the exact opposite of everything I thought I wanted?

An image flashes through my mind, and it's not Savannah.

I see wild, pink-streaked hair, tattoos, and a smile that makes my heart race and my blood flow just south of the belt. She cares about her brother, is a talented artist to boot, and has one hell of a sassy mouth.

Funny, the woman I'm interested in isn't someone I'd ever expected.

She's better.

I wonder what BJ's doing.

It's the first real beautiful Sunday in April, and I can't wait to spend a little time outside in my yard. After I change from work clothes into a rare T-shirt and khaki shorts, I dig the mower out of the small shed in the corner of the lot and get ready to service it for the summer season. Before I use it for the year, I change the spark plug and oil and make sure the blades are sharpened.

Okay, fine.

Jameson will be here in fifteen minutes to do it.

I spot Jeb stepping out onto his patio and offer a quick wave before heading his way. "Gorgeous day," I say as the only pair of tennis shoes I own hits the pavement.

"Isn't it? I figured you'd be out here after work. Busy day?" he asks, taking a seat in one of his chairs.

"It usually is after the church crowd." I take the seat next to him and kick my feet up on the table. "How is your day going?"

He nods, sipping his sweet tea. "Good. Where's that pretty young lady at these days? I haven't seen her around much."

"You mean since the night you showed up at my back door to snoop?"

The old man just grins. "Potato, potahto." He glances up at the sky. "You still seeing her?"

I open my mouth, but nothing comes out. How do you answer that question? Yes, we're still seeing each other, but not in the traditional sense. I highly doubt someone like Jeb would understand or approve of the arrangement BJ and I have.

"Don't let that one go. I can tell she's a good egg."

I study my neighbor, the man I consider a friend. "We're still seeing each other, but it's pretty casual right now." I don't know how else to word it.

"So it's all great sex, huh?" he asks, making me choke on the air I breathe. "Don't pretend like you're shocked I'd say something. Good sex is important in a relationship."

Relationship.

I sigh. "It is."

"Everything else comes over time. But if the sex isn't any good, the relationship won't flourish. And I could tell it's good."

I almost don't want to ask, but for some reason, I do. "How?"

"Well, besides the fire surrounding you the time I saw you together?"

"Yeah, besides that."

"I heard just how much she appreciated your attention to detail."

A blush spreads up my neck. I can feel it burning my cheeks. "Uhh..."

He cracks up laughing and takes another drink. "Don't be embarrassed. If I were you, I'd be pretty damn proud of myself," he says, raising his tea glass in salute.

Jesus.

I'm saved from having to continue this incredibly awkward conversation when I hear the rumblings of Jameson's Harley pull into the driveway.

"Is that the Tankersley boy?" he asks, making me chuckle.

"That *boy* is about to turn thirty-three."

"You boys will always be boys to me."

Jameson steps around the corner of the condo and heads our way. "Hey. Hi, Jeb."

"Good to see you," the old man says, nodding toward the mower. "You going to help our boy here get ready for summer?"

Jameson tosses his leather jacket onto my chair and pushes up the long sleeves on his black T-shirt. "He'd be lost without me," my friend teases, winking at my neighbor before he turns his attention to me. "Mind if I get started? I gotta run over to my sister's house and do the same, even though she insists she's more than capable of changing the oil in her mower."

I can almost picture exactly how that conversation went. Instead, I ignore the reference to BJ and hop up. "Sure. I picked up all the stuff you told me to get."

We head over to the shed and pull out everything we need. Jameson grabs the old piece of cardboard he's used the last few years, as well as the tire ramps. I watch as my friend gets it all set up and retrieves the push mower. Once it's set on top of the ramps, he places an oil pan beneath it and drains the old oil.

While he does his thing, I move around the few things in the shed and make sure they're ready for the season. The leaf blower and hedge trimmer are both electric, so all I'll need to do is plug them in and they're ready to go. Once they're set aside, I pull the rest of my lawn furniture out and set the pieces in the middle of the yard.

"How was work today?" Jameson asks without taking his eyes off his task.

"Good. Busy until about two, and then I left them to it."

"I'm surprised you're not still there, actually. Usually you pull a full day on Sundays."

I can't help but smile. "I could say the same about you."

Jameson doesn't reply right away, just starts to add the new oil to my mower. After it's finished, he wipes his hands on a shop towel and drops a bomb right in my lap. "I think my sister's seeing someone."

"BJ?" I stammer, my throat suddenly too dry to speak.

"Yeah," he starts, turning to face me. "She's been all...I don't know...happy lately."

Happy?

Why does that thought make me want to pump my arms in victory?

"Happy's good, right?" I ask, keeping my hands busy with the extension cord from the shed.

"Yeah," he states. Suddenly, he moves and he's standing right next to me. "I'm cool if she's dating. I just want her to be with a good guy who treats her right. Not some douchebag who makes her pay the tab every time they go out to dinner."

Annoyance creeps in as I turn to face my friend. "That's happened?"

He nods. "Yeah. A few years ago, she dated this asshole who conveniently forgot his wallet to almost all of their dates," he practically growls in disgust. "Then there was the guy who asked her to do his full back tattoo for free. They'd been seeing each other for about a week."

I shake my head, surprised by this revelation. I mean, she told me she doesn't do relationships, and I can see why. She's had her fair share of shitty dates. "Wow, sounds like some losers."

He nods. "There were. I've really only liked one guy, and that really happened after they stopped seeing each other. I thought he was my friend, but then found out he was messing around with Beej. It pissed me off."

All I can do is blink. She dated one of his friends? Clearly, not Jasper or Walker, so who? How long ago? And why does the thought of her dating someone he considered a friend make me a little jealous?

"Anyway, they broke it off and he apologized to me for messing around with her. It's crazy because I was the one who introduced them," he recalls, staring off at the yard. "All right, I'm out of here. See you tomorrow?"

My mind is reeling, and even though I have a thousand questions to ask, I have no right to ask them. So, instead, I reply, "Of course. Tomorrow."

"Later." Jameson grabs his leather jacket off the chair before disappearing around the side of my place. A few seconds later, his Harley starts up and he takes off down the road, heading to the one house I wish I was headed to as well.

Maybe I'll reach out to her tonight and see what she's up to. Not because I'm curious about the other guys she's dated or the fact her brother is picking up on her increased delight, but because I really want to see her.

I want to see that smile.

Because when she flashes it my way, it makes me happy too.

I just won't think about why.

BJ

Isaac: What are you doing?

Me: Getting ready to go for a walk. You?

He doesn't reply right away, and just as I slip my phone into the pocket of my leggings, it chimes with his reply.

Isaac: Bored.

Isaac: Want company or would you prefer to walk alone?

Me: Meet me at the entrance to the trails in fifteen?

Isaac: I'll be there.

Smiling, I return my phone to my pocket and run and brush my teeth. No, I wouldn't have done it before I invited Isaac, but now that he's going, a little kissing might be in order. Once my mouth is minty fresh, I slip on my favorite runners and grab my keys.

There's an extra spring in my step as I head down the steps and jump in my truck. She purrs like a kitten as I back out of my driveway and make my way to the biggest city park in Stewart Grove. Stretched across thirty-four acres, the park houses a community center, public swimming pool, camping and picnic area, three playgrounds, and some walking trails. I've never been a runner, but I do enjoy hiking through the trees and breathing in the cool air.

When I pull into the parking lot closest to the trails, I spot a couple of vehicles in the lot, including Isaac's Maxima. I park beside it and hop out, catching my first glimpse of the man I can't stop thinking about. He's wearing gray joggers, a long-sleeved white T-shirt, and black tennis shoes. He looks positively yummy.

"Hey," I say with the slip of a smile and an awkward wave.

"Hi." He shoves his hands in his pockets, which somehow seems to draw attention to the bulge below the waistband of his sweats. They're loose yet leave absolutely nothing to the imagination. I can see the outline of his cock, which makes my mouth water. "Are you objectifying me?" he asks, grinning widely from where he stands.

I look up, meeting his sexy hazel eyes, and offer my own smile. "Actually, I am."

He steps forward, eating up the space between us. "Funny, I'm doing the same." His eyes drop to my crewneck sweatshirt, and I'm certain he can see my pebbled nipples through the thicker material.

I clear my throat and glance around us, checking to see if we're alone. We're not, of course. A family of four is heading toward a minivan just a few parking spots away. "Ready to hit the trails?"

"Lead the way," he replies, waving his hand to where the dirt path starts.

We're quiet as we begin our walk, the ground mostly flat and clear of debris. The sun is dropping, as is the temperature. I take a few deep, cleansing breaths, letting my lungs fill with the early April evening air. "So, how was your day?" I ask as we round the first bend.

"Good. Worked for a while, then went home and got the mower ready for the season," he replies, his arm brushing against mine. That damn electricity zips through my blood, which is so wild, considering we're both clothed.

"*You* got your mower ready?" I ask, the teasing tone evident in my question.

"Well, Jameson did, but I was there," he states with a big smile.

"He did mine too, even though I told him I'd do it myself. There are some things he just insists on helping with."

"That's because he's a good big brother," he replies, and I catch something in his tone.

"You have a sister, right?" I ask, more curious about Isaac's family than I've ever been with any guy I'm...well, whatever it is we're doing.

"Two, actually. Amelia and Tabitha."

"Wow, I didn't realize that," I say, as we continue to walk along the path. Jameson isn't exactly a talker, only sharing what he feels is pertinent information.

"I have four nieces and nephews with another on the way."

"That's cool," I tell him, carefully stepping over a log on the walkway. "I probably won't have any," I add, almost absently.

"You never know. Jameson is really good with Lizzie. He'd make a great dad."

I nod, completely agreeing. "He is, but he's always sworn he'd never have kids. I hope he changes his mind when he meets the right woman, but honestly, I don't know. He still has a lot of unresolved issues from our childhood," I confess, only to feel guilty for talking about my brother so openly.

As if sensing my uneasiness, Isaac stops beside me and reaches for my hand. "Hey, anything you say doesn't go any further, okay? I'd never tell anyone, including Jameson. Your secrets and your feelings are safe with me," he says, squeezing my hand with his.

His hazel eyes are full of sincerity, it makes my heart skip a beat. I've never had someone completely in my corner before, at least someone I'm not related to. But I sense his loyalty and feel the truth in his words. "Thank you."

He nods, and we continue to walk, hand in hand. "I'm actually going to my older sister's house in Anderson this Wednesday. She and her husband have a work thing, so I'm going to watch their two kids." He pauses for a beat before adding, "Would you like to go with me?"

Now it's my turn to stop walking. "What?"

He shrugs and runs his other hand through his hair, causing it to stand up a little. "I'm sure you work, but I just thought you might enjoy getting away for a bit. Betsy is six and Alan is three, and they're complete animals when their mom and dad are gone," he says, wolfish grin spread across those sexy lips. "I love it."

I find myself grinning automatically, as the idea of going with him takes root and starts to bloom. I really want to go. "Okay."

"Yeah?"

Nodding, I add, "I have early appointments that day, so I only scheduled a few afternoon ones. My last client is at four, so I'd be able to leave around five, unless you need to go before then."

"No, that's perfect. I have to be there by six thirty, and since it's about an hour's drive, that works great. I'll pick you up at your house."

"Sounds good," I reply, slowly starting to continue our walk. It surprises me a little how excited I am to go watch his niece and nephew, because even though this feels like a huge step—meeting the family, or at least part of it, when you're really just messing around—it feels right.

But are we?

Just messing around?

The big thumping organ in my chest says no.

"So tell me what's on your schedule for tomorrow," he says, pulling me out of my own head.

"Well, I have the second of three sessions on a large back piece that'll take a big part of my early afternoon and a cover-up of an old tattoo from someone's spring break to Florida from 1997."

Isaac snorts. "See? That's why I've never gotten a tattoo. I'd be afraid I'd eventually regret it."

"Well, the key is to pick something that represents you, and never do it on a whim. Take your time to think about the design and location, because while it can be covered up, it will only cost you more money in the long run, and the new piece usually takes up more real estate on your skin."

"Hmm," he hums, gently swinging our joined hands between us. "Good advice. If I ever get one, I'll be sure to put a lot of thought into it."

I can't help but snicker just a little. "Yeah, I don't see you getting one."

"No?" he asks, more curious than anything else. "Why not?"

Again, we stop and face each other. "Well, you're not really the tattoo kinda guy. You're clean-cut and straitlaced, and I don't mean that as an insult. It's just not who you are."

He seems to really consider my words. "A few weeks ago, I definitely would have agreed with you, but now..." He looks at my arm for a few seconds where my tattoos hide beneath my sweatshirt, as if considering his words. "Now, I guess they don't seem so bad. They seem a little *sexy*." He steps forward, releasing my hand, and slides his hands up my sides, easily slipping beneath my sweatshirt.

"Yeah?" I take a slight step toward him and press my chest against his. I can feel my nipples already pebbling against my sweatshirt, aching for those hands to work their way up for some attention.

"You know what else I think is sexy?" he asks, glancing over his shoulders and making sure we're alone.

"What?"

He leads me into the tall foliage and presses me against a tree. "I think seeing you against this, my hand down the front of your pants making you come on my fingers, might be sexier."

Air escapes from my lungs in a loud whoosh as he rocks his hard cock against my core. "We should probably find out."

He smiles that mouthwatering grin. "Like an experiment. I like the way you think, beautiful."

His mouth moves against mine, his lips devouring and his tongue delving. A fire burns deep inside me as he slips his hand down the front of my leggings. He finds my core completely bare and wet, which clearly catches him off guard.

"Fuck, you shaved?" He grits against my mouth, nipping at my swollen bottom lip. Big fingers easily slide against my pussy before a single finger pushes inside. "This is the sexiest thing ever."

I have no idea what he's referring to. The fact his finger is buried inside me or because he discovered me completely bare just moments before—or both.

Yeah, probably both.

Isaac uses his body to cage me against the tree. One hand moves right where I need him most, while the other cups my breasts and toys with the nipple ring. My body is on fire, the flames burning every square inch of me from the inside out. But there's no time to focus on anything but the sensations. They race through my blood as my body climbs higher and higher.

The amount of time it takes for me to come is embarrassingly short, but I don't care. All I can do is enjoy the ride. He slips a second finger into my body and curls them upward, sliding easily over my clit and piercing. The result is like a detonation, an explosion of blinding white light and electricity.

I sag against the tree, grateful it's there to hold me up. "Wow," I whisper, trying to catch my breath.

"You know, I really appreciate your lack of bra and panties," he says, removing his fingers but not his hand. He seems to enjoy cupping me in his hand, because he leaves it there as he kisses me once more.

When he releases my lips, I confess, "It definitely does have its advantages."

Isaac smirks. "Just as long as I'm the only one with this vantage point." He flicks my nipple ring just to punctuate his statement.

"Oh, most definitely," I mutter, trying to clear the lust from my brain. "You know," I start, sliding my hands across his T-shirt-covered abs, "there's one particular vantage point that I loved too."

His Adam's apple bobs as he swallows. "Yeah? Which one's that?"

I lean in and whisper against his ear, "The one where I'm on my knees in front of you, sucking you off."

He makes this throaty groan noise and pushes back, righting my clothes as best he can. "What a coincidence. That just so happens to be one of my favorites too."

"Maybe I can give a little demonstration," I say, walking my fingers down his abdomen to where his sweatpants tent in front of him.

Before he can reply, we hear voices approaching on the trail. "Shit," he mumbles, adjusting himself. Unfortunately, in sweats, it's not possible with a cock that big and amazing.

We return to the path just as the other couple passes. There's no missing their smirks as they offer quick greetings and hurry by. Isaac's trying to hide behind me until his erection subsides, and his shirt is rumpled from my hands.

When he meets my gaze, he starts laughing. "What's so funny?" I ask.

He reaches up and plucks a stick from my hair. "They totally knew what we were doing," he proclaims. "Your face is flushed, and your eyes are wild in that *I just had an epic orgasm* way."

"Epic, huh?"

He shifts one eyebrow upward in question. "It wasn't?"

I hug his chest and sigh. "Oh, it was, and so will the next one."

"The next one?" he asks with another laugh. "Someone's sure she's going to get me naked soon."

"I'm not?"

He presses his lips to my own. "Oh, no, you definitely will. The second we get back to my place. Your clothes are coming off the moment the front door is closed."

"Keep talking," I say, taking his offered hand as we turn and head back the way we came, following the trail back to the parking lot.

So he does. He describes in great detail all the dirty things he wants to do to me the moment we get to his place, so when we finally reach the end of the trail, I'm soaked once more and aching with need. All I can think about is getting back to his house and doing all those things he just shared.

Unfortunately, that's all pushed aside when we spot the lights flashing on top of the cop car.

Seventeen 17

Isaac

"Good evening, officer," I say the moment I notice the cop getting out of his car.

"Evening," he replies, rounding his trunk and approaching.

The moment he steps under the streetlight, recognition sets in. "Oh, Marty. Good to see you," I say, holding out my hand—thank God it's not the one that was just down BJ's pants—to one of the first men I met when I moved to town.

"Isaac," he replies, shaking my hand. When he sees BJ beside me, he nods. "Billie."

"Hi, Officer Downy. What brings you out to the park this evening?" she asks casually, as if she's not in the least worried about seeing a police officer standing in front of us.

He leans against the trunk of his squad car, crossing one ankle over the other. "Well, we had a call with a noise complaint, and they sent me here to check it out."

Noise complaint?

"Oh re-really?" BJ stammers, quickly glancing over her shoulder at me.

"Yeah, the caller thought there were teenagers out here. You know, up to no good about a quarter of the way down the walking path."

I swallow hard as embarrassment creeps up my face. "No good, huh?" I ask, running my hands through my hair.

"Yep. That's what the caller said. And heard." He shakes his head and levels me with a serious look. I swear the corner of his lip twitches. "You didn't hear or see anything back there, did you?"

"No," I insist, unable to hear the sound of the birds in the trees over the rushing blood in my head. "We didn't hear anything."

BJ turns and gives me a look that screams *calm down, you psycho.* "No, I'm sorry, Officer Downy, but we didn't hear or see anything. We did pass another couple along our hike, though. Maybe if you head down to the opposite end of the trail, you'll catch them when they're coming out of the trees."

He considers her words a moment before he smiles. "Maybe I'll do that. Thank you for your time," he says, heading back to the driver's side of his squad. "Oh, and Isaac?" When I look up, he adds, "You have something on the front of your pants."

I look down and find moisture on the front of my sweats, right over where my cock was hard and seeping not long before our night was interrupted by the police. A groan spills from my lips as I close my eyes and wait for the ground to open and swallow me whole.

"Night," Marty hollers before getting into his car and driving away.

"Well, that was embarrassing," BJ states the second the car disappears from the lot.

"I'm pretty sure he knew we were the ones up to no good," I add.

She turns and gives me a big grin. "Oh, definitely. He was trying not to laugh the whole time."

When we reach our vehicles at the end of the lot, I can't help but ask, "So, are you still interested in coming back to my place for a bit?"

She turns hungry eyes my way. "Are you kidding? The vantage point, remember?"

My cock twitches in excitement. "Yes, I do recall some discussion about that."

Her grin turns absolutely wicked as she runs her hand down the front of my sweats. "No time for discussion. Only demonstration."

Am I nervous to take BJ to my sister's house? Hell yes.

Savannah has accompanied me to family dinners or holiday gatherings over the years, but never one of my babysitting gigs. She always had some excuse, usually work related, as to why she couldn't go. Looking back now, I don't think she's a fan of kids. Even when we were around Lizzie, she always kept her distance and her nose in her phone.

I should have recognized that sign long before now because I've made my stance on having a family perfectly clear. I want one. Big, small, I don't care. I just see a child or two when I think about what I want from life. Looking back, I realize that every time I brought it up, she'd change the subject or take off her clothes. She was good at distracting me.

I pull into BJ's driveway, and before I can get out of my car, she steps out the front door and heads my way carrying a plastic container. "Hey," she says, slipping into the passenger seat and placing the lidded dish on her lap.

"Hi. What's that?" I ask, nodding to her lap and the container she guards carefully.

She seems nervous as she replies, "Uhh, I made cookies."

Instantly, I smile. "You did? They're gonna love them."

"Well, they don't look very pretty. I'm a decent cook, but not much of a baker. They might not even taste very good," she rambles, getting it all out without taking a breath.

I reach over and grasp the corner of the lid. "May I?"

She nods insistently as she pulls it open. "Yeah, sure. You probably want to make sure they aren't going to get sick or anything," she says with an awkward chuckle.

"No," I insist, lightly touching her cheek until she meets my gaze. "I'm just starving and wanted a snack. I'm sure they're delicious, and the kids will love them. Thank you."

Her eyes soften, changing from worried to appreciative, which makes me want to kiss her, but I know once I start, I won't want to stop. So instead of thanking her for thinking of my niece and nephew the way I want, I just give her a smile and steal a cookie. One bite in and I know I have a new favorite sweet treat. "Wow, these are delicious."

"Really?"

"Definitely, and chocolate chip is the kids' favorite. You did good."

She sags in relief against the seat. "Oh, thank God. I was so nervous. What if they don't eat chocolate—"

"Wait, who doesn't like chocolate?"

She shrugs. "I don't know. Some parents don't let their kids have sugar."

I snort and finish off my cookie. "Amelia isn't one of those moms, believe me. They're going to love these."

"Okay, well, if you think so."

Throwing my car in reverse, I reply, "I know so. And if they don't, then there's more for me."

We make small talk the entire trip to Anderson, which seems to calm whatever nerves she has, but the moment I pull into my sister's driveway, they return in full force. "Hey," I say, turning to face her the second I shut off my vehicle. "It's going to be fine. I promise."

She swallows hard, her eyes a little wide. "I've just...I've never met someone...well, someone I'm sleeping with's family before. Not like this. There was the time a guy's mom came in for a tattoo, but I didn't know it was his mom until the end of the appointment."

A gentle smile spreads across my lips as I cup her cheek once more. "BJ, everything's gonna be fine. We're going to go inside, feed the monsters pizza, have cookies, and watch a movie. It's just a few hours, and I won't leave your side the entire time."

She nods. "Okay, yeah. I'm sorry I'm a little freaked out, but this seems so...huge."

"That's what she said," I sing, making her laugh. The worry lines around her eyes disappear and I don't think I've ever seen her more beautiful. "You ready to go in? If we don't move, the monsters will come looking for us."

"We better go then, huh?"

I bring her hand to my mouth and kiss her knuckles just as the front door to my sister's home flies open and the two heathens make their escape. Before I can climb out, a little face is plastered to the driver's side window, leaving fingerprints and a wet smear from a tongue. "You ready?" I ask, reaching for the handle.

"Let's do this."

The moment I step out, my niece and nephew launch themselves at my legs. "Uncle Isaac!" Betsy bellows, squeezing me tightly in a fierce hug.

"Hey, guys!"

"Who dat?" Alan asks, peeking at BJ from between my legs.

"This is my friend, BJ," I answer, lifting the smaller of the two kids into my arms. "Can you say hello?"

"Hi," they both sing together.

"You have pretty hair," Betsy says, pointing up to the pink streaks.

BJ smiles down at the little girl. "Thank you. I really like your pink bow."

My niece grins widely, missing her two front teeth, and takes BJ's hand. She's practically jumping up and down. "Can we do each other's hair?" Betsy asks, the anticipation almost too much to contain.

"Of course we can."

"Yay!" Betsy hollers, pulling BJ along as she runs for the front door. "Mommy, this girl is gonna do my hair!"

Before our feet land on the porch, my sister, Amelia, and her husband, Collin, appear in the doorway. "Really?" my sister asks, taking in BJ before turning her shocked eyes on me.

"Hey, Meal," I say, leaning in and kissing her cheek. "This is my friend, BJ. BJ, this is my bossy, big sister, Amelia, and her saint of a husband, Collin."

Amelia steps forward, grinning like a lunatic, as she reaches for BJ's hand. "BJ, it's so wonderful to meet you. Please come in," she says moments before she drags BJ through the entryway. Once we're inside, she adds, "So, my brother didn't mention he was bringing a friend."

"Be cool, Meal," I warn, setting Alan down on the floor.

Her mouth opens and she places her hand over her heart. "What? I'm totally cool. I mean, just because you rarely bring friends home doesn't mean I'm going to do something embarrassing, like tell her about the time you went to school without underwear."

"Amelia!" I groan, running my hands through my hair. Turning to BJ, I quickly add, "It was preschool, and I had pants on."

"Yes, but how did Mom find out about the no underwear?" my horrible, awful sister asks, leading me straight to the mortifying punchline of the story.

Sighing, I close my eyes, surrounded by the dead silence of everyone waiting for me to answer. "Because I pulled my pants down to pee on the tree."

Amelia giggles, and a quick glance at BJ confirms she's trying not to laugh. "The tree was in the middle of the playground."

"Okay, now that you've shared a very embarrassing story about me, can you go?" I ask, kissing my sister's forehead and practically pushing her to the front door.

"Yes, we do need to go. Pizza is ordered and will be delivered around six thirty. Make sure you cut Alan's up or he'll try to shove the whole piece in his mouth, and Betsy isn't to touch the makeup in my closet, despite how much she begs."

"We'll be fine. Enjoy your banquet thingy," I say.

"Okay, we'll be back by nine," Collin says, escorting his wife out the door and toward their minivan.

When the door is shut and locked, I turn to find both kids holding BJ's hands. "All right, monsters, what's first?" I ask, clapping my hands together in anticipation.

"Makeup!"

"Matchbox cars and LEGOs!"

"How about we pick out a movie to watch after we eat," I reason, picturing the Matchbox and LEGO scene—and by scene, I mean mess.

"Okay!" they both proclaim, running for the living room.

"You all right?"

BJ glances into the living room, where the hellions are tearing apart the entertainment cabinet, pulling all the DVDs from the shelves. "I'm great, actually." Her smile is small but genuine, which makes me happy.

"Good. Now, come on. We better get in there before they play *Weekend at Bernie's* again."

"Your hair is so pretty," BJ says, brushing out Betsy's long, dark hair.

"Yours too. I want to put pink in mine," my niece replies from the love seat where she's patiently waiting for BJ to finish her hairdo.

"When you get bigger you can."

"Or when Mommy says so," Betsy replies.

"That's right," BJ agrees, smiling as she starts some weird braid thing.

After we ate pizza, we started a children's movie they picked out together. When we hit the halfway point, we took a quick intermission for cookies and milk. Both kids ate two chocolate chip cookies, swearing they were the best cookies they'd ever had. The smile on BJ's face was priceless. Now, we're making our way through the second half of the movie and braiding hair. Well, not Alan. He's sitting beside me, using my leg like a dragstrip for his little toy car.

My attention isn't on the television, but on the woman doing my niece's hair. Betsy sits perfectly still, chatting openly about her day in kindergarten. The way my heart races when I look at her, how I can see so much more than what meets the eye is pretty startling. The future I always saw, the one I tried so damn hard to stuff Savannah in, isn't the one I now see before me. In fact, the picture is clearer now than ever before.

I see BJ.

I see her smiles and the way her eyes light up when she's excited. I want more nights with her falling asleep beside me and more mornings with her waking the same way. The daily text to check in and the surprise visits just to steal a few kisses. But that's not all I see. She's artistic, determined, and loyal, and any man who dates her is better because of it.

The only problem is...that will never be us.

She doesn't want anything serious. The future I see doesn't align with her vision.

Frankly, that sucks.

"All done," BJ declares, fastening the pink bow into place and grabbing a handheld mirror to show Betsy.

"Thank you!" the little girl bellows, throwing her arms around BJ's neck and hugging her tight.

BJ closes her eyes, holding the girl against her chest, the faintest smile on her lips. "You're welcome." When she looks down, I can see tears gathered in those beautiful caramel-colored eyes, and the sight kills me.

"BJ, would you mind helping me in the kitchen for a minute?" I ask, carefully standing up and sending two Matchbox cars flying to the floor. "We'll be right back, okay?" I say to Alan, picking up the toys and placing them on the couch. "Don't cause any trouble."

He laughs.

Laughs.

But I have no time to think about it, because all I want to do is find out why she's crying.

The moment we step inside the kitchen, I take her in my arms and just hold her. "What's wrong?"

"Nothing," she insists, waving off the show of emotion and trying to hide behind her hand.

"No, tell me. You're crying," I implore, searching her face for information.

"It's just," she starts, sniffling and wiping away the moisture beneath her eyes, "Well, I just really had a great time tonight with them. They're amazing kids. I don't have a lot of experience, and I never really knew if I wanted them or not because of my own parents and the struggles Jameson and I endured growing up, but after spending just a few hours with them," she continues, waving her hand toward the living room, "I realize I do. Eventually, I want kids."

I smile and pull her into my chest. "You'll make a great mom someday."

She sniffles, and I'm pretty sure she wipes her nose on my button-down. But instead of freaking out, I just grin and hold her closer. "Someday. Not now though. I guess it's just good to know it's not completely out of the question, you know?"

Pulling back, I look down at those shining brown eyes. All I do is smile, gazing at the most stunning woman I've ever known, and I'm not just talking physically. She's a truly beautiful person on the inside too.

My lips are on hers moments later, because I can't see myself *not* kissing her in this moment. Unfortunately, the kiss is short-lived and interrupted by the approaching sound of four running feet.

"Uncle Isaac, look!" Betsy hollers, running into the kitchen with her brother hot on her heels.

I release BJ and jump back, turning to see what the urgency is. My heart stops beating, dropping down to my shoes. "What did you do?" I ask, ignoring the markers in their hands and taking in the scribbles all over their faces and arms.

"We have tattoos too! Like BJ!"

BJ

"Thank you for taking me to meet them," I say for the third time—or is it the fourth?—since we began our drive back to Stewart Grove.

Isaac raises my hand to his lips and brushes them across my knuckles, sending waves of desire through my veins. "You're very welcome. You don't have to keep thanking me though. I'm glad you were able to go. The kids had a great time."

"I did too," I reply honestly. But I know there's more I want to say. I'm not sure when the last time I cried was, and I can't believe I did it in front of a guy. "By the way, I wanted to apologize. For the waterworks."

He glances away from the road, but only for a quick second. "You don't have to apologize for that. That's what friends are for, right?"

I swallow, trying to push back the way the word *friends* makes my chest feel tight and my breathing a little shallow. "Yeah. Sure."

He offers me another grin as he passes the city limit sign. "So, I was thinking," he starts, stopping at the first light in downtown, "What do you think about going back to my place?"

"I don't have my truck."

"I can drive you back to your house in the morning on my way to work."

"I don't have any clothes."

The grin he gives is full of dirty promises. "I'm pretty sure you're not going to need them for what I have planned for you."

I'm able to completely push all other thoughts out of my head and focus on the one thing we can both agree on right now: sex. "Better hurry," I reply, sliding my hand down his leg and boldly grabbing his hard length.

He presses down on the gas and makes it back to his condo in impressive time and pulls directly into the garage. He practically pulls me from the car, presses the button to lower the garage door, and drags me inside. Of course, it's not really considered a drag when you willingly go with him, right?

Inside, he twists me around and presses me into the door. He cages me in place, his big, warm hand coming up and gently cupping my neck. His eyes roam my face before dropping to where he holds me. Suddenly, he starts to laugh.

"Something funny?"

Isaac sighs and holds up his hands. They're covered in marker from when he tried to wash Alan after their homemade tattoos. Apparently, Alan had another marker on him, and the moment Isaac turned his head, the little boy decided to give his uncle some nice, colorful artwork too. He even got it all over Isaac's white button-down.

"I should go shower," he says, shaking his head and smiling.

"Your shirt is probably ruined," I state, running my fingers along the blue doodle on the cuff of his shirt.

Isaac shrugs. "Believe it or not, it's not the first shirt the monsters have ruined."

"You'd think your sister would buy washable markers," I note.

"Oh, she does. These permanent ones were in her office. Probably even hidden in a desk drawer."

I can't stop touching the markings on his shirt. It seems so out of character to see him with marker all over him. I guess I've always pictured Isaac as a man who carries one of those bleach or stain removing sticks with him for times like these. Of course, I doubt one of those laundry sticks would have met its match on this permanent blue marker. "They took it well. The mess."

He snorts a laugh. "Amelia and Collin are used to special surprises left by their kids. They have the patience of saints, that's for sure."

"As do you."

He shrugs and kisses my forehead.

"Why don't you go get in the shower and wash it off? Maybe I'll join you in a few minutes," I suggest, running my finger down the buttons on his shirt.

"Yes, I do think I'll need some assistance, you know, making sure my back is clean." A wolfish grin spreads across his lips, making my thighs clench.

"I'll be in there in a few minutes," I say, placing a quick kiss on his lips and watching his ass as he walks away.

I stop by the kitchen and grab a glass of water before making my way to his bedroom. Once the water is running, I slip out of my clothes and toss them in a heap on the floor, knowing it'll drive him crazy when he sees them. Then I grab the lighter lying on the dresser and ignite the jar candle.

Vanilla.

Such a plain, boring scent.

I make a mental note to buy him a better one. Maybe something with lavender or amber in it. At least then it's subtle and not overpowering like apple cinnamon.

Just as I set the lighter down, a noise catches my attention. *Was that the front door?* I look around the room, listening for the sound I thought I heard. After a few seconds, I definitely hear something again. I make a mad dash for the shirt tossed over the chair in the corner. It's the doodle shirt, but I don't care. I slip my arms into the holes and move toward the front of the house. Part of me wonders if I should go to the bathroom and alert Isaac that someone's here, but what if I imagined it all? How embarrassing would it be to pull him from the shower to check out a noise at the front door, when there wasn't even a noise?

I hurry through the condo, fastening a few buttons, and peek through the drawn curtain. There's a small car in the driveway, but I don't recognize it. The fact it's not my brother's or any of his other friends is good. The last thing I'd want is to have one of them discover me here. Just as I move to the door and go to look through the peephole, a knock sounds, making me yelp in surprise.

"Hello?" comes a voice on the opposite side of the door.

Clearly having heard my noise, I unlock the door and pull it open, revealing a very surprised Savannah on the other side.

"Who are you?" she demands. Her eyes narrow as she takes in my appearance from head to toe. When they settle back on my face, she spits out, "I know you."

I don't reply right away, just stare at her. "May I help you?"

"What are you doing here?" she asks, then seems to reconsider her question as her gaze drops to the shirt I'm wearing.

The one that clearly doesn't belong to me. She rolls her eyes dramatically and flips her hair over her shoulder.

"I could ask you the same question."

She stands up straight and narrows her blue eyes. "Listen...BJ, is it?" she asks with a bit of nastiness in her tone, clearly recognizing me from around town. "I just stopped by to gather my things."

"At almost eleven at night?"

"Well, he wasn't here earlier when I stopped by. I told him I was coming for my things. I need them." She's clearly annoyed, which gives me a little delight, if I'm being honest.

"I'm sorry, I'm not sure where your things are."

She huffs out a deep breath. "Where's Isaac? I know he's home."

"In the shower. It's been a long night," I say with a big smile, throwing the spiteful insinuation out there, even though I probably shouldn't have.

"Listen, *BJ*," she practically growls, "Isaac promised to give me my things, but hasn't."

"Well, *Savannah*, I'm not sure where your belongings are located. If you call him tomorrow during normal person daytime hours, I'm sure he will arrange a convenient time for you to claim your shit. Until then, get lost," I say, trying to close the door in her face.

Her hands fly forward, keeping the door from slamming in her face. "It appears Isaac is slumming it in my absence."

My eyebrows pull together as I glare at her through the opening of the door. "Your absence?"

"It's temporary," she says with another hair flip. "I'll be back in his bed soon, and you can head back to the trailer park."

"Excuse me?"

"Oh, don't be all sensitive. Besides, we all know whatever you have with Isaac will be brief. He's clearly just going through a phase of some sort. Before you know it, we'll be back together like always."

I lean against the door, keeping her outside. "Yet, I'm the one in here, and you're out there."

"I give it one week. He'll be done with your weird stringy hair and your dirty tattoos. You're the last thing Isaac wants, believe me. He has a very distinct taste, a clear image to maintain, and I guarantee you don't fit the mold."

"If you say so," I say, trying to sound completely aloof, yet hating the bubble of self-doubt that rises in my chest. So what if he gets back with her eventually? It's not like what we're doing doesn't have an expiration date on it, right? Friends with benefits? Keeping it casual? Sex without the relationship?

Sound familiar?

"Now, if you'll excuse me, I think I heard the shower shut off," I say, pushing the door closed and throwing the lock. "Jesus," I mutter, rubbing my hand over my forehead.

"I was wondering where you ran off to."

I quickly turn around, startled to hear Isaac behind me.

"What's wrong?" he asks, heading my way with concern in his eyes.

My eyes drop to the towel around his hips, hanging dangerously low. That delicious V evident, even in the dark room. "Umm, you had a visitor."

When he reaches me, he asks, "Who?"

"Savannah." He seems surprised by my response, so I quickly add, "She stopped by to gather her things."

"Seriously? At this hour?"

I shrug, running my palm up the ridges of his abs and scraping my nails through his dark chest hair. “I told her to come back another time.”

“So we’re alone?”

I nod.

“And you’re wearing my shirt?”

Again, I nod.

“Hmm,” he practically hums in appreciation, tracing a finger down my chest to where the first button is secured. “I like it on you.” When his fiery eyes meet mine, he pulls me against his body and lifts, my legs wrapping around his waist.

The towel falls away.

His lips are demanding as he takes mine in a bruising kiss. His tongue delves deep, tasting and teasing me in the best way possible. When I’m breathless and gasping, he pulls back and grins.

“Yes, I definitely like it. Let’s leave it on.”

I step into the office, finding Jax sitting behind his desk. “How’s it going?” I ask, flopping down into the chair across from him.

“Good. Just doing some paperwork. Jesus, I fucking hate this shit,” he mumbles, shuffling a stack of papers together and setting them aside. “What’s up?”

“Not much. Just finished an appointment and waiting for my next one,” I say before taking a drink from my water bottle. “So…what’s going on with the Amanda situation?”

"Amanda situation?" he asks, shifting uncomfortably in his chair.

"Don't play dumb with me. Have you asked her?"

He holds my gaze before glancing away. "No. I don't think I'm going to."

"Why not?"

Jax sighs deeply and leans back, looking up. "I don't want to risk losing a good employee."

That surprises me. "Really? But you had no problem risking my employment status? Was I not a good employee?" I ask with a big teasing grin.

"It wasn't like that for us," he says somberly. "What we had, that was different. We both knew it had no future."

Even though he's right, his words hold a slight sting to the ego. "True."

"So, tell me. What's going on with you and the suit?"

I shrug, not really wanting to talk about Isaac or the fact he's meeting his ex-girlfriend right now to return her box of belongings.

I mean, everything's fine, really. We woke up this morning to his cell phone ringing, and when he grabbed the device, it was Savannah's smiling face on the screen. He answered it, and all I could hear was her bubbly, over-the-top chipper voice on the other end. And her giggles. Fuck, in a one-minute phone call, she must have giggled a dozen times, annoying me more than I've probably ever been in my life.

"You know, he isn't who I'd picture you with, but now that I've met him, he's not so bad."

"Seriously?"

He lifts his shoulders. "He seemed like a nice guy," he replies, referring to the night I drew on Isaac's chest with the markers.

"He is, but don't get too attached, okay? It's just a thing."

Jax openly gazes at me with curiosity. "A thing?"

"You know, fun."

He studies me for several long seconds before leaning forward and resting his elbows on his desk. "That wasn't a guy having fun, BJ."

"What are you talking about?"

"The looks. When you were focused on his tattoo, he was completely focused on you."

What?

"Excuse me? How would you know that?" I ask. I drew on him after everyone had left for the night.

He gives me a sheepish grin. "The cameras. If you want to...entertain, you should probably pull the curtain closed."

Cheese and rice!

The cameras! We have three of them installed in the building so we can monitor activity while we're occupied. The main one is in the waiting area, with one pointed down each of the two hallways. It gives us the vantage point of seeing who's sitting in the chairs until the curtains close. I'm so used to them I don't even think about the fact they're there anymore.

"Oh God," I groan, closing my eyes, recalling exactly how I climbed onto his lap and kissed him. And how our clothes came off moments later for one fast, hard ride.

Jax's chuckle is slow and deep. "Don't worry, I didn't watch anything. Once I realized what was happening, I turned it off."

"Well, this is embarrassing," I mutter, feeling the start of a headache.

"Don't worry about it. Not anything I haven't seen before, right?" he asks with a hearty laugh. "Besides, you're not the only one to use the chair for extracurricular activities. Remember that woman who inquired about getting her boyfriend's dick pierced when she got both her nipples done about two years ago?"

"Yeah," I reply, unsure of where this is going.

"Well, we got talking about it. She asked a bunch of questions about the pleasure and how it felt, and I showed her those pictures of mine on the wall. The boyfriend was pissed, said no way was he getting his junk done."

"I remember. They got in that big fight."

Jax smiles. "She returned later that night, *alone*. Wanted an up-close-and-personal view of said piercing."

"And let me guess, you gave it to her?"

"We'll call it research, BJ."

"Jesus, Jax," I reply, laughing. "You're horrible."

He shrugs, brushing off my comment. "There was nothing horrible about it."

"I hope you used plenty of Clorox Wipes," I tease.

"As many as I'm sure you used after you and your friend were done."

Before I can say anything else, a knock sounds at the door and draws our attention. "Hey, guys. Beej, your next appointment is here."

I hop up and wave to the chair I'm vacating. "Why don't you sit, Amanda, and take a break. I'm sure Jax would love your help in prepping for his quarterly tax appointment next week. He gets all stressed out when he has to pull everything together, but I'm sure if you were here, helping, he'd feel much more at ease."

I don't look at his face as I leave, but I definitely notice the smile she gives him as I pass by. "How can I help?" my best friend asks, joining him in the office.

I can picture his annoyed, yet completely excited face, and I'm sure he's going to have something to say later about me sticking my nose in his business.

But I didn't just do it for him, I did it for my best friend too. I love her like a sister, and I want her to be happy. If Jax is that man, then so be it. I've always thought he'd be the most loyal, caring boyfriend, if he'd ever take the chance and actually date a woman for more than a few quick romps between the sheets.

And don't get me started on Amanda. She's the very best kind of woman too, and the more I think about it, the more perfect they are for each other. They would balance each other out. His intensity and abrasiveness with her sincerity and kindheartedness, who happens to straddle the line between sweet and wild.

They might be made for each other.

Just call me Cupid.

Nineteen 19

Isaac

"What are you all doing Sunday?" Jasper asks as he places food in front of each of us to start our Monday owners' meeting.

"Going to Aunt Edna's but I'll be done by midafternoon," Walker declares, shoving a few fries in his mouth.

"Working for a bit," I state, even though I'm not sure I'll put much time in. Lately, I've been enjoying working less hours and spending more time with a certain tattoo artist.

"Don't know. Why?" Jameson asks, making sure there's no onions on his burger before taking a huge bite.

"It's Lyndee's birthday, so I'm making dinner at the house. You're all invited."

"What do you want us to bring?" Walker inquires between bites.

"Nothing. I've got it covered, and Dustin and Dana are in charge of the cake," Jasper says, taking the fourth seat for himself.

Jameson practically shovels half his burger in his mouth as he asks, "What time?"

"Any time after four. We'll probably eat around five thirty. Oh, and Jameson, you're welcome to bring your sister, if you want. I haven't seen her since the night she had dinner with Numbers, but if she's not doing anything, you can bring her with."

My throat is suddenly too dry to swallow the food I'm chewing. I can feel Jameson's eyes on me from across the table, and when I glance up, it's confirmed. They're slightly narrowed, not completely menacing, but enough to make me sweat.

Be cool. Don't make any major movements. Don't show weakness.

Once I get the food down my throat without choking, I quickly say, "The night you were sick, and she stayed at the brewery until I got over there. I bought her a burger as a thank-you for helping us out."

Jameson stares at me without giving anything away. Honestly, I'm not sure if it's a good thing or a bad one that I can't read his mind right now. Something tells me I'd not like what's running through his head.

Fortunately, I'm saved any more worry when he lifts his chin. "Thanks for buying her dinner. I appreciate her stopping by and helping me out." To Jasper he quickly adds, "I don't think she's around this weekend, or I'd bring her. She's got some tattoo gig in Chicago for a band."

I try not to act completely shocked by the news. She's going to Chicago this weekend? Why hasn't she said anything?

"What band?" Walker asks.

"Toxic Energy. The bass player is from here and went to school with Jax. He invited them to come to the show and give them some ink to celebrate their latest album going Platinum."

"Damn, that's a big honor," Jasper adds.

Jameson nods, but doesn't elaborate further.

While everyone continues to eat, a sense of pride fills me. I'm so damn proud of her for accomplishing what she has in such a short amount of time. But I also can't ignore the feeling of jealousy that she'd share something so big with her brother and not me. I know we're just...whatever we are...but I would have thought she'd still at least mention it to me. It wasn't that many hours ago I was licking chocolate off her naked body. Perhaps she was just too distracted to tell me something so big and exciting.

When all our plates are clean, we switch gears to discussing the restaurant, bar, and brewery, and I'm able to push thoughts of BJ out of my mind. Since Jasper started dating Lyndee, his mood swings are a little more bearable, so employee turnover in the kitchen hasn't been as high. Thank God. I'm not sure there are many people left in Stewart Grove to hire.

Finally, I gather my papers, ready to go back to my office and work—not think about the one woman I can't stop thinking about and the news she didn't share with me.

"Oh, and, Isaac?" Jasper says, grabbing my attention before I hit the back hallway that leads to my office. "You can bring her Sunday."

My mouth falls to the floor before I can stop it. "Excuse me?"

"The woman you're seeing," he states casually, making my blood run cold with dread.

Jameson spins around and glares. "Savannah? You're back with Savannah?"

Before I can answer, Jasper jumps in. "No, not Savannah. Someone else."

I swallow hard over the lump of dread in my throat. "I, uh," I stammer, searching for words, but coming up empty.

Jasper laughs at my uneasiness. "Relax, you don't have to if you don't want to. I ran into Jeb yesterday at the grocery store, and he mentioned you had been entertaining a pretty girl, and specifically said it wasn't the decorator girl."

I sigh in relief, grateful BJ and I weren't just exposed. I mean, I knew that we could reach the point where we'd have to confirm the fact we were hanging out, but I really didn't want to do it now, at work, and surrounded by all three of my friends.

Specifically by Jameson.

Who might want to pound his fist into my face.

Knowing I need to say something, I reply, "We're not really there yet. We've just been getting to know each other." It's not a lie. We aren't.

He seems to buy my excuse and nods. "Okay. Well, just know she's invited too."

"Thanks," I reply, eager to get the hell out of there and back to my office.

As I head upstairs, my mind is reeling with the news of her going to Chicago to tattoo Toxic Energy. I'm definitely excited for her, even if it hurts a little she kept that news to herself. It just goes to prove we're not at *that* place. Not that I expect us to get there. I mean, we did agree to a short-term friends with benefits arrangement, right?

Keep telling yourself that.

Once I leave work, I fully intend to head home. Yet, for some reason, my car drives toward Xpress Urself Tattoo. I park in front, noticing the small lot is still pretty busy for a Monday evening. Honestly, I should go home. I should not take my keys from the ignition, not get out of this car. Stewart Grove is a small enough town that someone is going to notice my extra attention toward BJ, and I really need to be prepared for that to happen. Jeb has already outed me to Jasper, and it won't be long before everyone figures out her name. When that happens, all hell will break loose.

Yet, that doesn't keep my ass in my car.

I slip from my Maxima and head for the front door of the studio. The heavy beat of metal music greets me as I step inside. There's a couple sitting in the waiting area, and the front desk where Amanda sits is empty. I stay for a few minutes before deciding to venture down the hall and peek into BJ's room.

There she is, leaning against the counter and talking to Amanda. The first thing I notice is her hair. It's completely different today than it was a few days ago. Instead of blonde with pink streaks, it's a darker color, and thanks to being pulled in a ponytail high on her head, I can see the rich purple color on the underside.

She's stunning.

"Oh, hey!" Amanda greets when she notices me standing in the doorway.

"Hi," I reply with a nod, glancing over to meet BJ's gaze. She's smiling, which calms any apprehension I may have felt about just stopping by here.

"I have some amazing news to share," she says, coming over to where I stand.

"I'll give you two a few minutes before I bring back your next client," her best friend says before leaving the room.

BJ steps forward and presses her hands to my chest, her lips to my own. “Guess what?” I hum, not wanting her to move her lips. Unfortunately, she pulls back, but keeps her hands where they are. “I found out this morning I’m going to Chicago this weekend to meet Toxic Energy.”

I grin, and not just because of the excitement radiating from her, but because she only found out today and is sharing her big news. “Really? How cool is that?”

“Right? So, the bassist went to school with Jax, and he called him last night to see if he’d come do a few tattoos. They got to talking and Jax offered to bring me too, since there are six guys. Isn’t that amazing? We’re going to the show on Saturday night at the United Center and then doing matching tattoos on all six guys to celebrate their latest album. Can you believe that? I’m going to tattoo Toxic Energy,” she proclaims, giggling like a young girl who just heard she’s meeting her favorite boy band.

“Wow, that’s great,” I say, kissing her forehead.

“I know. We spent the whole afternoon rearranging our schedule so we can leave Saturday, but we were able to get it done. I’ll have to work later than normal through Friday, but that’s okay. It’ll be worth it.”

I give her a hug, loving the way her body fits so perfectly against mine. “I’m so happy for you,” I say as Amanda steps back into the room.

“Thank God you’re cool, Numbers. Not everyone can handle their girl heading off for the weekend with her ex,” Amanda says with a chuckle. I feel BJ tense in my arms as Amanda adds, “You ready for Gio?”

Pulling back, I meet her gaze, my mind spinning. “Your ex?”

She clears her throat and shoots Amanda daggers. "Uh, yeah. Jax and I…we dated. A long time ago. Just for a bit," she replies with a shrug.

My heart is racing as I try to piece together the new information. She's going to Chicago…with Jax. Her ex-boyfriend. Jealousy sweeps in, gripping my chest tightly and making it hard to breathe.

"You okay?" Concern fills her gorgeous brown eyes.

"Oh, yeah, sure. Fine. I guess I didn't realize you and Jax…dated."

She gives me a small grin before confirming, "It was a long time ago. Years ago, actually."

I nod, not really sure what to say. I mean, I know she's dated in the past, but I guess I never considered she was with her boss at one point. And they still work together? So closely?

Amanda clears her throat before saying, "I'll give you another minute," and slowly backs out of the room.

"I'm sorry I never mentioned that," BJ says, messing with her hair awkwardly.

I wave off her concern and paint on an indifferent face. "It's fine, really. We're just, you know, messing around, right? It's not like I didn't know you had dated."

"Yeah, but I probably should have said one of them was Jax."

The pieces slowly slide into place. "He must have been the one your brother was friends with."

"Yeah," she verifies.

"Hey, Isaac, right?" Jax says, filling the doorway with his large, tattoo-covered body. "Did Beej tell you her news?"

Which news? The fact she's going to Chicago with you or the part where you two used to fuck?

Clearing my throat, I confirm, "She did. That's pretty great."

"When I told Kale about her work and how brilliant she is, he insisted we both come," Jax adds, offering BJ a warm, proud smile. "Anyway, I overheard Amanda. Your next appointment is ready, so I'll get out of your hair. Later," he says, slapping me on the back as he goes.

"Well, I should head out too. You have an appointment."

BJ steps forward, crowding my personal space. "Are you okay?"

"Yeah, of course."

She holds my gaze as she whispers, "Are *we* okay?"

I want to ask more questions about her and Jax, but I realize it doesn't matter. Her past is her past, right? There's nothing I can do about it, and there's no point in stressing. It's not like I can change mine with Savannah or anyone else I've dated. All I can do is learn from it and move on.

Leaning forward, I kiss her sexy lips. "Yeah, we're okay."

The slowest grin spreads across her face. "Good."

With one more kiss, I pull back, my fingers sliding through the ponytail. "I really like this."

"Yeah?" Her eyes light up.

"It's gorgeous. Like you." Then with Herculean strength, I back completely away and move to the doorway. "Can I call you later?"

"Sure," she replies, just as Amanda delivers the couple from the front waiting area to BJ's room.

"Gio's ready," she says, glancing between her friend and me, as if to make sure there aren't any issues.

"Have a good one," I reply, shoving my hands in my pockets. "Later, Amanda."

Outside, I head for my car, trying not to let the jealousy creep back in. I've never really felt this crazed before. Why now?

Why her?

You know why, you just refuse to see it.

Probably because I know this is going nowhere, even if the idea of something more with BJ feels right. That's not what she wants, what we agreed upon.

So, I'll take what I can get, enjoying our time together while we have it.

That's all I can do.

"Hello?"

"Hey, are you home?"

"Just got here," BJ replies, tossing what sounds like her keys onto the counter. "How was your night?"

"Good. I ran a few sales reports for the brewery."

She snickers. "Numbers running numbers, huh?"

I'm instantly smiling. "It's what I do. So, how did your appointment go?"

"Really good. My client, Gio, was adding some detail to a wolf tattoo on his upper arm, and it turned out gorgeous."

I love hearing the satisfaction in her voice. She's so damn talented. I can see why people come back to her time and time again. If I were ever to get ink, I'd only let BJ do it. "I'm glad."

"Me too. He brought his girlfriend with him for this appointment, and she talked the entire time," she recalls with a yawn.

"I can let you go. I'm sure you want to eat and get cleaned up before going to bed."

"No, I'm okay, as long as you don't mind me eating chicken wings in your ear," she replies with a chuckle.

"Chicken wings? Plain or with sauce?"

"Caribbean Jerk, the only way to eat them," she states.

"I should have known. You with that spicy food."

"And let me guess, you eat boneless with honey barbecue?"

I'm quiet for a few seconds, mostly because she guessed right. When she laughs, melting my heart at the sound, I kick my feet up on the coffee table and lean back on the couch.

"So I'm right."

"You're right," I confirm. "And you probably eat them with the bone-in."

"Duh! That's how you get the best flavor," she says, making a slurping noise. I can picture her licking the sauce off her fingers, which causes me to get hard. I seem to find myself in a perpetual state of arousal lately.

"I wish I could watch you eat your food," I mutter absently, not meaning to say it aloud.

"I have an idea."

Then she hangs up.

"Hello?" I ask, glancing at the phone screen to see the call time has stopped.

Suddenly, it rings, BJ's beautiful face filling the screen. "Hey."

"Sorry about that, but I thought this would be like you're right here with me," she replies, somewhat shyly.

"Great idea. Now I can watch you gnawing on that chicken bone and sucking spicy sauce off your fingers."

She sets the phone down, leaning it against the wall, and digs into her food. "It's so good."

"Where'd you get them from? We don't serve wings," I tease.

"The bar on Adams. They have the best wings. We order them all the time at the shop," she informs, reminding me of the fact she works with a man she used to sleep with.

"I'll have to try them sometime."

"You should. They'll even do your safe little boneless honey barbecue ones." BJ flashes me a quick smile with sauce covering her lips.

Why am I so turned on?

"What's wrong? You're all twitchy and your cheeks are flushed," she asks, sticking her thumb in her mouth and sucking.

I stare at her hand, my cock throbbing in my trousers, and suddenly, I wish I were right in front of her, taking that damn thumb and shoving it in my own mouth.

"Isaac?" she asks, her voice all husky and raw.

"Hmm?"

"What are you thinking about?" She holds my gaze and slowly lifts her index finger, the tip of her tongue slipping out and swirling it around and removing the sauce.

"Nothing." My voice doesn't even sound like my own.

BJ leans forward, getting closer to the screen. "Isaac? Show me your lap?"

I can't help but smile. "My lap?"

"Yeah. I just want to see something for a second."

I shift the phone so she can see how hard I am beneath the black pants. "Happy?"

"No," she says, pushing the food aside and picking up the phone, carrying me away.

"What's wrong?"

A seductive grin spreads across her lips. "Nothing. I want to see your hard cock. Take it out," she demands, setting the phone down on her nightstand and positioning it toward her bed.

"What?" I gape, so fucking turned on I can't think straight.

BJ lies on her bed and spreads her legs. "Let me see. Go to your room and set the phone on your dresser."

I don't waste any time jumping up and practically sprinting to my room, my eyes glued to the screen the entire time. BJ strips off her leggings and shirt, suddenly naked before me.

"Jesus, Billie," I mutter, my mouth watering to taste her skin.

She meets my eye as she says, "I like it when you say my name like that. I've always hated it, but when you say it, it's not so bad."

I set my phone on my dresser and step back, unbuttoning my pants. "Your name is as beautiful as you are."

She grins at the compliment and runs her hand down her chest, toying with the nipple piercing. I can't get naked fast enough.

"Have you ever done this?"

"Sex via video chat? Can't say I have," I confirm, sitting back on the bed the moment my pants are down to my ankles.

"Good. I kinda like the idea of being your first video sex."

All I can do is smile and watch the incredible show.

Me too, BJ. Me too.

BJ

"Your nine o'clock piercing appointment canceled for tonight, so I called someone on the waitlist who could come on short notice. I hope that's okay," Amanda says over my shoulder as I finish up a sunset piece on a man's shoulder blade.

"That's fine. As long as they know what they want. I still have that small butterfly tattoo at nine fifteen, right?"

"Yep, that's still on the schedule. And the woman I just added is a belly ring, so in and out in fifteen minutes."

"Perfect," I reply, adding a little more golden yellow and orange colors to the glowing sun.

I keep my focus on where it needs to be, even though I really want to think about Isaac. But that's the problem. I've been allowing the man to monopolize way too many of my thoughts lately. Sure, the occasional flash of Isaac's dirty mouth or an image of him in one of his sexy suits might creep into my mind, setting my blood on fire, but that's not what worries me. It's the fact I crave more than just sex with him. I want to talk to him, find out about his busy day, and share the details of designs I completed throughout mine. I want to have dinner and breakfast and everything in between. I wonder if he's going to drop by to say hello and steal a few kisses between clients.

And *that's* the problem.

I want more.

I want it all.

"You're all set," I announce, wiping off the new ink and moving the arm rest so my client can stand and look at his new tattoo in the mirror.

"Damn, BJ, that's sick," he says, studying his shoulder blade and smiling fondly.

"I'm glad you like it," I reply as I gather my supplies to cover the design.

"Like it? This is exactly why I recommend you to everyone. You're a fucking wizard with that gun," he states with a chuckle.

"Well, I definitely appreciate the recommendation. Word of mouth is the best form of advertising," I say, repeating the phrase Jax says on a regular basis.

I walk him up front to where Amanda waits and go over the care instructions, even though he's visited me five times over the years. At this point, he's a pro, but I always go through the steps for care with everyone, despite the number of times sitting in my chair.

Once he leaves, Amanda turns her attention to me. "I'm going to take a quick break and buy a new suitcase for this weekend. Do you need anything from the department store?"

"No, I'm good, but if you stop for food, will you grab me something?"

"Sure," she agrees, grabbing her purse from the filing cabinet beside her desk. "Any requests? Burgers, perhaps?" Amanda waggles her eyebrows, making me roll my eyes.

"Stop it. I'm not picky. Just grab me something," I reply, pulling some cash from my pocket.

She waves me off though, and heads for the back hallway. "Jax, you want food?"

"Yep. Grab me anything," he hollers over the hum of his tattoo gun.

"I'll be back in less than an hour," she says, heading for the rear entrance of the building.

I spend the next few minutes cleaning my room and prepping for my final tattoo of the evening. Until then, I have piercing appointments back-to-back, including a cartilage, nose, and belly ring. It's funny how they come in spurts. Some days, I feel like I do more piercings than tattoos, while others, I don't do a single one.

My first one is the ear conch for an eighteen-year-old young woman. Once she picks the earring and approves the placement, I grab my instruments and finish the piercing. "Let's go up front and go over the care instructions. I also like to make sure to tell you to keep your hair clear of the jewelry. I've seen a few cases where hair gets tangled around the earring and causes an infection."

"I'll do that," the woman says, taking the flyer I hand her. "Thank you."

"You're most welcome," I reply, taking her payment and walking her to the front door.

My next appointment is the nose ring, and that almost goes as smoothly as the previous one. This woman, however, can't seem to make up her mind when it comes to the jewelry she wants. She goes back and forth between two different styles of studs, one with a diamond-like jewel and the other with a purple amethyst. After video chatting with three different friends to get their opinions, she finally settles on the purple stone.

I'm still standing at the front counter after she leaves when Amanda returns. "Hey! I got a new carry-on-sized suitcase with palm trees on it, and it came with this matching waterproof makeup pouch." She holds up the small bag, her small body vibrating with excitement.

"Adorable. What'd you bring for dinner?"

She sets the big white bag down on the counter and pulls out the first of three Styrofoam containers. "The burgers sounded good, so I called in an order. Paradise by the Dashboard Lights was on special, so I just got three of them."

"Perfect, thanks," I reply, taking the container and pulling over a stool.

"Let me run this back to Jax, and I'll join you," she says, hurrying down the hall to deliver the third container of food.

"So, how did the piercings go?" she asks the moment she steps back into the front waiting area.

"Fine. The nose couldn't make a decision without calling everyone she knew, but we finally got it done." I take a bite of my burger and moan. "Holy shit, this is good."

"Yeah, I had one a few weeks ago for the first time. I never would have thought a meatloaf patty would be so good, but it really is." We eat in comfortable silence as Jax wraps up his work in the back. After a few minutes, she leans back, clearly having something on her mind.

"What's up?" I ask.

"I think I want to get my tongue pierced."

Her statement catches me off guard. "Really?"

When she wipes her mouth, she replies, "Yeah, I've been putting a lot of thought into it."

"But, Amanda, you won't even get your belly button pierced. Now, you want to get your tongue done?"

She blushes a bit and shrugs. "I think it'll be fun. And sexy."

I'm taken aback a bit. "What? Seriously?"

Jax walks out at that moment, his burger in his hand. "What are you serious about?" he asks, taking a huge bite.

"Amanda wants to get her tongue pierced."

He stops and looks at the petite redhead. "Really?"

She nods eagerly. "What do you think?"

He seems to choke on either his food or air or the desire I see swirling in his eyes. "I think," he starts, clearing his throat, "it would look pretty fucking cute on you."

She beams brightly. "Then let's do it!"

"When?" I ask, eating a few fries.

"How about now? Your next appointment isn't until nine, so we have about twenty minutes," Amanda informs.

Even though I'm totally surprised she wants to do this, I'll happily pierce her tongue. "Okay. And I do agree with Jax. I think you'll look totally cute with a bar." I glance over at Jax and see him studying my friend intently. I want to tell him just to get off his ass and do it—ask her out already!

The moment our food is gone, we head for the piercing room. "You gonna watch?" I ask my boss and friend.

He nods and trails behind us quietly. Inside the room, he goes over and grabs the bars, finding the perfect size for Amanda's tongue. I pull out the rest of the supplies I need and set them on a tray, listening intently as he explains the process to her. By the nervous look on his face, I think he's going through it more for himself than for her. Amanda's been around dozens of piercings over the last couple of years. I'm pretty sure she's very knowledgeable on the steps.

"Ready?" I ask, grabbing the clamp that'll hold her tongue flat while I pierce it.

She nods, not even a flinch of nervousness.

I set the clamp and grab the marker. She nods in agreement when I ask for her approval. Then, I grab the needle. The whole process takes less than thirty seconds, and before I know it, my best friend is sporting some new jewelry.

"All done," I say, taking off the latex gloves.

"Thanks!" she says, wiggling her tongue around, as if getting used to the feel of having something else in her mouth.

"You're welcome." I go to turn around, and that's when I notice their hands. They're joined and he's squeezing gently in support.

Smiling, I spin around and place my supplies in the sanitizer, giving them a moment for whatever *this* is. The thought of Jax and Amanda is really growing on me, and suddenly, I'm really rooting for them. I know his feelings on her, but I've never had a conversation with her about him. Maybe I should talk to her this weekend when we're in Chicago.

Help prod this along.

Just as Amanda hops off the chair—with Jax's help, of course—I hear a voice holler from the front room. "Hello?"

"That must be your nine o'clock. I'll go grab her and bring her back," Amanda says, scurrying off.

I glance over at my boss and grin. "You okay there, big guy?"

He crosses his tattoo-covered arms. "Of course. Why wouldn't I be?"

"You just seemed a little...concerned."

Jax sigh and shakes his head. "I'm fine." He glances over his shoulder before he adds, "You did good with her."

"Thanks. Like I'd give my bestie a bad tongue piercing."

He grumbles under his breath, "I wasn't saying that."

"I know." My devil horns sprout up as I add, "It's going to be totally hot when it heals, isn't it?"

He tenses, which makes me grin even more. "Yeah. Listen, I'm gonna go prep for my last tattoo. See ya later."

He disappears just as Amanda returns with a blonde hot on her heels. "Uhh," my best friend says, panic written all over her face.

Before I can ask what's wrong, the blonde steps around the corner and enters the room. "Well, isn't this exciting."

Savannah.

What the hell is she doing here?

As if sensing my panic, Amanda says, "Savannah is here for the belly ring appointment." She also mouths, "I'm sorry, I didn't know!"

With a sigh, I turn to Isaac's ex-girlfriend. "What are you doing here, Savannah?"

She smiles a perfect pink, put-together grin. "Well, I've decided to get my belly button pierced, and you had an opening."

Sighing, I grab the tray and start placing my supplies needed for the belly ring. "Whatever. Lie on the bench, please."

She does as instructed, and wordlessly, I prep for the job. Savannah picks a small hoop with a pink gem, which doesn't surprise me in the least, considering she's wearing a pink business suit. It's like something out of the movie *Steel Magnolias*. Her colors are blush and bashful too.

I disinfect and clamp her belly, not bothering to warn her there might be slight discomfort from the pinch. When I grab the marker, a part of me wants to make it off-center, but the professional in me won't let that happen, even in spite. Instead, I make sure I'm one-hundred-percent happy with the placement and ask her to approve it.

Then, I pierce her belly button.

"All done," I say, pulling off the gloves and tossing them in the trash.

"I love it," she says, standing up and glancing at her super-flat stomach in the mirror. "I can't wait to show Isaac!"

That catches my attention.

"Excuse me?"

She smiles sweetly. "Oh, poor girl. He hasn't told you? We've been talking again, ever since I met up with him to retrieve my things. He's the one who suggested I get this pierced," she says, gazing at her stomach in the mirror once more. "He said I have the perfect body for it."

I swallow over the lump of pure jealousy lodged in my throat. She's doing this on purpose, right? Getting under my skin and making me second-guess myself and my relationship with Isaac?

Except…there isn't a relationship.

We're having fun, right? That's what we agreed upon. Fun until it's not fun anymore, and even though I'm still enjoying myself, that doesn't mean he still is.

"Anyway, he's working until close tonight, so I wanted to surprise him later," she says, malice rolling off her in waves.

God, I hate her.

"Let's go up front and Amanda can get you checked out."

She blabbers on and on the entire way—about what, I have no clue because I tune her out—but thankfully, it's a short trip to the front counter. "Here's some information about care," Amanda says, slipping the document across to the blonde.

"Savannah, let us know if you have any issues," I add, turning to head back to the room.

"Thank you, BJ. I'm sure everything is going to turn out just the way it's supposed to." Her underlying message is clear. She expects to be back with Isaac any day now.

I nod, refusing to discuss Isaac with her anymore. "Have a good one," I say, leaving her standing at the counter.

Once I clean the piercing room, and Amanda comes in to apologize again for not realizing Savannah was *the* Savannah, I move to my tattoo space to prep for my final appointment of the night. I pull out my phone, only to find a blank screen. A part of me says to send him a message, but Savannah's words about talking to him again come back to me, and the last thing I want to seem is desperate for his attention.

I slip my phone back into my pocket and push thoughts of Isaac out of my head. Now isn't the time to stress over something I can't control. Now is the time to focus on my job. The rest of the cards will fall as they may.

"I can't believe we're headed to see Toxic Energy," Amanda says, practically bouncing in her seat as she tries to buckle her seat belt and get comfortable between Jax and me.

"You didn't even know who they were," I tease. When Jax told her we were going and invited her to go to Chicago with us, she had to download some of the music. Heavy metal isn't exactly her preferred music genre. It's not really mine either, but it doesn't bother me, and I know Jax loves it, so there are plenty of times he plays it at the shop.

"But I do now," she insists, messing with the tray table on the back of the seat in front of her.

"Stop that. You're like a toddler messing with everything. Have you never flown before?"

My best friend turns wide eyes toward me. "I always drive to my parents' house. When I was growing up, my mom was afraid of flying, so we always drove everywhere."

"You've never been on a plane before?" Jax asks, just as surprised as me.

"Nope. Why? Should I be nervous?" she asks, pinning him with a nervous gaze.

"No way, darlin'. You'll be completely safe."

"Okay good."

I pull out my earbuds and phone, getting ready for the short flight to Chicago. "I can't believe I didn't know you've never flown before."

She shrugs, retrieving her own earbuds and phone from her bag. "It's just never come up. I've always wanted to, but never really had a reason. It's not like I go on long-distance vacations by myself."

"We should do a girls' trip. Somewhere warm and beachy," I insist, realizing I rarely get out of town myself. Sure, I've been to a few tattoo conventions over the years, but I've only traveled on a plane for work.

It's time I change that.

"Yes! Let's!"

"If it's a girls' trip, then I don't get to go?" Jax asks with a laugh, reclining his seat well before we're allowed to, considering we haven't taken off yet.

"Nope, sorry, big guy. The only dudes around are gonna be the cabana boys who bring me rum drinks," Amanda replies as the flight crew starts going over their safety demonstration.

I click on my text app and scan over the last text I received from Isaac early this morning.

> **Isaac**: Hope you have a great time at the concert and give some kickass ink. I'm proud of you. Maybe we can get together when you get home.

Hope bubbles in my chest as I reread the words. Even though we haven't been able to connect hardly at all this past week because of our work schedules, knowing he wants to see me when I get back to Stewart Grove eases a bit of the worry I've been carrying. Ever since Savannah showed up at the shop two nights ago, I've been stressing a lot more than I ever have about this thing between us.

Where's it going?

The more I try to tell myself this is casual, the more I realize it's not. Not anymore. Not for me. I want more.

I want him.

Isaac

"Happy birthday, Lyndee," I say the moment she opens the door.

"Thanks, Isaac," she replies, going up on her tiptoes and placing a kiss on my cheek. I hand over the bottle of expensive wine I bought from an alcohol vendor. He sold it to me from his personal collection, assuring me it's one of his favorites he purchases from a winery in Italy. "You didn't have to do this," she adds, checking the label on the bottle. "Wow."

"I figured living with Jasper calls for the good stuff."

Lyndee laughs as the man himself steps into the foyer. "Hey, I heard that."

"Don't be all sensitive. You know you're a bear," I reply, winking at my friend as I hand over a small bag.

"Something for me too?" Jasper asks, glancing inside and gasping. "Holy shit, is this gorgonzola?"

"Gorgonzola Dolce," I confirm.

"The sweet cheese. I've never had it before. Notice the blue-green veins running through it?" he asks, holding the wheel of cheese delicately, as if he were holding a precious gem. He looks up and smiles. "This is spectacular. You're officially my favorite friend."

I bark out a laugh just as Walker, Mallory, and Lizzie enter the house.

"I'll pretend I didn't hear you say that," Walker states, kissing Lyndee on the cheek. "Happy birthday."

"Thanks," she replies right before she turns her attention to Mallory and her growing belly.

"Isaac!" Lizzie bellows, taking a running leap into my arms.

"Lizard. How's my favorite little lady?"

"Dood! I gots my brush and ponies," she proclaims, holding up the little pink bag filled with whatever goodies she decided to bring.

"Really? I bet Jameson would love a pony with a pink bow," I insist, making the little girl smile.

She nods in understanding. "I tink so too. Bye, Mommy! I gots to find Tank!" she says moments before taking off to go find the grumpy one who will do anything for this child.

"He's going to punch you," Jasper states with a grin.

"He deserves it," I say, following behind the ladies as they head for the kitchen, chatting.

When we reach the large kitchen, we find Jameson already sitting on the floor while Lizzie does his hair. The sight would make anyone grin. The big, tattooed biker letting a little girl brush his hair. Hell, it wasn't that long ago I found myself in a similar situation with a tiara and wand, which is why I grab my phone and snap a quick picture.

"I saw that," Jameson mumbles, facing in the opposite direction.

"You're dunna be pweddy, Tank!" Lizzie proclaims, pulling sections of his hair into her little fist for a ponytail.

"Oh, he's definitely pretty," Jasper teases, uncovering two trays of appetizers.

"You're next, isn't that right, Lou?" Walker asks the little girl.

"I brungdid a purple pony for you, Jasper!"

"Excellent, Lizzie. Purple is Jasper's favorite color," Lyndee says with a giggle, earning her a glare from her boyfriend.

While everyone chats around me, I check the photo I took of Jameson and Lizzie on my phone, except I'm not really looking at that photo. It's an excuse to look at the other two I saved to my device. Late last night, BJ sent me two pictures from the Toxic Energy concert she attended. The first one is an image of her and Amanda, smiling widely backstage together and looking like they're having the time of their life.

The second one is just of her. She's staring off at the stage, the softest grin on those full, sexy lips. I can practically see her swaying her hips to the music, singing along word for word. She looks carefree, like nothing could touch her.

Damn, I miss her.

"Hey, Jameson, have you talked to your sister? Wasn't that concert she went to last night?" Walker asks, popping a stuffed pepper in his mouth.

"Yeah, she sent me some pictures this morning. I guess they were meeting the band at their hotel room at two o'clock. Each tattoo will take about an hour and a half, and she's got three to do," he says, standing up and grabbing Lizzie, propping her on his hip.

He pulls out his phone and hands it over to Walker. "Damn, I can't believe she's hanging out with Toxic Energy," he says, flipping through whatever photos are on the screen.

I try to school my features as the phone is passed around, eventually making its way to me. I click on the first picture and can't stop the noise that falls from my lips. It's part groan, part growl, and I try to cover it with a cough, but I know it doesn't work. Everyone heard, including Jameson, who's now standing directly beside me. "You okay?" he asks.

"Yep, fine. Just a tickle in my throat," I insist, throwing him a reassuring grin before glancing back down at the phone.

My heart jumps in my throat as I stare at image after image of BJ with members of the band. Sure, some of them have Amanda too, but a few are just her and some guy. When I get to the sixth and final image, I have to close my eyes and pretend I'm looking at something else. No way do I want to see the photo of BJ and Jax, his arm thrown over her shoulder and his tongue on her cheek.

Like he's licking her.

Like he's fucking licking something that doesn't belong to him.

She's mine.

Once again, jealousy rears its ugly head, blinding me with an uncomfortable anger I'm not used to experiencing. I'm the calm one of the group, yet the rage I'm feeling right now is anything but calm. I feel like Jasper after his assistant chef let them run out of sauteed onions.

"You sure you're all right? You look a little...pissy," Walker mumbles beside me, looking at me like I'm one second away from snapping.

"Yeah, I'm good. Just tired. Worked late last night after we closed and was back at it again this morning," I reply. It's the truth, but I leave out the part about missing BJ and being slightly jealous over the fact she's with her ex at a hotel in Chicago for the weekend.

He seems to buy my tale and turns his attention to Lizzie, who comes running with her hairbrush and a bright green scrunchie. “Isaac, you too!” she broadcasts, waving the brush and smiling widely.

Just as I take a seat on the dining room floor, Jameson’s phone buzzes. The brush runs through my hair from back to front, and I can tell any attention I gave my hair this morning is being completely undone. However, I don’t mind. I’d let Lizard dye my hair purple and pink if she wanted to.

Which makes me think of BJ once more. I bet Lizzie would get a kick out of BJ’s purple locks, and knowing BJ, I’m sure she’d let the little girl do anything she wanted to her hair, much like she let my niece a week and a half ago.

“Check it out,” Jameson says, handing his phone over once more to Jasper and Walker.

“Dude, that’s sick,” one of them declares, passing the phone across the counter to where the ladies snack on appetizers.

Eventually, the big broody one brings his device over to me and shows me the image. It’s of the coolest tattoo I’ve ever seen. The Toxic Energy logo, and it looks like it’s on fire. The detail is exquisite, as if the flames are burning the skin. “Shit,” I mutter, noting the realism of the piece.

“Good, huh?” he states proudly, the smallest smile on his lips. We rarely see Jameson show emotion, unless it’s anger, so it’s good to witness it now as he talks about his sister’s work. “She says they’re all done for the day. They each did three tattoos, and now they’re all going to dinner or something.”

“When do they fly home?” Mallory asks.

"Tomorrow morning, but they gave themselves no time to rest. The shop opens at three, so they will jump right back in," Jameson confirms, shaking his head.

"Sounds like someone else I know," Walker says, grinning at the big man.

He snorts in acknowledgement of the comment but doesn't say any more.

The fact is we all work our asses off, which means we often work crazy hours. I've worked seven days a week since day one, as have my friends. It wasn't until the business became more established that we started cutting back a bit.

Well, everyone but Jasper.

Now he's dating Lyndee, so he does try to relinquish some of his control to the evening chef so he can be home with her at night. With her bakery, she's more of a morning person, and with his insomnia, that can be a challenge for them, but they make it work.

Walker might still work some evenings, but he tries to limit those to just Friday and Saturday nights. If he has to work a later shift during the week, Mal and Lizzie always come in for dinner to see him. Otherwise, he's home as much as he can with his new wife and young daughter, making sure to establish a routine as much as possible.

Jameson still works his ass off, but his focus has switched. Instead of being at the bar twenty-four seven, he's next door at the brewery. I'm just glad he has George to help him, and hopefully soon, another brewer. Even though he still plays music Friday and Saturday evenings, he seems more content than I've ever seen him.

Then there's me, who wants to leave work early just to see BJ. Even when I was dating Savannah, I think the times I called it an early night was more out of necessity than want. I enjoyed spending time with her, but I can look back now and see there were things missing from our relationship. Things I ignored so I didn't have to be alone or step outside of my comfort zone. It's probably why I put so much time and energy into making sure our business was a success.

BJ helped me see that.

Now, all I want is to call her, see her beautiful face, hold her in my arms. She's all I can think about, even though Savannah has been texting me lately. There's no way we'll get back together. Not ever. Not after I've experienced life with a woman like BJ.

We may not have a future, but she's shown me how to sit back and just enjoy the little things. I feel like I'm not stuck in the same rut, the same ol' situation, over and over again.

It's because of Billie Jean Tankersley.

The woman I'm falling for.

The woman who'll never want me the way I want her.

Later that night, I'm lying in bed, staring at the image on my phone. She's so fucking beautiful it hurts. When this is over, I don't know what I'll do with myself. Except be sad. I'll definitely be sad.

My phone vibrates and a text notification pops up at the top of the screen.

BJ.

Instantly, I smile, and the heaviness in my chest lifts.

BJ: Did you know there's a box at the Willis Tower that's made of glass? It's like you're standing out on the clouds, overlooking the entire city.

Me: I have heard that, but you couldn't pay me a million dollars to walk out on that thing.

BJ: No? Chicken?

Me: Absolutely. Terrified of heights.

BJ: That's too bad. You wouldn't even go out there with me? I'd hold your hand.

Another grin tickles my lips at her teasing.

Me: Well, as long as you hold my hand.

BJ: I'd definitely hold...something. *insert smirking devil emoji*

Relief sweeps through me at how quickly we fall into a familiar bantering. Before I can reply, the phone rings.

"Hello?"

"Hey," she replies, the exhaustion evident in her voice.

"How are you?" I ask, turning on my side.

She sighs or yawns, I'm not really sure which. The time displayed on the alarm clock says it could be either. "Have you ever been surrounded by so much excitement, but not really seen any of it?"

"Yes," I reply without hesitation.

She's silent for a few seconds before she continues, "There's people everywhere. On the streets, at the concert, at the restaurants. It's nothing like Stewart Grove here, that's for sure, and all I can think about is what's happening at home, you know?"

"I get it. The good news is you're coming home tomorrow morning, right?"

"Yeah."

I'm greeted with more silence, and I can tell something's bothering her. I hate that. I wish she were here, sitting beside me so I could see her eyes. I've always heard they are the windows to the soul, and I completely agree. Her light brown eyes are so expressive, so vibrant, and I can get lost in them time and time again.

"Hey, Isaac?"

"Yeah?"

"What are you wearing?"

Her question catches me so off guard, when my brain finally catches up, all I can do is laugh. "Jesus, I miss you."

I don't mean to say it out loud, but I'm not sorry I did. Besides, there's no taking it back now. The words are out, and there's nothing I can do about it.

Fortunately, BJ must not read too far into them, because she giggles lightly and sighs. "I miss you too."

Something hangs between us, loud and heavy, but neither of us draw attention to it. Instead, I redirect the conversation back to where we're both comfortable, light, easy banter. "Oh, I almost forgot. I have to show you something." I slide my finger across the screen and send her a quick text.

BJ snorts when her phone chimes with my message. "Is this the part where you show me what you're wearing? Or *not* wearing?"

"No, it's better than me in my fancy Valentine's Day boxers."

There's a pause on the other end of the line. "You're wearing Valentine's Day boxers?"

"Red ones with little white hearts. It's laundry day, and I was feeling lazy. I actually left clothes sitting down in the dryer without folding them."

"Wow, look at you, living on the edge."

I chuckle. "Smart-ass. Now open your picture."

"I'm not sure I want to," she starts, but stops when she must click on the image. "Holy shit, this is great!" she bellows, bursting into fits of laughter. "Does he know you took this?"

"Oh, he knows. I'm not exactly his favorite person right now."

"Because you took this picture?"

"No, because I sent it to Walker and Jasper," I confess, recalling the moment Jameson heard the shutter click on my phone right before our friends' devices chimed with a message alert.

"Oh my God, that's brilliant. You know, he looks really good in pink. It softens the eye daggers he's trying to throw at you," she says, referring to the pink scrunchie Lizzie was able to secure at the top of his head.

"He's a good sport. He'd let that little girl do anything she wanted to him, including painting his toenails, which I did not see, but heard all about it from Lizard."

"You know, when I was about thirteen, he let me paint his toenails too. Don't you dare tell anyone I said that though, or he'll kill us both."

I smile, knowing her brother wouldn't do anything to harm even a hair on her head. "Your secret is safe with me."

"Good. Now, let's talk about this," she says, right before my phone chimes with an alert.

"What?" I ask, bringing up the screen and clicking what she sent me. The moment the picture is displayed, I bust up laughing. "That asshole."

"I'm pretty sure he sent that to everyone too," she confirms. "I really like the green ribbons."

I shake my head at the image. I'm sitting on the floor, long green ribbons pinned in my hair, which looks like I stood in front of a jet engine for about thirty minutes beforehand. The best part is the bright pink plastic jewels hanging around my neck. "Lizzie says the pink really brings out my eyes," I say offhand, trying not to laugh.

BJ giggles. "She's right. It really complements your skin tone too."

"Not every guy can pull that off, you know."

"Oh, I'm sure." She sighs once more. "Isaac?

"Yeah?" I ask, all humor pushed aside.

"You'd make a very pretty woman."

We both die laughing, which is pretty much what we do for the next thirty minutes. Lots of talk and laughter until her yawns grow closer together and I know she's fading fast. "I can let you go. You have an early morning."

"Yeah," she replies through another yawn. "We have to be to Midway Airport by seven."

"Text me when you land."

"I will. Man, I didn't realize it was getting this late. I'm surprised Amanda and Jax aren't back yet?"

"Where'd they go?"

"Sightseeing. Amanda's never been on a plane before and her travel experience isn't very lengthy. So after the band left tonight for Philly, Jax took her to see the Bean, Navy Pier, and Willis Tower."

"You didn't go?"

"No, I was ready for a little quiet. Besides, there's no way I'd go up on that glass deck floor."

This surprises me. "What? I thought you went earlier."

"Fuck no. Heights don't usually bother me, but I'm not stupid enough to walk out into a glass box a mile and a half in the air."

"It's not a mile and a half up. It's only about a quarter of a mile up."

"How in the world do you know that?"

I change positions and lie on my back, one arm beneath my head. "Sorry, I know all sorts of useless information."

"Don't be sorry. That's one of the things I like most about you."

"Yeah? What's something else?"

"Your keen fashion sense. And I'm not talking about the suits and ties, Mr. Valentine's Boxers."

I can't help but laugh. "You should see the Christmas tree ones I have too. My younger sister, Tabitha, thought it'd be funny to get me crazy boxers a few years ago for my birthday."

BJ yawns again. "I'd love to see them sometime."

"That can definitely be arranged." When she yawns yet again, I add, "I'm going to let you get some sleep."

"Okay," she whispers.

"I'm glad you called."

"Me too."

"Night, BJ."

"Night, Isaac. Maybe I'll see you tomorrow," she practically mumbles before signing off.

I set my phone on my nightstand and make sure it's plugged in to the charger before getting comfortable once more. I feel much better having talked to her. In fact, it's one of my favorite parts of the day.

I don't know what I'm going to do when that's gone.

BJ

"We stopped at this amazing little bar on Michigan Avenue and had the best chili cheese fries," Amanda gushes for probably the third time, and all I can do is shake my head.

Ever since she returned to our hotel room late last night, she's talked nonstop about her sightseeing with Jax, and now that we've returned to Stewart Grove, it doesn't look like her excitement is waning anytime soon.

"Hey, I wanted to talk to you before Jax gets here," I say as we make our way to the front counter.

Our plane landed around eleven this morning, and we had just enough time to run home, drop off our luggage and grab a fast bite to eat, and then get to the shop by the time it opened at three. Jax should be here any minute, and with a packed schedule all week, thanks to taking this past Saturday off to go to Chicago, this may be one of my only opportunities to chat with her openly.

"What's up?" she asks after placing her purse in the filing cabinet.

I take a deep breath, trying to determine how I want to approach this conversation. "You and Jax seem to have had a great time."

She grins, her long auburn hair pulled back in a high ponytail and her green eyes shining with eagerness. "We did. He was a great tour guide, never once complaining about the fifty thousand pictures I made him take or the questions I asked at every stop we made."

"He's a good guy, despite the rough and tough persona he puts out there. That's kinda what I wanted to talk to you about," I start, leaning against the counter.

"What? He's not a good guy?" she asks, seeming confused by my words.

"No, he is." I take a deep breath. "I guess I just wanted to say, you know what Jax and I had is in the past, right?"

She nods. "Of course."

"We're just way better friends."

"I know."

"Okay," I reply, nodding. "I just wanted to make sure you know that. *And* that I want him to be happy, no matter who that's with."

Her eyes narrow and she considers my words. "Why are you acting all weird?"

"I'm not," I insist, even though I really am. "Okay, listen, what I'm about to say just stays between us. I talked to Jax not that long ago, and he may have confided in me he has a crush on someone."

Her eyes sparkle as she slightly leans forward. "Really? Who?"

Gosh, I fucking love her. She's an amazing person, and anyone would be lucky to have her. Deciding to just rip off the Band-Aid, I reply, "You."

Amanda blinks several times before whispering, "Me?"

"Yes, you. And I need you to know that if anything were to transpire between the two of you, I'd be okay with it."

"M-me and Jax?" she stutters, her eyes so wide, it's almost comical.

"Yes," I confirm, reaching over and squeezing her hand. "And I'm being serious when I say this, okay? If there's a chance you like him even half as much as he seems to like you, I want you to go for it. I don't want you to discount any feelings you may have, just because I used to date him."

"Wow," she mutters, staring off over my shoulder. When she finally meets my gaze, she asks, "So…he has a crush on me?"

I nod in confirmation, yet still say, "Yeah."

She clears her throat and opens her mouth but nothing comes out. I seem to have caught her completely off guard and left her speechless. Before I can continue, the back door of the shop opens and Jax's distinct heavy boots hit the tile floor. "Listen, I hope I haven't overstepped here," I start, but Amanda cuts me off.

"Pfft, please. Of course you did. It's what best friends do. We overstep," she replies with the faintest of smiles on her lips.

"Hey, guys," Jax hollers right before he walks into the front room.

"Hi," I reply, flashing him a quick grin.

He looks between Amanda and me before he asks, "Everything okay?"

"Yeah," Amanda replies instantly. "We were just reviewing today's schedule."

"Okay." Jax goes over to the sound system and turns on some music before heading over to flip the open sign. "Holler when my first appointment gets here."

"Sure thing," Amanda says, watching as Jax heads down the hallway to his room. "What do I do?"

I sigh, closing my eyes. "I don't know. What do you want to do?"

Amanda seems to need a few minutes to think, so I don't say a word until she's ready. "I wish I knew. I've never looked at him like that before," she whispers, even though I'm sure our boss can't hear us from his room.

"I get it. And you don't have to do anything about it right now anyway. I just wanted to make sure you knew where I stood, you know, in case you wanted to give it a shot."

She rests her chin on her fist and sighs. "I'll think about it, okay?"

"That's sounds like a good plan," I state, scanning my afternoon schedule to make sure there aren't any changes since last Friday. Mondays aren't usually very busy, but today is full.

Just as I turn to go to my own room to prep for my first appointment, my best friend says, "You know..." I stop and turn around. "He is pretty cute."

I smile. "He is."

"And that single dimple in his right cheek? It's kinda adorable, isn't it?"

I'm already nodding. "Totally."

"And the tattoos? I never thought I'd find them so...sexy."

"Look at you. First a tongue piercing, and now attracted to the bad boy."

She grins and averts her gaze. "I still don't know if I'll do anything about it, but I promise I'll think about it...*if*," she says, drawing out that last word, "you consider having more with Isaac."

Now it's my eyes that widen in surprise. "What?"

"Oh, come on. Stop being all *we're just friends who have incredible sex all the time but don't want anything else*. That's not factual."

"Factual?"

My best friend rolls her eyes. "Yes, factual. I can tell. You want more."

"I—"

"And the reason I know this is because I know you better than anyone else in the world, and I've seen how happy you are since you two started 'hanging out,'" she says, using air quotes.

I can't argue because I know she's correct. I have been pretty happy lately, and I'm not dense. I know the reason why.

Isaac.

It's so easy being with him. He's easy to talk to and makes me feel like he's truly listening to what I say. Of course, the *other* stuff is amazing too. It turns out, Isaac is anything but boring or routine when it comes to sex.

"All I'm asking is that you think about it, like me."

I swallow over the lump in my throat. There's something terrifying about putting yourself out there for someone else to either deny or accept. I mean, he can tell me to get lost at a moment's notice, not wanting to take things between us any further than they are now.

Or he could take me in his arms and tell me he wants more too.

"Okay," I concede, agreeing to put some thought into talking to Isaac about us.

Our conversation is cut to an end when my first appointment of the day arrives, followed very quickly by Jax's. No time to think about Isaac. Or what I want. Or the future.

Time to shut off that part of my brain and focus on the only thing I can control.

My work.

It's almost eleven by the time I get out of work. Amanda left shortly after we flipped the closed sign at ten, but my afternoon slowly started to get backed up when my four o'clock appointment was late, followed by my five o'clock one changing part of their tattoo design. It seemed like setback after setback, and now I'm finally turning off the lights and heading for my truck.

"Did you say something to Amanda tonight?" Jax asks, walking me to my vehicle. Even though our town is fairly safe, he never leaves me alone this late at night.

"What?" I ask, pretending like I didn't hear him.

He shoves his hands in the pockets of his jeans and rocks back on his heels. "I don't know, she was just...different tonight."

"How do you mean?" I ask, guilt reaching out and grabbing a hold of me.

"Well, it's probably nothing, but she just seemed a little, well, flirty, I guess."

I have to fight the smile. "Really? Isn't that a good thing?" I ask, tossing my bag onto the passenger seat.

"It is," he confirms, looking completely uncomfortable. "I guess I just wasn't expecting it. That's all."

I give him a smile and step forward, reaching out and squeezing his arm. “If she’s flirting, maybe that’s a sign. Just go with it, okay?”

His Adam’s apple bobs as he swallows hard. “Okay.”

“You know, for such a confident, slightly arrogant man, seeing you all nervous is refreshing,” I tease.

Jax rolls his eyes. “I’m not arrogant.”

That makes me laugh. “Sure you’re not. Anyway, I’m heading home. It’s been a crazy long day.”

“It has,” he confirms, quickly adding before I get into my truck. “And, Beej?” When I turn and meet his gaze, he says, “Thank you.”

I step forward, go up on my tiptoes, and place a kiss on his cheek. “Just be good to her, okay?”

He nods. “Promise.” I pat his arm and climb up into my truck. “Oh, and, Beej?” When I look his way, he says, “Go for it with the numbers guy. I think he really likes you, and if you’re worried about Jameson, don’t be. If Tank can forgive me for, well, you know, I’m positive he’ll understand with his friend.”

I don’t tell him my brother is the least of my worries.

Possibly it’s the fact I’d be changing the rules after we started playing the game. We decided to have fun and move on, and suddenly, I’m thinking about asking him to forget all about the terms we set and embark in a real relationship.

But maybe the game *has* changed.

I know I’m not exactly in the same place I was all those weeks ago when we made our little arrangement. The thought of dating once felt suffocating, but now it feels like the only option. Weeks ago, he wasn’t ready for anything yet, having just broken up with his girlfriend mere hours prior. But now, well, maybe that's different too.

Perhaps we've both changed.

And that's okay.

I just have to figure out how to tell him how I feel.

But not tonight. It's late and I'm exhausted. Even though I'd love to stop by his house and fall asleep in his arms, I just don't have the energy to do anything but drive home and pass out, hopefully in bed. My conversation with Isaac is going to have to wait.

For now.

Maybe I can give him a call tomorrow morning after I wake. Or surprise him with lunch at the restaurant. Of course, since my brother will most likely be nearby, that might be a little tricky.

Tomorrow. I'll meet up with Isaac and have the talk about us.

Let's just hope there's still an *us* when we're done.

Isaac

All I can do is stare at her truck as it pulls out of the back lot behind the shop. When she turns to the left and disappears, the only other remaining vehicle in the lot starts up and heads right.

Jax.

She just kissed Jax.

Granted, it was on his cheek, but still. They were chummy, all laughing and touchy feely in a way that spoke volumes for the relationship they've had.

And probably still have.

The realization that we're no longer on the same page is like a knife to the chest. It burns with a fierce pain, making it hard to breathe. I don't know why or how, but this moment feels so much worse than every breakup I've ever had with Savannah.

Combined.

I pull from the lot, heading…nowhere and anywhere at the same time. My original plan of surprising BJ and inviting her back to my place was just thrown out the window the moment I saw her kiss another man.

Now, I don't know what to do or where to go, so I just drive. Part of me wants to go to her house, to demand to know what's going on with her and Jax, but to be honest, I'm not sure I'm ready for that truth. Because even if it was nothing more than a friend kissing another friend on the cheek, the fact still remains that our time together is on a deadline, and always has been. It was never designed to last. We agreed on fun, until the moment it's no longer fun and one of us is ready to move on.

I grab my phone, ready to call one of two people I know are still awake. One, I can't call because, well, how do you talk to the brother of the girl you've been sleeping with, when he doesn't know you've been sleeping with her? So I ignore Jameson's contact information and move to the next name.

Jasper's insomnia is probably keeping him up. However, if it's not, I don't want to be the asshole who wakes him. And I definitely don't want to be the asshole who wakes up his girlfriend, especially since she gets up so damn early in the morning. So instead of calling him, I decide just to drive by. If he's awake, he'll most likely be in the kitchen and I'll be able to see the lights from the street. Maybe. If they didn't close the curtains in the dining room.

Jesus, I'm a mess.

Yet, here I am, driving down his road and looking for light. When I see it spilling through the window, I pull into his driveway and park. But I don't get out. At least not right away. I sit here, trying to decide if I want to go knock or just start up my car and head home. I don't need to bring my problems to his door.

Just as I go to restart my car and head home, the front porch light turns on and Jasper steps out, his hands shoved in the pockets of his sweats. With a sigh, I slowly get out and walk his way. "Hey."

"Everything okay?" he asks.

"Yeah, I...was just in the area."

He snorts and glances at his watch. "Wanna come in?"

"If I'm not interrupting anything," I reply, following him to the door.

"No, come on in. Lyndee's sleeping so we have to be quiet, but I was just hanging out in the kitchen," he says, gingerly shutting the front door behind us.

"Baking or cooking?" I ask when we hit the kitchen.

"Baking. I wanted to try a blueberry cobbler recipe I found online," he says, checking the dish he's prepping on the counter.

"Online?" I quip, taking a seat on the barstool across from where he's working.

He smiles. "Fine, I changed pretty much the whole thing, but I kept the blueberries, okay?"

I chuckle and reach for the bottle of water he slides across to me. "Or does this conversation call for something a little stronger?"

I twist off the top and take a drink, watching as he completes his cobbler and slides it into the oven.

"So? Are you going to tell me why I found you sitting in my driveway at eleven thirty at night?"

Sighing, I close the lid and rest my elbows on the cool, hard marble. "It wasn't eleven thirty," I reply lamely.

"Okay, fine. Eleven fifteen." He props a hip against the counter and crosses his arms. "Does this have anything to do with the woman Jeb mentioned?"

"How do you know?" I ask, looking up and meeting his gaze.

Jasper snorts a low laugh. "Are you kidding? No one understands the confusion a woman causes a man more than me. So, tell me about it."

I take a deep breath, deciding to unload the weight on my shoulders. "Over the last several weeks, we've gotten to know each other, even though I've technically known her a few years. She's…great. Funny and smart and so fucking sexy," I mumble, closing my eyes and instantly picturing her smiling face.

"So what's wrong?"

"Well, when we started *hanging out* it was with the understanding it was just temporary. You know, fun. I had just broken up with Savannah and she wasn't interested in a relationship, so we agreed to keep it simple."

"But now it's not so simple," he deduces, shifting so he's leaning his elbows on the counter in front of me.

"No."

"Because you want more."

"Yes."

He sighs. "And you're sure she doesn't?"

"Well, the fact she was kissing her ex-boyfriend right before I got here is pretty telling."

He whistles and shakes his head. "Yeah, that's probably not a good sign."

I shake my head, trying to get the image of her going up on her tiptoes and kissing Jax's cheek out of my head. Sure, it might not have been a *kiss* kiss, but her lips were definitely on someone else's face. Someone who wasn't me.

"Anyway, it's probably for the best anyway, right? Better to know now before I fall for her and really get my heart broken," I state, feeling said organ clench in my chest.

Probably because I know I've already fallen.

He raises a single eyebrow, like he doesn't buy it. "You know, Numbers, I'm probably the last person you'd want to get relationship advice from, but, from personal experience, I do know what not to do."

I can't help but chuckle, recalling how Jasper messed up his relationship royally with Lyndee and it took him forever to get his head out of his ass. "I recall."

He grins, as if my teasing doesn't bother him. Probably because he actually got the girl. "Listen, it doesn't surprise me you'd be the one searching for the deep, meaningful relationship. Ever since I met you in college, that's what you've done. It's why you kept taking Savannah back, even though you knew in your heart she wasn't right for you."

I can't argue with him because I know he's right.

Dammit.

"Well, how do I know if she's the right one? I guess I don't exactly trust my gut, considering it kept telling me Savannah was the one over and over again. How did you know Lyndee was the one, that she was worth taking the risk?"

He sighs and gives me the slightest grin. "I guess, well, I guess you just know. I knew it in my heart, felt it in my soul. I wasn't whole without her. Does that make sense?"

I nod, knowing exactly what he means. "Yeah."

Except my story doesn't have the happy ending like his does.

Knowing what I have to do, I decide to switch gears and get my mind on something else. "So, when are you going to make an honest woman out of her?"

He finally twists the top off his own bottle of water and takes a long drink. "I'm not sure yet. I mean, don't get me wrong, I love her and want to spend the rest of my life with her, but it hasn't been that long, you know? We really only got together officially about two months ago, right before Walker and Mal's wedding."

"But she's living here," I argue.

"Not officially. She's been here almost every night for the last month, but she still technically lives in her condo with Dustin."

"But you want her to live here with you." It's not a question.

"Of course I do," he confirms.

I shrug. "Then ask her."

"To move in? You don't think it's too soon?"

"Maybe for someone else, but for you and Lyndee? Hell no," I state, taking another drink of my water.

Jasper relaxes, as if needing to hear someone say the words, and I can't help but wonder how long he's been stressing about it. He struggles to sleep anyway, but with something bothering him like that? Hell, he probably hasn't gotten any real sleep in days. Maybe even weeks.

"Yeah. Maybe. I just worry, I guess."

"About you and Lyndee? You don't have anything to worry about, man. You're both on the same page, willing to put in the time and energy it takes to make the relationship work."

"No, not about that. I'm worried she'll worry about Dustin, and her moving in here will create extra anxiety and stress for her."

"Don't you think you should talk to her about that?"

"Yes, I think he should definitely talk to her about it." The feminine voice comes from the side, and we both startle and turn to find Lyndee standing in the doorway.

"Hey," Jasper says, heading her way. "Did we wake you?"

"No," she replies, wrapping her arms around his neck and returning his hug. "I rolled over and you weren't there, so I thought I'd come down and see what you were working on."

"Blueberry cobbler."

She gives him the softest grin before turning her attention to me. "Hey, Numbers."

"Hi, Lyndee. Sorry to drop by so late."

She waves off my comment and heads for the oven, peeking in to check on the contents. When she's done, she turns and pins my friend with a look. "So, you're worried about what I'd say if you were to ask me to officially move in with you, huh?"

I really should go, but I can't seem to make myself move.

"Yeah. I know how much Dustin relies on you," he replies, reaching out and taking her hand.

"What if I told you I have already had this conversation with my brother?"

Jasper seems completely shocked by the news. "Really?"

"Yeah," she says, stepping forward and pressing her cheek against his chest. "He was the one who brought it up, actually. He wanted me to know he was okay with me moving in with you, because he wants to ask Dana to live with him."

"Wow," he replies, incredulously.

"Yeah. He knows how I worry about him, and even though he insisted he'd be fine on his own, he realizes he's ready to take the next step with Dana."

"That's awesome," I state, really liking Dustin and Dana together. She's patient and caring in regard to his cerebral palsy, always encouraging his independence, but doesn't let him overdo it and get overly tired.

"Isn't it?" she says, flashing me a beaming smile before turning her attention to Jasper. "My point is, *if* you were to ask me to move in with you officially, I'd say yes."

He grins and wraps his arms around her shoulders. "You would?"

"I would."

"How quickly can you move in?"

"I'm off Sunday," Lyndee replies with a shrug.

Jasper kisses her hard before glancing my way. "You're helping Lyndee move in here Sunday. Tell the others."

I scoff and shake my head. "What if I have big plans on Sunday?"

He gives me a pointed look, letting me know he's not buying whatever I'm trying to sell him. "You do. Moving Lyndee's stuff here."

Then, he places his lips against hers and deepens the kiss. I actually have to look away because I feel like I'm intruding on a private moment, especially when he mumbles a quick 'I love you' and she follows it up with an 'I love you too.'

"I'm gonna head out," I finally say, sliding from my stool to give them peace.

"What are you going to do about…you know?" he asks, tucking his girlfriend close to his side.

Sighing, I hate that I already realize the answer to that. "I'm going to have to end it. We're not on the same page anymore."

He nods slowly in understanding. "I'm sorry, Numbers."

I shrug and shove my hands into the pockets of my trousers. "It is what it is. I'll be fine."

Jasper's gaze is full of pity. "You will be."

"Congratulations, you two. I'd be happy to help on Sunday," I confirm, heading over to give Lyndee a quick hug before I go.

"I'll make you some of those little cheesecakes you like."

"Make sure you put cherries on them," I say, moving toward the front door.

"But Jameson doesn't like cherries" she says, stopping at the doorway.

A big smile stretches across my lips. "I know."

Jasper chuckles and holds the door open for me. "See you tomorrow?"

"I'll be there," I confirm, slipping out the door and heading for my car.

The mid-April night air is still cool, so I turn on the heat to ebb the chill, but it really doesn't help. My body is numb, my heart sad. I'm going to break things off with BJ, and no amount of artificial heat can offer me comfort from the cold I feel in my chest.

This sucks.

Plain and simple.

When I get home, it's just after midnight. The moment I throw my keys on the counter, I wonder what BJ's doing, because even though I have to let her go, I can't stop the want. The desire to call her, to talk about my crazy day and to ask about hers, is great. So much so I leave my phone in the kitchen with my keys before I move to my bedroom.

I run through the shower, replaying what I saw earlier like some lovesick fool. No, the kiss wasn't terrible and can probably be explained easily, but deep down, I know it's more than that. We want different things. I want to take our relationship public, and she wants to be friends with benefits. There isn't much room for gray area anymore.

When I finally climb into bed, even though I'm exhausted from a long day, I can't calm my mind. I recall the first time she stayed here with me, and every time she's been in my bed since. Has it really only been a month? It feels so much longer than that, like we've been together for months, or hell, years. I know her body better than I know my own and can picture it in vivid detail every time I close my eyes.

But her body isn't the only thing I'm attracted to.

Her head and her heart. For a woman who puts up a rough and tough exterior, she's the sweetest, most caring and loyal person I know.

And do you know what? Her ever-changing hair and her tattoos only add to her beauty. Never—and I do mean never—would I ever had thought I'd find them so fucking sexy, but I do. Dammit, I really, *really* do. So much so, I'm hard and throbbing in my pajama pants just thinking about the delicate lines and vibrant colors adorning her skin.

And her piercings?

I could come just thinking about the first time I saw that little bar through her nipple and stumbled upon the one above her clit. Sexy. As. Hell. Throw in the noises she made while I was exploring them with my mouth and I'm pretty sure I'll be hard for the rest of the night.

Probably a good thing I can picture it all so brilliantly. After I tell her it's time for us to move on, I'm going to need those recollections to get me through the lonely nights that follow.

In the dead of night, I can hear my phone chime in the kitchen. A part of me says to stay here, to try to get some sleep, but a much bigger part lets me know it could be BJ reaching out. So like the sad sucker I am, I practically jump up from my bed and run to retrieve my phone. The moment I see the name on the screen, I groan, wishing I wouldn't have wasted my time getting up.

Savannah.

I glance at the clock, and even though I don't feel anything for her whatsoever, I worry something's wrong. She's never texted me at this hour, which is why I end up inputting my passcode into the phone and pulling up her message.

Savannah: Just thinking of you. I miss you, Isaac.

A deep sigh resounds through my entire body as I stare at her message. Before I can set the device down, bubbles appear.

Savannah: I see you're still up and read this. Listen, I was hoping I can drop by tomorrow for a few minutes. I have something we need to talk about.

Me: What could we possible have to talk about?

Savannah: Us.

Me: There is no us. Not anymore.

Savannah: I know that, but I think we've made a mistake.

Me: No.

It feels really fucking good to type that, so I keep going.

Me: We're over, Savannah. I'm tired of being jerked around. I deserve better.

Savannah: I know you do! I realize that now. I just love you so much, Isaac!

I rub my forehead, hating the headache I feel coming on. I really don't want to get into this, but maybe that's exactly what we need to do. Maybe I need to have this meeting, face-to-face, and be done with it—and her—once and for all. I'm ready to find love, but not with her. I know that for a fact. BJ helped me see it.

Me: We can meet tomorrow. Can you come to my office on your lunch break?

Savannah: Yes, of course! I can't wait! I love you!

I ignore the last part and type out one final reply.

Me: See you tomorrow.

I toss my phone back on the counter, actually looking forward to having this conversation. Even if things aren't happening with BJ, I know this is the right decision for me. I do deserve better, like my friends have been telling me for a while.

It's time for me to do this—to live—for me.

BJ

Even though I slept like crap, I'm full of excitement and energy today. Of course, that could be the four cups of coffee I had, but whatever. The point is I'm anxious to see Isaac and talk to him about us.

It took everything I had not to text him last night. I really wanted to. Hell, I almost drove to his house. But I was practically the walking dead, desperate to catch up on a little sleep, and thanks to almost eight hours of blissful rest, I feel much better today.

I decided to catch up on a few things at my house before heading over to Burgers and Brew. I finished three loads of laundry, including washing my sheets, cleaned the bathroom, and even ran the vacuum and dusted the whole house. It felt good to be so productive on a Tuesday morning.

Now, I'm parking on the street in front of Burgers and Brew. I can't use the back entrance, since I don't have a security code, which means I'm walking in through the front door. The silver lining is my brother is next door at the brewery, so at least I won't run into him and have to answer questions I'm not ready to answer yet. I don't want to say anything to him until I find out if a relationship with Isaac is really possible.

I'll cross that bridge with Jameson when I get there.

And I really hope I get there.

I decide to go in through the bar entrance, since it appears the lunch rush has started. I'm hoping I can just slip down the back hall and up the stairs to Isaac's office.

Though, perhaps showing up unannounced isn't the best idea either. What if he's busy? He could be helping with the onslaught of orders or dealing with a staff issue. I guess if that happens, I'll leave and text him later.

The moment I step inside the door, the familiar sights and sounds of my brother's booming business settles around me. I can't help but smile at all he and his friends have accomplished in the nearly six years they've been open.

"Hey, BJ!" Mallory hollers, loading up her tray with drinks at the bar. "Are you here for lunch?"

"Actually, I was hoping I could have a quick word with Isaac, but I see you guys are really busy. I can come back later," I insist.

She waves off my comment. "I'm pretty sure he's upstairs in his office. You're welcome to head up."

"Okay, thanks," I reply, heading in that general direction.

Mallory gives me a warm smile before lifting her tray and moving toward the dining room. I watch her go, noticing how easily she moves, even pregnant. Longing reaches into my chest and squeezes my heart, which is nuts. Sure, I've always wanted kids...someday. Suddenly, it feels so much closer, just within my reach.

Another image of Isaac fills my mind and makes me grin. Do I want kids with Isaac? I don't know, it's way too soon for that talk, but for the first time in my adult life, the thought doesn't scare me to death. Maybe it's because of him, the man who makes me want things I've never wanted before.

I move through the bar area, finding most of the pub tables filled with patrons, and head for the back hallway that leads up to Isaac's office. Just as I'm about to round the corner, I smack into someone. I quickly jump back, worried it's a server, but when my eyes collide with hers, I realize it's not someone who works here.

It's Savannah.

"Oh, it's you," she snips, adjusting her fancy fitted suit jacket and narrowing her eyes.

"Uhh, sorry, I didn't mean to run into you," I reply politely, even though I would much rather tell her off and go about my day.

"If you're looking for Isaac, he's busy. We just had lunch together before he deals with payroll. Though, I guess now is the perfect time to tell you our news," she states, lifting her chin and flipping her long hair over her shoulder in that annoying way I seem to hate.

"News?"

"Yes, big news. We've decided to get back together, only this time, it's going to stick. We're already talking marriage."

My brain seems to hear her words but not fully comprehend them, so it takes me a few seconds before I can reply. "Wow, that is big news. Congratulations."

She flashes me a perfect smile. "Thank you. I knew it'd come to this. We're meant for each other. Both career driven and focused. We complement each other greatly," she says, glancing down at my ripped-up jeans and Chucks, "unlike you. You're nothing but a good time to him, and that's over now."

Savannah isn't spewing anything she hasn't said before, but for some reason she hits the mark a little harder today. I want to roll my eyes, to call her on her bullshit, but I can't ignore the fact she's here, coming down from Isaac's office like she owns the place.

I turn my back to her and round the corner, heading up the stairs. I hate how easily she can get under my skin, which is another reason I despise this woman so much. She has the ability to make me question myself, something I've never let happen before. Usually I don't care what someone thinks of me. I don't care what they say.

Yet, with Savannah, she makes me feel second best every time she's near.

When I reach the landing at the top of the stairs, I notice his door is half closed. A part of me wants to turn around, not bothering him if he's busy, but the bigger part is anxious to see him. To talk to him. It's been over a week since we were face-to-face, and I'm more than ready to feel his arms wrap around me, his lips pressed against mine.

I knock lightly as I push the door open. Isaac is sitting at his desk, holding a paper in his hand, yet staring off into space. "Hey."

When his tired, worried eyes meet mine, there's a flash of excitement before he quickly pushes it away. "Hi."

"You busy?" I ask, stepping into the room farther and shutting the door behind me.

"No, not really," he says, setting the paper down and shuffling his work aside.

When he doesn't come around to greet me, I take a seat at one of the two guest chairs across from him. My eyes are drawn to the cabinet to my left, where two empty food plates sit. Apparently, he really did have lunch with Savannah.

Wow, okay. I wasn't expecting that.

"How have you been?" I ask, my foot tapping nervously on the floor.

"Good. You?"

I nod. "Fine. I thought I'd drop by to talk before I went to work, but I can come back another time if you're busy."

He takes a deep breath and closes his eyes. When they open, they're a little hard and I can't read them. "No, this is okay. Now is probably as good of a time as ever."

"Okay," I start, wanting to have a conversation too, yet suddenly feeling like it's not the same type of talk. It's in his body language and the way he's distancing himself from me, both physically and emotionally. I can feel it. I shift to the front of my seat, waiting.

"When we started…hanging out, it was with the decision we'd continue until it stops working for one or both of us. No questions, right?"

I nod, already dreading where this is going.

He levels his gaze on me and drops the bomb. "Well, I don't think it's working for me anymore."

My heart drops to my shoes, my gut twists with hurt. "Oh, okay," I reply quickly, trying to cover my shock. "That is what we decided," I add, swallowing the acid taste in my mouth.

"I've had a lot of fun with you, BJ, I hope you know that."

"Yes, of course. I've had fun with you too."

There it is. That *F* word again. Usually, it wouldn't bother me so much, but I guess I just thought it was more than that. It *felt* like it was more than that, at least for me. But now hearing him talk, with so much distance already put between us, I realize how very wrong I was. We weren't on the same page. Hell, we're not even in the same chapter anymore. He's already flipping the page and is moving on.

With Savannah.

He gets up and comes around to where I sit. Even though my legs feel like they're lead, I stand as well. The arms I've longed to have wrapped around me do as I wished, yet it doesn't hold the power and meaning I had longed for. His hug feels final.

Absolute.

Like goodbye.

"You're an amazing woman, Billie Jean Tankersley," he whispers. As our eyes meet once more, I don't miss the slice of hurt staring back at me in those hazel orbs.

Pain radiates through my chest as his words dig like a knife to the chest.

Apparently, not amazing enough.

I give him my best 'I'm fine' smile and reach up to adjust his necktie, ignoring the tremble in my hands. "You're not so bad yourself, Isaac Thompson."

He doesn't return my grin, just watches me with those soulful, deep eyes. It's as if he's memorizing me, memorizing our last moment together. He opens his mouth but stops himself. Instead of speaking, he leans forward and presses his lips to my forehead.

I love it and hate it at the same time.

Needing to get out of here, I clear my throat and take a step back. My action severs our connection, the instant void like a knife to my lungs, my heart, my soul. "I'll let you get back to work," I state, so fucking proud of myself for keeping my cool and remaining passive.

I will not cry until I'm alone.

"Goodbye, Numbers," I say, using his nickname like a buffer between us.

He notices. I can tell by the glimpse of pain I spy on his face. But I push that aside, needing to get out of this office. Needing to get away from Isaac.

He shoves his hands in the pockets of his trousers and nods. "Goodbye, BJ."

I give him a lame wave and turn to exit the room. His scent is too strong, too potent, and even though I'll never forget it, I can't be surrounded by it right now.

He doesn't stop me. That realization is like the final nail in the coffin for my heart. I hurry down the stairs and through the bar. I ignore the bartender and even Mallory, who hollers a farewell as I make my hasty retreat. The moment I step onto the sidewalk, my heart clenches in my chest.

Painfully.

I'm able to make it to my truck before the first tear falls. I'm not a crier. Even as a child, I learned to just push all of my emotions and feelings to the back of my mind, to build a protective wall around them. Well, now I've done it. I actually let someone in, allowed those carefully constructed walls to shift, exposing my heart.

The consequences suck, because this fucking hurts.

I wasn't one-hundred-percent certain of how things would transpire when I went to his office, but I was hoping that wasn't it. I thought I'd get to tell him I was falling for him, to ask him if he was interested in giving a real relationship a try.

Unfortunately, that's not what happened at all.

Apparently, he's decided who he wants and it's not me.

Whether he goes back to Savannah or not doesn't really matter, even though I really hope he doesn't. He deserves someone who'll treat him like he matters, not as an afterthought. He's such a good person, loyal, caring, and a hard worker, and she doesn't appreciate it. She uses him until something or someone better comes along. The thought of him going back to her and repeating the cycle just hurts.

He deserves so much better than her.

He deserves someone like me.

I'm so fucking glad I didn't say anything like I had planned. Can you imagine how dumb and desperate I would have looked, telling him I want to be with him officially, only to have him dump me anyway?

I start my truck and take off toward the studio. It won't open for a couple of hours yet, which is for the best. I'll be able to lick my wounds in private before two of my best friends get there and probably read me like a book. That gives me two hours to cry and then get over Isaac Thompson.

Shouldn't be too hard, right?

I'm just glad I didn't fall completely in love with him before I found out he didn't feel the same way.

Yeah, right. Keep telling yourself that.

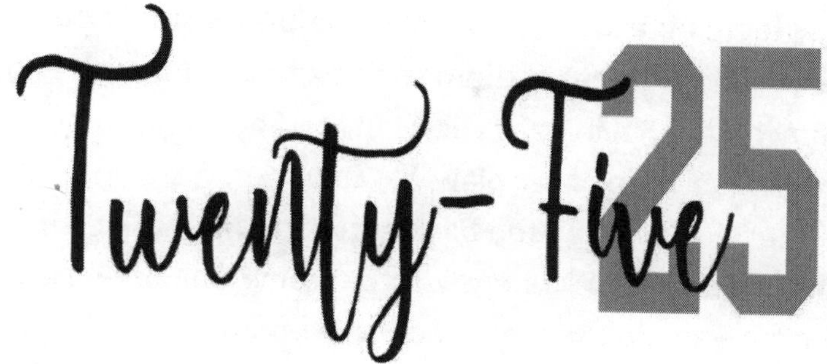

Twenty-Five

Isaac

I run my hands through my hair once more, staring at the closed door. Why do I wish she'd come bursting in, telling me I'm wrong? That we do belong together.

But that door doesn't open.

Instead, I'm surrounded in silence and heartache. I keep picturing how stoic and unaffected she looked when I told her our time together had run its course. But why would she be upset? From the very beginning, we were on a timeline. The end was always looming in the distance, just over her shoulder. I knew it was coming, but that doesn't make it any less painful.

This is exactly why a friends with benefits relationship is a bad idea. Somewhere along the way, one of the parties starts to have real feelings and ends up getting hurt.

That someone is me.

I make my way back to my desk, but it's too hard to focus on what I need to do. Instead, I need to get out of here. I can still smell her subtle perfume. It lingers in the air, like a curse.

I jump up and grab the two dirty plates sitting on the cabinet and head down to return them to the kitchen. I wasn't expecting to have lunch with Savannah when I invited her to stop by to talk, but apparently, she had other plans.

Pushing through the back entrance for the kitchen, I take the plates to where Patrick works on restocking the dishwasher. "Here's two more," I say to the man who has worked here since we opened.

"Thanks, boss. How was your food?" he asks politely, placing the two plates inside the unit.

"Good."

Not wanting to hang around and disrupt his work, I spin on my heel and prepare to exit the way I came in. Except when I turn, I almost slam into Jasper's chest. "Got a minute?" he asks, his arms crossed over his chest.

I nod and follow him into his office at the back of the kitchen. "What's up?" I ask when the door is closed.

"What was Savannah doing here, grabbing two plates for lunch?"

I sigh, shaking my head. "I asked her to come so we could talk. I didn't know she was going to stop by the kitchen and grab food."

He seems to consider my words and flops down in his chair. "I thought you were done with her." There's a hint of accusation in his question, not that I can blame him. It was just last night I told him I was severing ties with the woman I was seeing, and now all of a sudden my ex was here, getting all chummy.

"I am," I insist, taking the chair across from his desk. "I told her we were over, for good. I don't love her, not anymore."

How can I love her when I'm in love with BJ?

"How'd she take it?"

"Oh, she was pissed. Threw my stapler at me."

Jasper chuckles, steepling his fingers in front of his mouth. "I wish I could say I'm torn up about that."

I snort. "You wanted me to get hit with my stapler?"

"No, not that. The other part. I'm glad you're done with her."

I sigh and kick back in the chair. "Me too. I just wish I didn't have to be done with the other one."

Feeling his gaze on me, I glance up. "When are you going to do that?"

Closing my eyes, I recall the pain I felt, saying those words. "It's already done. She actually stopped by right after Savannah left."

Jasper's eyes widen. "So you broke two hearts in one lunch?"

"Pretty much," I confirm, even though the second heart wasn't BJ's.

It was mine.

"Damn, rough day. How'd the second one go?"

I shrug. "Fine. She didn't throw objects from my desk at me."

"That's always a good thing." After a few long seconds, he asks, "So, are you okay?"

I open my mouth to tell him I am, but the lie just won't slide off my tongue. Instead, I go with, "I will be."

He nods in understanding. "Sorry it didn't work out. If you need anything, let me know."

I stand up and stretch my arms over my head. "I will. I'm gonna finish payroll and then take off for the day a little early. You okay with that?"

"I got you. Jameson's next door if I have any issues," he agrees, walking around his desk and opening his door. Before I step out, he squeezes my shoulder in support. "Holler if you need anything, okay?"

"I'll be fine, but thanks for the offer."

I head out of the office and return upstairs, determined to focus on my job. Payroll takes me twice as long as it normally does, considering I'm so damn distracted, but eventually, I get it complete. As soon as it's printed and locked away in the safe, I shut down my laptop and prepare to leave. I don't even pack a bag of work stuff to take home. I just stand up, secure my office, and head for my car.

Ready to put this shitty day behind me, yet knowing every time I look back, it'll be BJ's face I see.

I pick up my phone no less than a dozen times, wanting to call her. Even though I know she's at work.

How sad am I?

I'm the one who officially ended it, yet all I can think about is her. I wonder if she's hurting like I am or if she's grateful so she can move on. Perhaps it's somewhere in between, or at least that's where I hope she is. Not happy we're over, but not miserable like me, because I wouldn't wish this on my worst enemy.

Well, maybe on Savannah, but that would mean she'd actually have to give a shit about someone other than herself.

The TV is on, but I'm not actually watching it, so when I hear a car door shut, it's easy to identify. Yet, I still don't move. Not until the knock sounds on my front door.

I jump up, my heart racing with the prospect of finding BJ at my front stoop. But as I rip open the door, it's not the woman I want to find standing there. My disappointment must be evident when Mallory smiles. "Expecting someone else?"

"Sorry," I reply, stepping back and allowing her to enter. "How are you?" I glance over her shoulder, surprised to find her alone.

"I'm good," she states with a smile. "How are you?" Her green eyes filled with concern.

"I'm fine," I lie.

Apparently, she doesn't believe it and gives me a skeptical look. "Sure you are. Busy?"

"No, just watching some television."

Mallory looks over at the TV and laughs. "*Steel Magnolias*? It's a favorite of mine too."

I run a hand through my hair and sigh. "Fine, I just turned it on. I wasn't even watching it."

She exhales deeply and faces me head-on. "Talk to me. Jasper says you were seeing someone, but it ended?"

Now it's my turn to exhale. "Want something to drink?" I ask, not answering her question and heading to the kitchen.

"Just water, please. This baby likes to tap dance on my bladder, so if I drink too much, I'll spend the entire time in the bathroom, and we don't want that."

"We don't?" I tease, grabbing two bottles of water from the fridge and placing them on the table.

Mal takes a seat and twists off the top, taking a small drink of the cold liquid before turning her attention back to me. She looks at me expectantly, as if waiting for me to finally respond to her previous statement.

"Yes, I was seeing someone, but it was nothing serious," I finally confirm as I sit across from her. I feel her eyes on me, but keep mine on my water bottle, as if it were the most fascinating thing I've ever seen.

"No? Then why do you look like someone kicked your monkey?"

"My monkey?" I ask, the corner of my lips turned upward.

Mal shrugs. "We watch a lot of Curious George movies right now. You know what I mean. Why are you so gloomy?"

I don't want to answer her, but I will. She's been a great friend, even before she started dating and eventually marrying one of my best friends. "I guess I just started to like her more than she liked me."

She pulls a face. "That's the worst. I'm sorry."

"It's okay. I'll survive."

"Of course you will, but that doesn't mean it doesn't suck balls."

She would be correct. Ever since BJ left my office, I've felt numb and incomplete. It definitely sucks balls. Deciding to give her a little more info, I add, "We were pretty casual, but I was starting to want more."

"And she didn't?" she gathers.

"From my vantage point, I'd say she did not."

Her head tilts to the side just a bit. "What do you mean? You didn't ask her?"

"I didn't have to ask her," I state, sitting up straight in my chair. "I saw pictures of her and a few male friends, looking very *chummy*. And then I saw her kiss her ex."

"On the lips?" she demands with outrage.

"Well, no, but still."

"Wait. Where did she kiss him?" she asks, confused.

"On the cheek." My gut tightens with the memory.

"I kiss you on the cheek."

Now it's my turn to be confused. "So? We're friends."

"Exactly. We're *friends*. Why do you think there's more to her and her ex? Did she tell you there was?"

It's hard to swallow over the lump in my throat. "No. I saw it."

She closes her eyes and sighs. "Listen, Numbers, I'm going to ask you a question, and I want you to think about your answer before you say it, okay?" When I nod, she continues, "Are you certain there's something between her and her ex?"

Doing as she asks, I stop and think back to everything BJ has said and done regarding Jax. There's a handful of shit that was just annoying and made me jealous, but I suppose nothing damning.

Do I have this all wrong? Could I have misread the kiss and the photos I saw on Jameson's phone? My head pounds with a headache, which makes it hard to think. "I don't know, Mal. I mean, I don't know for certain she's interested in her ex, but dammit, I didn't like seeing BJ in pictures with Jax's arms around her shoulders and his tongue on her cheek or watching her kiss him." I didn't mean for my voice to raise, but the jealousy was doing something to increase my agitation level.

She blinks once, twice, three times before she replies. "BJ?"

Shit.

Now it's my turn to sit dumbfounded, wishing I could take my words back, yet knowing I can't.

"You were seeing BJ? Jameson's sister?" she whispers, her eyes wide with the realization.

A growl rumbles my chest, and I know there's no going back now. "Yes."

"What? When? How? When?"

"You said when twice," I mutter.

"I know. It's an important question. Tell me all about this," she demands, leaning forward as to not miss a word.

With a heavy breath, I tell her everything, from the night of the open house, our decision to keep it casual and have fun, and the conversation we had earlier today that ended our time together. When I'm finally done, she just shakes her head. "Holy shit, I can't believe none of us picked up on this."

"Well, that was kind of the point," I mumble, shifting in my chair. "Not that we were trying to hide it from everyone, but we didn't want to complicate it any more than it already was by bringing her brother and all you guys into it."

"Wow, you think you know a guy, and suddenly you find out he's in love with someone you least expect."

"See? Even you know it was a bad idea," I argue.

Mallory shakes her head. "Whoa, whoa, whoa, I didn't say it was a bad idea, I just said I wasn't expecting it."

"Because of how she looks?"

She glares over at me, clearly offended by my question. "Are you kidding me? Of course not because of how she looks. All I meant was I didn't think you two knew each other that well, and that has absolutely nothing to do with her appearance. Which, I might add, is completely beautiful. Her tattoos are gorgeous and completely tasteful. In fact, Lyndee and I have talked about getting one. And her hair? I'd kill to have that kind of body and texture. My hair is limp and flat now that I'm pregnant."

"You're stunning," I tell my friend, reaching over and squeezing her hand. "Walker is the luckiest bastard on the planet."

Mallory tears up, waving her hand in front of her face. "And the hormones! I'd do anything not to see a puppy commercial and break down crying. He's going to throw me out of the house soon."

I hold her hand in mine. "Never gonna happen. He worships the ground you walk on. We all see it. It's a little nauseating, but no one deserves it more than you two. Please don't ever doubt his love and loyalty to you, okay?"

She nods and wipes her cheek roughly. "I know. I'm just all crazy right now. I don't mean any of it. I know he loves me."

I can't help but smile. "So much."

She lets out a long breath and places her other hand on top of mine. "You know, you're an incredible man, Numbers. BJ would be lucky to have you."

I shake my head slightly. "But it's not meant to be."

"I don't know about that. I think if you were to take a little time and think about it, you'd see the picture a little clearer."

"What the hell does that mean?" I ask with a laugh.

"Just that you're all emotional and raw still. Give it a few days and then reexamine your relationship with her. I think you'll see everything from a whole new perspective."

"I think you're talking in riddles."

She disagrees completely. "Men are stubborn and a little stupid. Just give it a few days and call her, okay? You need to talk to her and find out how she feels, not how you *think* she feels."

I lean back in my seat and consider her words. "I can do that. But when she tells me she's dating Jax again, I'm going to tell you I told you so."

She snorts and rolls her eyes. "If she tells you she's dating Jax, I'll name the baby after you."

I feign shock. "You mean you weren't to begin with?"

"Only if the baby comes with your fashion sense," she says, releasing my hand and standing up. "I should get home."

"Where does Walker think you are?"

Moving toward the front door, she doesn't even glance over her shoulder when she says, "He knew I was coming here. I told him I was going to check on you and would probably have to smack some sense into you." She meets my gaze. "Like you did for me not too long ago."

I nod, recalling the conversation we had about Walker after the drugs were found in his house. "I didn't tell you anything you didn't already know, Mal."

She grins. "I know. And I haven't told you anything you don't already know either. Talk to her."

I pull her into a hug, carefully smashing that cute little baby bump into my own stomach. "You're a good friend."

"As are you," she whispers. "Now, don't be stupid. Call her."

I roll my eyes and release my hold. "Yes, boss."

She grins widely, placing her hands on her hips. "I like that. You can call me that from now on."

"Not happening," I mutter, opening the door and walking her to her SUV.

When she's safely inside and rolls down her window, she pins me with another glare. "I mean it. Don't be stupid."

"I promise," I insist, holding up my hands in surrender.

"Good. Now, I'm gonna run through the ice cream shop drive-thru and eat a large chocolate cone before I head home. If you tell on me, I'll name the baby Isaac...but only if it's a girl."

"Jesus, you're ruthless," I tease, feeling lighter than I have all damn day.

She laughs and starts the car, throwing it in reverse and carefully backing out of my driveway. Mal honks as she takes off, no doubt heading for that ice cream she spoke of before she heads home. When her car is completely out of sight, I go back inside, locking the door behind me.

I return to the living room and turn off the TV before making my way down the hall to my bedroom. Maybe a shower will help clear my brain a little, but honestly, I doubt it. It's all jumbled together, and I can't make heads or tails of anything.

I have a feeling this is going to be a very long night.

Twenty-Six

BJ

Forty-eight hours.

That's how long it's been since I walked out of Isaac's office and felt my heart break. Ever since, I've gone through the motions, going to work, returning home, and barely sleeping. Barely eating.

Barely living.

When Jax and I broke up, I didn't feel an ounce of this kind of pain. Hell, when I walked in on Jimmy Stern, my first love, boinking my former roommate on the couch, even that didn't hurt like this.

This is hell. Truly.

Amanda and Jax know something is up. Amanda has tried a dozen times to get me to talk, but I'm not ready. If I talk, I'll break, and the last thing I want to do is cry again. And I'm not sure I have any more tears left.

That's why I'm pissed.

It's been two days, and now I'm just pissed the fuck off. Sitting here in my room, waiting for my next appointment, as the minutes tick by, I'm getting more and more angry.

I'm mad at myself, mostly, for falling in love with the one man who won't love me back. I'm mad at Isaac too, for choosing her. Especially because she's all wrong for him. She doesn't even realize how good she has it either. How sweet and giving he is. How he's so much more than just good with numbers. He's passionate and intense in a way I never expected from a man who wears expensive suits all day.

And he's so fucking good in bed.

How a woman like Savannah could have had him and let him go—repeatedly—is beyond me.

"Hey, your next appointment is here," Amanda says from the doorway, breaking through my thoughts.

"Okay, good. Any idea of what they want?" I ask, noting the last-minute addition to my schedule.

"He said he'd discuss it with you," she replies, turning to retrieve the client.

I grab another antibacterial wipe and clean the chair once more. It's been done since my last appointment left, but when I'm anxious, I have to do something with my hands. Usually, I draw or sketch, but this'll work just fine too for now.

"So this is what I have to resort to in order to see my sister."

I look up and my brother's large frame fills the doorway. "Jame?" He walks in and plops down in my chair unceremoniously. "What are you doing here?"

"I've sent you a few texts but you haven't replied. I dropped by last night, but you didn't answer the door, even though your truck was in the driveway. Have I done something to piss you off?" he asks, worry marring his light brown eyes.

"No, of course not," I quickly insist, rolling my chair so I'm directly beside him. "I went for a long walk last night. You must have missed me while I was gone. And as far as your texts, my phone died the night before and I didn't charge it until yesterday, and then, well, I guess I just forgot. I'm sorry." Guilt prickles my chest, replacing the anger I felt just a few minutes ago.

"I'm just glad you're okay. I was getting worried. I called here earlier and talked to Amanda. She said you were all sorts of pissy but didn't say why. I told her to get me on your schedule, if this was the only way I could talk to you."

I can't help but smile. "You can stop by here anytime without being on my schedule."

He shrugs and pushes up his T-shirt sleeve. "I figured, while I'm here, you might as well throw down some killer ink."

My grin widens. "Where? Your entire arm is already covered," I point out, even though that's not entirely true. He still has a few small areas I could squeeze in a little more ink.

"I was thinking here," he says, pointing to the back of his arm where the skin is more sensitive.

"Ouch, that's gonna hurt. You up for this, big guy?"

He huffs. "Does a bear shit in the woods?"

I shake my head and start prepping the area. "Do you know what you want?"

"Surprise me."

"I'd like a little direction, please."

He catches my gaze. "I trust you."

My heart flutters in my chest, a reminder that it still works and isn't completely broken, even though it feels that way. "You don't care at all?"

"Nope. Have at it," he says, popping earbuds in. I lay the chair back flat and have him get on his stomach, so I have better access to the real estate I'm about to tattoo.

I grab my phone and do a quick internet search for my idea. It's easy to find online, thanks to several musical websites. I verify it in three places, making sure what I'm looking at is genuine and right, and then grab my gun. I opt to freehand this one, like several of the others I've completed for Jameson.

My brother doesn't say a word, doesn't move for the next thirty minutes. He puts himself in a zone while I work, the heavy tempo of rock music spilling from his earbuds. Just as I'm nearing the finish line, he turns his head and removes his earpieces. "Do you want to talk about it?"

I keep my eyes trained on my work. "Not really."

"Anything I can do to help?"

I shake my head and risk a quick glance up. "No. I'll figure it out."

He nods and rests his cheek against the chair as I fire up the gun once more and add the finishing touches to his new piece. When I'm all done and it's wiped down, I move back and allow him to stand. Jameson goes to the mirror and looks in the handheld one I position just right so he can view his new ink. "Holy shit, Beej."

"It's the music notes for the chorus of 'Let It Be.' It slightly curves with your arm to fit between your other pieces."

He looks at my face, his eyes full of appreciation and gratitude. "Damn, it's fucking perfect. I love it."

I can't help but beam at the compliment. "I'm glad."

"No, seriously," he says, staring down at the image once more. "This means more to me than any other piece." His voice is thick with the emotion he rarely shows.

I wave off his comment. "You always say that." Reaching for my phone, I snap a quick photo of the tattoo for our social media pages.

"Yeah, maybe," he starts, grabbing my arm and halting my movements. When I look up, he continues, "but I really fucking mean it. You know..." he stops and clears his throat. "You know what this means to me."

I smile, proud that I was able to come up with something so perfect for the space on his skin. "I know. Now, let's get it wrapped up so you can get out of here. I imagine you have to get back to work."

He shrugs and sits on the chair, allowing me to add ointment and then cover the ink. "I'm off. I took the afternoon off to come see you."

My eyes soften as I glance his way. "You didn't have to do that."

"I know, but I was worried about you. You sure you're okay?"

I sigh. "Yeah, I'm okay. Just some stuff I have to work through, but I'll get there."

"Okay." He stands up and shoves his earbuds in the pocket of his jeans. "If you need me to kill him, just say the word. No one will find the body."

I'm almost startled by my brother's comment, even though I shouldn't be. He's protective to a fault, something he's been since I was a child. "No, it's nothing like that," I say, throwing in a good chuckle to let him know I'm all right.

His eyebrows shoot toward his hairline. "You sure, because I don't think I've ever seen you so sad before. I don't like it, and if a guy did this, I want to go beat his ass for making you this way."

I step forward and go up on my tiptoes. "I appreciate your support, but I promise I'll be fine. Eventually."

He practically growls. "I hate him."

"You don't even know him."

"I don't have to know him, Beej," he says, giving me a pointed look.

"I love you," I state, leaning into his chest and wrapping my arms around him.

He kisses the crown of my head. "Love you too."

"Now go. My next appointment will be here soon."

"Yeah, maybe I'll go check on Jax. See what he's been up to."

"Oh! You know what you should do? Ask him about Amanda," I whisper conspiratorially.

"Amanda?"

I nod in confirmation. "Apparently, he asked her out and she accepted."

"No shit? I guess I'm going to have to have the second *don't fuck with my little sister* conversation with the man."

I roll my eyes. "Amanda isn't your little sister."

"Close enough. You two have been as thick as thieves for as long as I can remember." Suddenly, he stops and gives me a look. "Are you okay with this? That's not why you're upset, is it?"

I wave my hand. "Pfft. Hell no. I'm super excited for them, and between you and me, really hope it works out for them."

"Are you sure? I mean, you and Jax...well, you know."

"I know, but I also know why it didn't last for too long. We're great friends. He's a phenomenal artist and mentor, and I really respect him. Our brief history has no weight on how I feel about him dating anyone, especially Amanda. In fact, I was the one who kept pushing him. Otherwise, he'd probably still be in his office with his thumb up his ass."

"I heard that," Jax says, stepping around the corner and filling the doorway.

"I don't care," I reply, shrugging off his gruffness.

"Hey, man," Jameson says, doing one of those bro-hug shoulder slaps, fortunately missing my brother's new ink.

"Stop by for some color?"

"Yeah, Beej threw some sick music notes on my arm," Jameson replies.

"I'll send you a pic," I tell Jax, firing off the images to both Jax and Amanda for her to upload to social media.

Jax stares down at the picture and whistles. "Damn, girl. That's sweet. I take it it's for one of your favorite songs?" he asks my brother, who nods in confirmation.

"All right, well, you two get out of here so I can prep for my next appointment."

"I'll stop by and pay Amanda."

"You know your money's no good here," I state, but he's already shaking his head.

"And you know I won't take your time without paying you for it."

"Whatever. Go."

He turns his whiskey-colored gaze my way once more. "Call me if you need anything. *Anything,* Beej."

It's hard to swallow over the lump in my throat. "I will. Promise."

He nods before disappearing down the hall, leaving me alone once more. The silence only lasts a few moments though, as my best friend comes barreling through my door. "Okay, listen up. I'm getting to the bottom of this whole Debbie Downer thing you've got going on. Jax let me go early, since the last appointment is at eight, so I'm going to get tacos and margaritas. I'll be at your house at ten oh five on the dot. We're gonna eat and get drunk and you're gonna tell me what's going on and who I need to kick in the balls."

I snort out a laugh. “You’re such a violent little thing. Does Jax know about this side of you?” I tease, waggling my eyebrows.

“Yes, he does, and I think he encourages it.”

“Of course he does.” I take a deep breath. “Okay, fine, but only if you promise to tell me all about what’s going on with you and Jax.”

“Duh,” she states.

“Fine. I’ll be there as soon as the shop closes.”

“Good. Now, get ready for your next appointment. This is the guy who wants the gauges in his ears and the bluebird tattoo on his ass.”

Twenty-Seven 27

Isaac

It's almost eleven when I finally shut down my laptop and stow it away in my cabinet. Exhaustion is settling in, and the numbers are starting to move on the screen. That's never a good sign.

It was a pretty busy Thursday night, but all is quiet now. Walker and Jasper went home shortly after the bar closed at ten, which has given me an opportunity to put in a little more time in silence. Not that I really want or need it. The silence is what's slowly killing me.

Just as I'm closing and locking my door, I hear the large outer one shut down the hall. At this hour, there is only a handful of people that could be, and I'm willing to bet money I know which one. "Hey," Jameson says, stepping into the dimly lit hallway.

"Hey, man. You're here late."

He nods. "I just finished up next door. We got a few applicants for that assistant brewer post, so I wanted to do a little research on them online. I saw your car still here, so I thought I'd see if you wanted to have a quick drink."

It's not unheard of for any of us to have a drink and visit after-hours, but I can't remember the last time it happened. Before Walker and Mallory got together, I imagine. "All right."

He leads the way into the bar, flipping on a single strip of lights over the stools. "What'll it be?"

I want to tell him to pour me something strong, but that just reminds me of the night BJ and I drank the tequila back at her place…and all the naughty stuff happened. "A beer would be fine."

"You care which?"

"Surprise me," I say, taking a seat as he pours two draft beers in frosty mugs.

He grabs the seat beside me and takes the first drink. "Damn, we do good work."

"We sure do," I agree, lifting my mug and enjoying the brew we created.

"How's everything been going?" he asks, glancing around at the empty room.

"Fine. I was working on our third quarter projections in comparison to where we stand right now in the second quarter. They're looking pretty solid," I tell him, detailing the figures between sips.

"Everything all right with you? You've been a little off the last few days," he finally says, changing the subject from sales figures to the one topic I really don't want to talk about.

"Yeah, of course. Just busy."

He makes a noise, but doesn't say any more, just sits there and drinks his beer. Finally, he asks, "So how's it going with the woman Jasper mentioned? The one you've been seeing."

Fuck.

"Oh, uh, it's over."

"Really?" he asks, turning his attention my way. "Why?"

I shrug and avert my gaze. "Just ran its course."

"That's too bad."

His statement catches me by surprise. "Why do you say that?"

He levels me with another intense gaze as he says, "Well, Jasper was right. You do seem a lot happier lately. Happier than I've ever seen you."

It's suddenly hard to get air down my tight throat, and I reach up and loosen my necktie. "Yeah, well, it's over now."

I can feel the heat of his gaze on me as I take another drink, wishing I had opted for the strong liquor right about now. "Do you want to know what I think?" he asks casually.

Do I? Probably not, but I know Jameson well enough to know he's going to throw his two cents in whether I like it or not.

"Uh, sure."

"Call her."

That's not at all what I expected him to say.

"What?"

"Call her. Or better yet, go see her. Get this shit figured out."

I sit back and watch his reflection in the mirror. "I'm not really sure that's an option."

"Bullshit." His eyes turn hard as he stares back at me. "She's fucking miserable too."

When his words finally register, I'm pretty sure my mouth drops open. "What?" I whisper.

Jameson rolls his eyes and drinks more beer. "You really think I didn't know?" he asks, the hard edges around his eyes softening just a fraction.

My throat is so dry, my tongue wants to stick to the roof of my mouth. “Know what?”

He sighs deeply and shakes his head. “You and BJ.”

The desire to run away is pretty strong right now. Mostly because I have no idea how this conversation is going to go. If there even is a conversation. Jameson could very well just beat my ass without saying a damn word.

Knowing the only way to do this is straightforward, I sag in defeat. “How long have you known?”

He laughs. The fucker actually laughs at me. “How long have I known my sister was seeing one of my best friends? Since the beginning.”

The beginning? The night we…you know.

“Do you really think my sister’s truck breaks down somewhere, a man gives her a ride home, and his car is parked in her driveway all night long in this town and no one talks about it?”

I open my mouth, but words don’t come out. What am I supposed to say to that anyway? Fortunately, I’m saved from having to talk, because he does it for us.

“The point is I think you should call her. She’s just as fucking miserable as you, and I don’t like it.”

I clear my throat, hating having this conversation with him, especially about BJ. “I don’t think we’re on the same page anymore. What we had was…casual.”

“Didn’t look casual from where I was sitting. She was a wreck. Amanda said she’s been miserable for a few days.”

But I don’t understand. Why would she be so miserable if she was interested in Jax again?

Then the conversation I had with Mallory a few nights ago comes back to me. Is she right? Did I have it all wrong where Jax and BJ are concerned?

"Let me ask you a question."

"Shoot."

"It's about BJ and Jax."

He arches a single eyebrow in question and waits me out.

"They dated. They're not still...you know."

"No, I don't know. Spit it out," he requests, not making this easy on me.

"Well, are they together? Like have they been off and on since they first dated?"

"You mean like you and the crazy blonde?" Before I can reply, he continues, "No, they're not like that. They dated for a few short months several years ago, and only have a professional relationship now. They consider each other friends, which they actually realized while they were still dating."

I close my eyes, the confirmation I was dreading blaring in my ears.

"In fact, he's starting to date Amanda. I guess he's had a crush on her for months now, and it was BJ who encouraged him to finally ask her out."

"Amanda?"

"Yeah. Amanda. *Not* BJ."

I groan and run my hands through my hair. "Mal's right. I'm such an idiot."

He snorts. "Well, she's not fucking wrong. My question is what are you going to do about it?"

I blink a few times, trying to wrap my head around the fact he's...helping me.

"Don't be so surprised, Numbers."

I can't help it. I am. "You're actually telling me to go after your sister?"

He levels me with the most serious look I've ever seen. "If there is anyone I trust with BJ, it's you."

Jesus, the emotion is lodged in my throat, stealing my ability to breathe. "I, uh, I don't know what to say."

"Do you love her?"

I glance back over at him, ready to tell him yes, but something has me holding back. "I don't think the first time I say those words should be to her brother."

Jameson smiles one of those rare, full smiles. "Good answer. Now," he says, slapping me on the back a little too hard, "let's talk about what you're gonna do to win back my sister."

BJ

"So, there's been a slight adjustment to your schedule tonight. Your ten o'clock appointment needed to reschedule, so I did a little shifting and he's going to be here at three. Then I filled the ten o'clock timeslot with a new guy. He's an ink virgin."

The corner of my mouth turns up in a grin as I add the finishing touches to a butterfly tattoo on a twenty-one-year-old for her birthday. "I do love virgins," I quip, making the young woman laugh.

"I figured. He specifically requested you too."

"Word of mouth is the best form of advertisement," I mutter, mimicking Jax and making my best friend laugh.

"That's what I've heard. Anyway, I'm going to order dinner around six. You have a piercing at that time, so you'll have a little wiggle room to eat some food."

"Sounds good. Get me anything. You know what I like."

Amanda agrees and disappears back up front. The rest of the Saturday afternoon flies by. We're packed with appointments, and

I'm able to slip in a couple of piercing walk-ins in between. When my friend returns with burgers from our favorite burger restaurant, I can't help the longing that hits me square in the feels. I haven't been doing too badly today, thanks to the full schedule, but now that I'm eating a gourmet burger from Burgers and Brew, the bone-deep sadness has returned. Even when Amanda joins me in the office to eat and does everything she can to make me laugh.

Fortunately, I don't have much time to focus on the ache in my chest as my next appointment arrives. I power through, putting all my energy into my work. It's what has gotten me through some really rough times, and it'll be no different with this. Isaac decided to go back to his horrible ex-girlfriend? Fine by me. I'll just kill this wolf tattoo, making sure the client is so happy, he comes back for more.

I take a quick break to rest my hand and prepare to study my final piece of the night, but since it's a new client, I don't have anything prepared. "Hey, Amanda? Did the last guy say what he wanted?" I ask, popping my head in the office where she sits with Jax.

"No, but he said it wouldn't be too big or detailed and he'd discuss it with you when he arrived."

I sigh and prop my back against the doorjamb. "I hate that. I wish they'd at least give you an idea so I can prepare a little."

"I know," she replies with an apologetic grin.

"Oh, my last client canceled on me. I think I'm gonna throw the closed sign for the last hour and take Amanda out for a drink," Jax states, shocking the hell out of me. Not because he's taking her out, but because he's leaving me alone with an unknown client. He rarely ever does that, even though I insist I'll be fine. Plus, there are times we'll have walk-ins during the last hour before closing, and it's not like Jax to turn down that opportunity to make a few extra bucks.

"Really?"

He shrugs and reaches his hand out for Amanda's. "Yeah. I mean, I'll stay if you want me to."

"No!" I quickly insist, not wanting him to cancel with her just to sit around and wait for me to finish. I'm a big girl. I can take care of myself. "I'll be fine."

"Okay," he says casually. "We'll make sure you're settled before we head out."

"Sounds good."

"I'll bring him back as soon as he arrives," Amanda insists, checking the clock on the wall. "Which should be any minute now."

I head to my room to make sure everything is ready and hear the bell above the door ring over the low thump of the music. Making sure my sketchbook is readily available, I glance through some of my latest designs, hoping something will inspire whatever it is I have to come up with on a dime tonight.

"Okay, your appointment is here. He's using the restroom real quick and will be in here in a few minutes. The front door is locked and the lights off. I even put a sign on the door about no walk-ins allowed tonight."

I glance over at my best friend. Is she sweating? Why does she look all fidgety and nervous? Before I can ask what's going on, she practically turns and bolts from my room.

"Jax and I will check in later. Bye!"

All I can do is stare at the space she just vacated. Did she really just leave some random guy in the bathroom, free to move about our studio? Why am I a little annoyed by this?

Just as I step into the hallway to watch for the mystery client, I slam into a brick wall. Strong arms wrap around me, as does a very familiar scent. My heart jumps in my chest, my eyes well up at the sudden rush of emotions the cologne invokes, and my pussy, well, she gets all wet and excited like the hussy she is when Isaac is near.

Except Isaac isn't here.

He's off with Savannah, probably celebrating their renewed relationship status and making it social media official by posting a selfie together.

"Are you okay?"

Okay, clearly I'm losing it, because this guy sounds just like Isaac too.

When I glance up, my heart literally clenches in my chest. The reason this guy smells and sounds like Isaac is because it *is* Isaac. "What are you doing here?" I ask, though the voice doesn't sound like me at all.

He gives me the slightest smile and adjusts his hands on my arms, as if he's holding me tenderly and refusing to let go. "I'm your appointment."

You could probably push me over with a feather. "You?"

He throws me that panty-melting grin, the one that I've come to love—and miss—so much. "Yes, me." He looks me over from head to toe. "Are you all right? You didn't hurt yourself when you ran into me, did you?"

Just my heart, but I don't vocalize that thought. "No, I'm fine." I carefully pull back, needing to put a little distance between him and me. Having him this close is messing with my brain, reminding me of how good we were together, even for just a short while.

"Okay," he replies, reluctantly releasing me and taking a small step back to give me space. He shoves his hands in his pockets, as if needing to put them away for some reason. I wish that reason was to keep from reaching for me, but I'm not holding my breath.

"So, you're my appointment?" I ask nervously, clearing my throat.

At least now I know why Jax and Amanda were so quick to leave me alone with him.

A big part of me wants to refuse the appointment. If he really wants a tattoo bad enough, he can reschedule with Jax, but a much smaller, yet incredibly loud part, wants him to sit in the chair, so I can touch and smell him for a short amount of time. Maybe he won't notice if I lightly graze my lips across his skin or stick my nose in the collar of his shirt and inhale.

God, I'm so weak.

Weak and pathetic.

"Are you sure this is a good idea?" I finally ask, glancing around the room to give me something to look at other than the gorgeous man standing before me.

"I can go if you'd rather, but to be honest, I would really like to talk to you."

I take a deep breath, the exhaustion of the last four days really starting to catch up with me. "Look, you can talk to me without making an appointment."

He flashes a quick grin. "Probably, but I figured this way, you can't hang up on me."

"But I can kick you out," I reason, raising my chin a bit in defiance.

Isaac nods. "You can, but I'm sort of hoping you won't."

With a long sigh, I step back and wave at the chair. "It's your money."

"Thank you," he replies, slipping off his suit jacket and releasing his tie. I try not to pay attention, but my vagina's calling the shots right now, and she's all about watching the show.

When he unfastens the small buttons on his dress shirt and slips it off his shoulders, I snap out of my trance. “What are you doing?”

His eyebrows draw together in confusion. “Are you going to tattoo me through my shirt?”

“Uh, well, n-no,” I sputter.

Jesus, BJ. Get it together.

He nods and slips the shirt off, tossing it onto the extra chair in the corner.

I clear my throat, determined to get down to work and be professional. “What location are you thinking?” I ask, doing everything I can not to stare at his amazing chest, the dark hair beckoning for my fingers to get tangled in it.

“Here,” he says, tapping his right pec.

“I’m going to have to shave you,” I state, noting the thick dark hair sprinkled over his chest.

“I figured. I’ve discovered I don’t seem to mind things *shaved*.”

His words catch me off guard. Is he flirting? Referring to me and my…shavedness?

He watches as I retrieve the trimmers, razor, and gel. “How big of an area?”

He makes a circle with his hands on his pec so I can see and then grab the trimmer to shave off the hair. Even though I’ve done this a thousand times before, there’s something more intimate and personal about doing it to Isaac.

While I work, I risk a quick glance up at his jaw. The five o’clock shadow is evident at this point, something he wears so well with his tanned skin and dark hair. My thighs clench at the memory of feeling that burn against my bare skin.

"Okay," I say, throwing the disposable razor in the trash and cleaning up the gel and water mess. "All set. So, what design do you want?"

He meets my gaze head-on. "Surprise me."

My heartbeat all but stops in my chest. "Excuse me?"

Isaac shrugs and gets comfortable in the chair, tossing his arm behind his head. "I mean, I want you to surprise me. No one knows me better than you do, BJ, so I give you full creative freedom to design my first tattoo."

It's hard to swallow as I gape at the man in front of me. "Why?" I ask hoarsely.

"Because I trust you."

My eyes burn, so I quickly avert them. He wants me to tattoo him with whatever I choose? Does he know this is permanent? It's not like the marker drawing I did all those weeks ago. This is forever.

"Are you sure?"

Hazel eyes hold steady as he whispers, "I've never been surer of anything in my life."

I don't know why I'm agreeing to this, honestly. This has disaster written all over it. I'd never tattoo a client without consulting with them about the design, except for Jameson. In most cases, a tattoo is extremely personal, an expression of oneself. But this is Isaac, and even though I'm terrified, I know I can do this.

I *want* to do this for him.

The man who I least expected to ever sit in this chair and endure the pain of getting ink. The one I could never imagine marring his perfect image, his pristine body. The guy I've fallen in love with, despite knowing the outcome would probably not go in my favor.

Nodding, I grab my sketch pad and phone and stare down at the blank page, sucking in a deep, cleansing breath. He doesn't say a word as my idea starts to unfold before my very eyes. In fact, he doesn't even look over to see what I'm drawing. I consult with Google to verify my information before adding a few touches of shading in all the right places. When the design is complete, I sit back and smile, loving what I see before me.

"You ready to see it?" I ask, holding my sketch pad against my chest.

"No need."

"Isaac," I argue, shaking my head in frustration, "you have to at least see the design to make sure you like it."

He reaches out and pushes a strand of hair off my cheek, lazily dragging his pinky finger across my jaw. "No need, love. I saw the passion and fire in your eyes while you drew it. I know it's perfect."

I shake my head, trying to clear the fog his touch creates in my brain. "You're sure? One-hundred-percent?"

"One-thousand-percent, BJ."

Unbelievable.

I place my design off to the side for reference and grab my tattoo gun and ink. Once my supplies are ready, I scoot close to his side, his familiar scent wrapping around me like a warm blanket. "You ready?" I ask, as if needing to hear his confirmation one last time.

"I'm ready."

Isaac

I try to ignore the sound of the tattoo gun and the sting of the needle piercing my skin by focusing on her. She's the poster child for professionalism and concentration, and even though a part of me is interested in seeing what she came up with, I refuse to look. I want to see it when it's complete and permanently on my skin forever.

"So, how have you been?" I finally ask, needing to focus my attention on something other than the burn.

"Fine." I can tell she's lying. "You?"

"Shitty, actually," I state, holding still as she pauses a moment to readjust her hand. The one that's pressed firmly against my chest, exactly where it should be.

"Sorry to hear that," she mutters, a touch of sarcasm in her words.

I can't help but snort a chuckle. "Something tells me that's not entirely accurate."

She doesn't say anything for a few long seconds, and I start to think she's not going to talk anymore, so when she finally speaks, it catches me by surprise. "No, that's not entirely accurate."

"Do you want to know why everything is so shitty lately?" I ask boldly, knowing I need to get all this out sooner rather than later.

She sighs and pushes that strand of hair back behind her ear once more. It's a mixture of the dark brown and purple coloring she added recently, and my fingers itch to touch those silky strands once more. "I guess, if you must talk."

"Well, I must," I start, carefully adjusting my hips in the chair. "It's been shitty because I made the wrong decision based on some sketchy information."

"Sounds like a problem," she mutters, keeping her eyes trained on her work. "But you're a smart guy. I'm sure you'll bounce back fast. Your sense of business is pretty keen."

"I'm not talking about the business," I reply softly, observing the gentle lines on her face as she tries to keep her concentration on the task at hand.

"No?"

"No. I'm talking about you."

The gun pauses and those whiskey-colored eyes look up. "Me?"

"Yeah, you. I thought I was doing the right thing and protecting my heart, but it turns out, I damaged it more."

She opens her mouth, but no words come out.

"I saw the pictures of you and Jax at the concert, and I got jealous. Then, when you returned, I saw you kiss him on the cheek, and I just freaked out. I kept telling myself we agreed this was temporary, so I thought I had to end it with you so I didn't fall for you further. Turns out, that was complete bullshit, because I was already madly in love with you."

BJ blinks several times, trying to keep the tears at bay. "You love me?" she whispers.

"More than anything in this world," I confirm, watching as the first tear spills down her cheek.

"But...but what about Savannah?" she asks, sitting back on her stool and severing the connection of her hand against my chest.

"Savannah? We're broken up," I state, even though she already knows this.

BJ shakes her head. "No, I saw her in the hallway before I went upstairs to your office. She said you two are back together."

"Uhh, no. She tried to sweet talk me into getting back together, but I told her we were forever done and over. I was in love with someone else."

She gapes at me. "You told her that?"

"She threw my fucking stapler at me."

"I...wow." She stares off into space for a few moments before returning her attention to me. "But you still broke it off with me."

Nodding, I reply, "I did. I had it in my head you wanted Jax, and since we were more casual, I wanted to end it before you did."

She sighs deeply and closes her eyes. "I don't know what to say, Isaac." When she opens them again, there's turmoil there, and I don't like it. "Jax and I, we're friends. That's all. Yes, we may have dated several years ago, but it hasn't been anything more than friendship since. I swear. He's actually interested in Amanda. They have their first official date tomorrow, and I'm so excited for them."

The slightest grin spreads across her lips before disappearing. "When he touches me or I kiss him—which was on the cheek, mind you—it's because we're still very close. He's one of my best friends and I love and respect him, both personally and professionally. I'm going to occasionally touch him and vice versa, but not sexually—never sexually. But you need to know, I won't give up my friendship with him for anyone, Isaac. Including you."

I'm already nodding. "I know that. This jealousy is on me, and I promise to work on it. Your brother helped me understand a little more about your relationship with him."

"My brother?" she asks, genuinely surprised by this revelation.

"Yeah, apparently, we weren't as good at hiding our time together as we thought," I reply with a shrug, noting the way my skin pulls on my chest.

"Wow, okay. I wasn't expecting that."

"So here's my question, BJ. Can you forgive me for being a dumbass and ending things when I wanted to do anything but? Knowing that if we do this, I'm all in, one-hundred-percent yours?"

Her grin starts small and slowly transforms her entire face. "I can live with that."

"And I have no intention of letting you go," I say, sitting up and reaching for her hand. "What I want from you won't be temporary or a friends with benefits arrangement. I want it all, Billie Jean Tankersley."

She moves forward and presses her lips against mine. "I can live with that," she replies against my lips.

"Good, because I can't live without you."

Then, I kiss her. After four days of personal hell, I kiss the only lips I ever want to kiss again, and feel the world seem to right itself instantly.

When we're both completely breathless and my cock entertains ideas of playtime, I pull back and stare into those gorgeous honey eyes. "I love you."

She sniffles and wraps her arms around my shoulders. "I love you too."

Unfortunately, the motion presses her against my chest, smarting the fresh ink. "Ouch."

BJ gasps and pulls back quickly. "Oh God, I'm so sorry," she says, wiping away the remnants of lingering tears.

"It's okay," I say, leaning back in the chair. "Are you ready to finish?"

She nods and grabs her gun off the stand. "I'm ready."

She spends the next twenty minutes finishing the work, and I'll be honest, it's almost twenty minutes too long. First off, it doesn't feel so great and is really starting to burn, but mostly because all I want to do is take her in my arms and kiss her right.

Then maybe take her back to my bed.

"All done," she says, leaning back and grinning. "You ready to see it?"

"Definitely." I push up the armrest and stand up, turning to face the full-length mirror on the wall. "Holy shit," I mumble, taking in the pink skin and the black ink stretched across it.

"I know it just looks like a bunch of numbers on there, but they mean something," she starts, grabbing her phone and displaying the image on the screen. "These are the latitude and longitude coordinates for Burgers and Brew," she informs somewhat shyly, as if she's worried about my reaction. "And the Roman numerals beneath it represent the date you guys opened."

All I can do is stare at the gorgeous ink on my chest. There's so much detail around the Roman numerals with shadowing, they look like they're leaping from my skin. "It's absolutely stunning," I tell her, finally pulling my gaze off the mirror to look at her. "I love it."

BJ awards me with a huge grin. "Good."

"Thank you," I tell her right before wrapping one hand around her hip and the other around the back of her neck and kissing her sweet lips.

"You're welcome. Let's get it covered," she says, reaching for the antibacterial ointment.

Once she has the pad taped over it, she turns and starts cleaning up her room. "So are there instructions I need to follow?"

"Of course," she replies casually before turning and facing me. "But I thought I'd take care of it personally, since I was hoping you'd come back to my place."

My cock twitches in my trousers. "Actually, I thought maybe you'd come back to *my* place."

She shrugs her slim shoulders and finishes sanitizing her space. "Doesn't matter to me, as long as there's a bed."

I press my hard cock against her ass and place a kiss against the side of her neck. "You know, if memory serves me correctly, we do pretty damn good without having a bed at all."

A shiver sweeps through her. "I recall, but I wouldn't mind a refresh."

"Done. You almost done?"

BJ finishes her task and makes sure everything is as it needs to be. "Done."

"Then let's go, so I can show the woman I love just how much I love her." I kiss her once more, though making sure to hang on to what little bit of control I have left.

"Yes, please." She stops in the middle of the hallway and turns to face me. "And maybe a little more of that tongue thing."

Taking her in my arms, I lick the lobe of her ear as I whisper, "Oh, there will definitely be a whole lot of tongue stuff."

"Excellent."

We practically sprint out of the shop, only stopping to make sure the lights are out and the door is locked, before we move to her truck. I don't even care about my car. It's locked, and I can get it tomorrow. All I want to do now is take this woman to bed and make love to her all night long, and by the look in her eyes, she's completely on board with this plan.

Which works out perfectly for me.

One night down.

The rest of our lives to go.

BJ

Six months later

"You ready?" Isaac hollers from outside my bedroom.

"Coming," I reply, grabbing the small purse I'm going to carry for the evening, considering my costume doesn't have pockets.

The moment I step into the hallway, Isaac gives me a devilish grin. "Well, you're not yet, but you most definitely will be later."

I snort and try to push past him, but he won't let me by. Instead, he wraps his arms around my waist and pulls me back against him. I can feel his hard cock.

"You better put that away or they won't let you into the trick-or-treat party," I tease.

"That's a surefire way of killing my erection. Hundreds of sugared-up little kids running around my restaurant and terrorizing the place," he says, cracking a quick smile.

I swat at his chest. "You love it, and you know it. Besides, it'll hardly be hundreds. Didn't they say this event usually draws about sixty to seventy kids?"

He nods and shifts his black cape. "Yeah. The Chamber does this trick-or-treat thing every year, but this is our first time participating." It actually worked out perfectly for Isaac and the guys. The Chamber blocks off the street in front of the restaurant, and kids will go from business-to-business trick-or-treating. Since Halloween isn't for a few more days, it gives the kids another opportunity to wear their costume and fill their buckets with treats.

There will be a DJ in the street and food available. Lyndee will have cookies set up in front of her bakery, while the restaurant is providing hotdogs and bags of chips to all the little trick-or-treaters.

Then afterward, when the youth event shuts down, Burgers and Brew is hosting their annual Halloween costume party. Isaac decided to dress as Dracula, while I chose Elvira. My costume is tight in all the right places, and if the look in his eye says anything, he's very appreciative of my efforts.

"We need to go," I mumble as he continues to explore my costume with his hands.

"No, we need to *come*," he retorts, nipping at the sensitive skin beneath my ear.

Lust bolts through my veins, and I know any fight I may have had is fruitless. I want him. I always want him, but right now, I want him even more. These hormones are completely out of control. "We can be a few minutes later, right?" I whimper as he carefully shoves his big hand down the front of my leather pants.

"Fuck, I love the fact you don't wear panties. And you're so wet."

I mutter something completely unintelligent before succumbing to the euphoria. Isaac Thompson is the master of my body, playing it like a violin. I come apart quickly, by just a few expert finger movements.

As I start to return from the blissful flight I was just taken on, I try to focus on those gorgeous hazel eyes. “Well, that was unexpected.”

Isaac smirks. “It shouldn’t be. You know I can’t keep my hands off you.”

I trail my hands down his white dress shirt, toward the zipper of his black trousers. “And what about you?”

He stops my hands. “We need to get going, love. I promised Jasper I’d help wrap hotdogs, but I’ll let you unwrap my hotdog later tonight when we get back home.”

A burst of laughter falls from my lips. “Oh my God, that was the cheesiest line I’ve ever heard.”

He places a hard kiss on my forehead. “But you’re very excited about it.”

I can’t even deny it. “I am.”

Isaac stops to wash his hands then leads me toward the front door. “Then let’s get this show on the road, so I can come home tonight and sink my teeth into you,” he quips, baring his fake vampire teeth and waggling his eyebrows suggestively.

Isaac

I can’t keep my eyes off her. Not only because of the tight Elvira outfit she’s wearing, but because she seems to be radiating with beauty. Her hair is black to fit the costume, and her glorious breasts seem to be overflowing from the top she's wearing, that's not even meant to be super seductive. I can't help it. She's definitely the sexiest Elvira I've ever seen.

"You keep staring," Walker says, stepping up beside me with his infant son in his arms.

"Can you blame me?" I ask, reaching down and placing my finger against Duncan's little hand. He instantly wraps his tiny hand around it.

"No, not at all." We stand there and watch as Mal, dressed as Mrs. Incredible, and BJ continue to chat and hand out hotdogs to the kids.

"That's a nice outfit, by the way," I tease, smiling widely at my friend in the bright red Mr. Incredible costume.

He shrugs, not seeming phased by my quip at all. "Lizzie picked them."

"And you'd do anything for her," I state, watching my friend track his wife with his eyes.

"Fuck yes I would. All of them, including this little guy," he says, gazing down at his six-week-old son with so much affection in his eyes, I can practically feel it seeping from his pores.

I can't help but smile down at the baby boy. He's wearing a red onesie with the Incredibles logo on the front, and even though he's covered in a warmer blanket and a cotton hat now, they made the cutest family picture earlier in front of the bar. "You're a lucky bastard, Walker Meyer," I tell my friend, carefully patting him on the back and squeezing his shoulder.

"I am," he says, glancing over to where Lizzie runs and jumps into her mom's arms, proudly showing her something in her Halloween bucket. "Because of them."

It's hard to swallow over the emotion in my throat. It's not jealousy, not this time. It's love and respect for my friend and his family. I'm damn proud of him for the life he's built, but it's also a reminder of how much I want that too.

With BJ.

Speaking of, I track her movements as she heads inside the bar, so I follow. Once she's inside, I spot her wave at her brother before she moves toward the back hallway and disappears around the corner.

I catch Jameson's attention who just shrugs, as if he has no clue where she's going. I take the stairs two at a time and find the woman I love sitting at my desk, her eyes closed as she relaxes. It gives me a few precious seconds to just stand there and watch her. I do that a lot, actually. If she only knew how much of a sick voyeur I am, she'd probably be a little freaked out.

"Are you just standing there, watching me?" she whispers, making me smile.

"I am," I confirm, entering my office and walking around to where she sits.

"Weirdo." She opens her eyes, and I can see the flash of exhaustion in them.

"You're tired. Are you feeling okay?" I ask, propping my ass against the desk and caging her legs between my own.

"Just a little tired lately, but it's no big deal."

"You sure?"

She nods and sits forward, taking my hand. "I've been doing some thinking."

"You know, I have been too," I reply, entwining my fingers with hers.

"You first."

"Move in with me." I don't hesitate, just ask the question I've been wanting to ask for weeks now.

"Okay, but I think we should move into my house. It has more room."

I've already considered that actually, but I didn't want to just invite myself to move in with her. I had hoped me asking would lead to more discussion over which place was better suited for us. "More room is good."

"More yard space too. We're going to need that," she says, standing up in front of me.

"Yeah? Planning some big parties?" I ask, loving the way she presses her body against mine.

"Yes. Plus, we'll need the space for a swing set and probably a sandbox someday."

That catches my attention, because I want to think she's suggesting these things for our own family's use but know she could also be talking about Lizzie and baby Duncan. "Those are always good to have," I comment, trying to manage my breathing.

"We can turn the second bedroom into your home office, and the third one into the nursery."

I jump right over the first part and focus on the second. "Nursery?"

She slides her fingers up my neck and into my hair. "You remember that time in my truck? The one at the beginning of the month when we forgot the condom?"

Oh fuck yes, I remember, but since my throat is suddenly Sahara-dry and my brain is short circuiting, all I can do is nod.

"Well, surprise," she finally says with a little giggle at the end.

"You're pregnant?" I ask, needing to hear the words.

"I'm pregnant."

She barely gets them out before I'm lifting her off the ground and spinning her around. "Holy fuck!"

The sweetest giggle hits my ear, but so does the realization she's pregnant and I'm spinning her around like a top. "Sorry," I quickly say, setting her down. "Are you feeling okay?"

She shrugs. "I haven't been sick yet but definitely more tired lately. Oh, and my boobs are tender and swollen."

A Cheshire grin spreads across my mouth. "I'll inspect those later."

"I'm sure you will," she says, rolling her eyes. Then she pins me with a worried look. "You're okay? With this?"

"Are you kidding? I'm more than okay. I'm ecstatic and can't wait to tell everyone else."

"Well, I thought maybe we could wait just a little bit. At least until the doctor confirms it in a few weeks."

I tuck her under my chin and hold her close. "That makes sense."

"I don't want to rush you, Isaac. You know, with the whole moving in thing."

"Oh, you're not, love. I'd marry you tomorrow if I had a ring," I insist, wishing I would have stopped at the jeweler and picked out a ring like I had planned. "But that's going to happen, you hear? So we do things a little out of order. So what? This is our story to tell."

She grins up at me before resting her cheek against my chest. "It is."

"I love you, BJ."

"Love you, Isaac," she says, squeezing me tightly.

This is my life, and it's more beautiful than I could have ever imagined. To think, if I hadn't gone inside her house for a drink all those months ago, none of this would be happening. I would probably have been stuck in the same ol' situation I had been in for months—hell, years.

But now, now my life has meaning. It's full and rich and beautiful, just like the woman who is carrying my baby. The woman I love.

The one I'll spend the rest of my life with, raising a family.

And that's worth more than any amount of money in the bank or possession I may own. I have love, support, friendship, and a real partner in life.

I have BJ, and soon, a child.

Now, I really do have everything.

THE END

Books by Lacey Black

Rivers Edge series

Trust Me, Rivers Edge book 1 (Maddox and Avery) – FREE at all retailers

~ *#1 Bestseller in Contemporary Romance*

Fight Me, Rivers Edge book 2 (Jake and Erin)

Expect Me, Rivers Edge book 3 (Travis and Josselyn)

Promise Me: A Novella, Rivers Edge book 3.5 (Jase and Holly)

Protect Me, Rivers Edge book 4 (Nate and Lia)

Boss Me, Rivers Edge book 5 (Will and Carmen)

Trust Us: A Rivers Edge Christmas Novella (Maddox and Avery)

~ *This novella was originally part of the Christmas Miracles Anthology*

BOX SET – contains all 5 novels, 2 novellas, and a BONUS short story

With Me, A Rivers Edge Christmas Novella (Brooklyn and Becker)

Bound Together series

Submerged, Bound Together book 1 (Blake and Carly)

~ *An International Bestseller*

Profited, Bound Together book 2 (Reid and Dani)

~*A Bestseller, reaching Top 100 on 2 e-retailers*

Entwined, Bound Together book 3 (Luke and Sidney)

Summer Sisters series

My Kinda Kisses, Summer Sisters book 1 (Jaime and Ryan)
~A Bestseller, reaching Top 100 on 2 e-retailers
My Kinda Night, Summer Sisters book 2 (Payton and Dean)
My Kinda Song, Summer Sisters book 3 (Abby and Levi)
My Kinda Mess, Summer Sisters book 4 (Lexi and Linkin)
My Kinda Player, Summer Sisters book 5 (AJ and Sawyer)
My Kinda Player, Summer Sisters book 6 (Meghan and Nick)
My Kinda Wedding, A Summer Sisters Novella book 7 (Meghan and Nick)

Rockland Falls series

Love and Pancakes, Rockland Falls book 1
Love and Lingerie, Rockland Falls book 2
Love and Landscape, Rockland Falls book 3
Love and Neckties, Rockland Falls book 4

Standalone

Music Notes, a sexy contemporary romance standalone
A Place To Call Home, a Memorial Day novella
Exes and Ho Ho Ho's, a sexy contemporary romance standalone novella
Pants on Fire, a sexy contemporary romance standalone
Double Dog Dare You, a new standalone
Grip, A Driven World Novel
Bachelor Swap, A Bachelor Tower Series Novel
Perfect Kiss, Mason Creek Series book 9
Waiting For Love, The Love Vixen Series book 11

Burgers and Brew Crüe Series

Kickstart My Heart
Don't Go Away Mad
Same Ol' Situation

<u>Co-Written with *NYT Bestselling* Author, Kaylee Ryan</u>

It's Not Over, Fair Lakes book 1
Just Getting Started, Fair Lakes book 2
Can't Get Enough, Fair Lakes book 3
Fair Lakes Box Set
Boy Trouble
Home To You
Beneath the Fallen Stars

I have the most amazing team to help me the journey of publishing!

My editing team – Kara Hildebrand, Sandra Shipman, Joanne Thompson, and Karen Hrdlicka. You ladies are THE best! I couldn't do it without you!!

The book team - Photographer, Wander Aguiar; Model, Zach Bradford; Cover Designer, Melissa Gill; Graphics Designer, Gel with Tempting Illustrations; Formatting, Brenda with Formatting Done Wright; and Promotions by Give Me Books. You each make this entire process easy!

Kaylee Ryan, Holly Collins, Lacey's Ladies, and my ARC team, thank you for listening, for your encouragements, and for your constant support.

To my husband and kids, thank you for always standing by my side and forgiving me when I submerge myself into my book world. It's not easy, but we make it work together.

To all the bloggers and readers, thank you, thank you, thank you. I hope you enjoy this story as much as I loved writing it.

About the Author

USA Today Bestselling Author Lacey Black is a Midwestern girl with a passion for reading, writing, and shopping. She carries her e-reader with her everywhere she goes so she never misses an opportunity to read a few pages. Always looking for a happily ever after, Lacey is passionate about contemporary romance novels and enjoys it further when you mix in a little suspense. She resides in a small town in Illinois with her husband, two children, crazy cat, and three rowdy chickens.

Website: www.laceyblackbooks.com
Email: laceyblackwrites@gmail.com
Facebook: https://www.facebook.com/authorlaceyblack
Instagram: https://www.instagram.com/laceyblackwrites/
Bookbub: https://www.bookbub.com/authors/lacey-black
Amazon: https://www.amazon.com/Lacey-Black/e/B00MW2UGZI
Twitter: https://twitter.com/AuthLaceyBlack
Goodreads:
https://www.goodreads.com/author/show/8414783.Lacey_Black

Sign up for my newsletter so you don't miss a single sale, reveal, or release!
http://www.laceyblackbooks.com/newsletter

Made in the USA
Middletown, DE
19 August 2024